Homeward Bound Hearts

by

Lee Ann Sontheimer Murphy

Copyright Notice
This is a work of fiction. Names, characters, places, and incidents are either the product of the author's imagination or are used fictitiously, and any resemblance to actual persons living or dead, business establishments, events, or locales, is entirely coincidental.

Homeward Bound Hearts

COPYRIGHT © 2024 by Lee Ann Sontheimer Murphy

All rights reserved. No part of this book may be used or reproduced in any manner whatsoever without written permission of the author or The Wild Rose Press, Inc. except in the case of brief quotations embodied in critical articles or reviews.
Contact Information: info@thewildrosepress.com

Cover Art by *Tina Lynn Stout*

The Wild Rose Press, Inc.
PO Box 708
Adams Basin, NY 14410-0708
Visit us at www.thewildrosepress.com

Publishing History
First Edition, 2024
Trade Paperback ISBN 978-1-5092-5917-5
Digital ISBN 978-1-5092-5918-2

Published in the United States of America

Dedication

For Granny and Pop, whose marriage brought a second chance in life for both and became the best grandparents in the world.

For Grandma who lost her sweet talking Southern husband too young but who carried on and gave me a grandpa to love.

For my late husband, Roy, who married me twenty years after we met in high school and gave me the best if brief second chance romance of all.

Chapter One

One minute Jeb sat tall in the saddle, hoping to last eight seconds on a bucking saddle bronc, and the next, he sailed across the fairgrounds arena in Tennessee. He landed hard in the dirt. Jeb struggled to find his feet and rise but couldn't. Pain shot through his body, centered in his back, so he waited for help. He'd been hurt many times before but this was different. Jeb had a hunch it might be the worst injury he ever suffered. It could prove to be his last.

Rodeo medics gathered like circling buzzards around a sick cow, but when they didn't jump into action with first aid, Jeb knew his injuries must be severe. Someone phoned for an ambulance. Jeb suffered the humble fate of riding a gurney to the rig in front of a thousand hushed fans.

"Well, folks," the announcer broke the uneasy silence. "The Hillbilly Hotshot, Jeb Hill, is down, but he's on his way to getting the medical attention he needs. Next up is Martin Magdaleno. If you're the praying kind, say a quick one for Jeb."

He didn't recall anything else until much later. Consciousness returned as he lay on his back, face up, in a hospital bed. His head rested on one pillow, with his feet on another. He managed to lift his right hand and wiggle his toes. Although the motion sparked pain, Jeb thanked God he could move. *At least I'm not paralyzed.*

His throat ached as he craved water. With effort, Jeb reached for the nurse call device looped around the bed rail. He pressed the center red button.

A speaker on the wall crackled to life. "May I help you?"

The voice lacked inflection and could have been a robot's. "I need a drink something awful," Jeb croaked.

"I'll send your nurse."

Jeb expected a woman but instead, a tall, muscular man wearing light-blue scrubs entered the room. "Jebediah, I'm Sam. I'll be your nurse on this shift. What can I do to help you?"

Why couldn't it have been a pretty lady? "I could use some water."

Sam maneuvered the bed upward at a slight angle. He poured water from a plastic pitcher into a lidded cup, then placed the straw within reach of Jeb's lips.

Jeb drank deep as the ice water trickled down his throat. "Exactly what are my injuries?" A sharp pain stabbed his lower back. Jeb winced. "Is my back broken?"

"You have a spinal fracture so yes, but no. The rest of your back and spine are fine. The break is in your lower back, vertebrae T10-L2." Sam took Jeb's wrist between his fingers.

"That means about as much to me as yesterday's lottery numbers." Jeb ignored an urge to pull away. "What are you doing now?"

Sam released his grip. "I was taking your pulse."

Jeb shifted his gaze to the monitor beside the bed. "I thought your fancy machine displayed pulse, heartbeat, and all."

"It does, but I like to check for myself. Machines can make mistakes. L-2 is the second of five lumbar vertebrae. We call it a burst fracture, and fortunately, yours is stable." Sam sat in the bedside chair. "What's your pain level on a scale of one to ten?"

"Twelve." Jeb shifted, which made his back hurt more. "I got pain down my legs, too."

Sam nodded. "That's normal with this type of injury. I can provide pain medication. For the first couple of days, the doc ordered a strong narcotic, but we'll wean you off to ibuprofen."

"Bring it on, then." Jeb bit his lip so he wouldn't groan. He'd hurt before many times, but not this bad. "Will I walk again?"

"No reason you shouldn't. You can talk to the doctor when he comes in, which will be soon. Dr. Ahmed is making rounds. I'll get your meds and be back. Don't go anywhere." Sam stood and winked.

If he could have, Jeb would have punched him square in the nose.

Before the physician arrived, the nurse returned and injected Jeb with morphine.

It dulled Jeb's pain to a tolerable level, but relief wasn't immediate.

Dr. Ahmed sauntered into the room in a confident fashion. His salt-and-pepper hair and beard indicated he wasn't young. He catalogued Jeb's injuries, outlined the treatment plan, and read the chart. "Have you been briefed on your injuries?"

"I got two questions—will I be able to walk and can I ride again?" Jeb clenched the edge of the sheet with his fingers. Both activities were important to Jeb. His future depended on those abilities.

"Walking shouldn't be a problem, not after rehab and physical therapy. Dr. Ahmed tugged at his tidy goatee. "Riding horses is more problematic. I don't recommend busting broncs or participating in any other rodeo events in the future. Although you'll recover from the fracture, your spine is compromised. You don't want any further injury because any future breaks are more likely to cause permanent issues."

The doctor's stern expression sobered Jeb. He tightened his jaw so hard it ached. If he couldn't ride, he would no longer be able to compete. With his career and livelihood at stake, Jeb drew a harsh breath as he steeled himself not to weep. "When can I go home?" Jeb pictured his quiet farmhouse back in Missouri. "And how do I get there?"

"You have two options." Dr. Ahmed adjusted his glasses and gazed down his nose. "We transfer you to a rehabilitation facility for six to eight weeks, then let you go, or we can arrange transport to your home, which I understand is several states away from Tennessee."

And more than six hundred miles. "I'll go with transport. I'm not ending up in some nursing home, no matter what fancy name it might have."

"It's up to you but it is expensive." The doctor glanced at the chart in his hands. "We'll have to check your insurance. If it doesn't cover costs, hospital social services can assist you in applying for financial aid."

Jeb lifted both hands and waved them in protest. He refused to become what he considered a charity case. "I can privately pay. I've got the bucks. Plus, I have insurance through my sponsor." At least, he hoped the major boot manufacturer wouldn't cancel coverage and refuse to pay. Rodeo and busting broncs had been his life for more than fifteen years. He might not hold the current championship ranking, but he'd hit the top ten every year for the past decade. His career was all he had and the only thing he took pride in. *Maybe he'd heard wrong or misunderstood earlier.* Jeb had to confirm what the doctor said. "Tell me the truth. Will I ride and compete again or am I finished?"

The doctor lowered his gold-framed glasses and peered over them. "I thought I made it clear. You might ride a horse for pleasure in the future, although I wouldn't recommend it. Injuries happen at home as well as in the arena. Competition, however, for you has ended. Your spinal injuries are severe enough that any future damage could result in permanent paralysis. Your rodeo career, Mr. Hill, is over."

At the age of thirty, Jeb's only job and lifelong passion vanished. His chest tightened as if a vice were clamped in place. When he tried to take a deep breath, he couldn't. Although he'd never had one, Jeb feared he might be in the throes of an anxiety attack. At least if he needed medical attention, he had a doctor in the room. He wanted to cry like a little boy but didn't. *Cowboy up. Take it like a man. It's not the end of the world.*

For Jeb, however, it seemed as if this was his personal doomsday. Jeb pulled his thoughts together and focused on the future. "I'm going home, even if I have to foot the bill. When do I get out of here?"

"Soon. You'll remain here as a patient for five to seven more days. I'll have social services start the dismissal process and arrange for transport. We'll also verify whether or not your insurance will cover the cost. Steff, our social services director, will set up home health care and physical therapy. Your qualified home nurse will make sure you get to your sessions." Dr. Ahmed paused. "You must be glad to return home. Do you have family?"

"I guess I am." Jeb failed to dredge up much enthusiasm since he had little choice. He spent some of the off-season at the farm each year, but he hadn't lived there since he was a teenager. He hadn't planned to return for good until he retired or got old. Home had been the rodeo circuit. "And I don't have any family to speak of. Not anymore." Jeb sighed. He had a couple of aunts and a few cousins. He wouldn't mention his estranged dad. "How long until I'm healed?"

"Full recovery will take two to three months. It could be more, depending on how hard you work on therapy." The doc scribbled on the prescriptions pad he pulled from his pocket.

"I'll work my tail off to get out of this place." Jeb sighed. He valued his mobility and freedom more now.

"Very good. I'll have social services start the process." Dr. Ahmed nodded and almost smiled. "I'll leave these two scripts at the nursing station."

Five days, multiple rounds of excruciating physical therapy, and too many tasteless meals later, Jeb left the medical center. Although he could hobble with a walker, he hoped to graduate to a cane once he reached home. A nurse prepared Jeb for transport, then left him to wait, staring at the bland walls of the hospital room. He wore sweats some of his rodeo friends had brought along with his gear. The clothing he'd worn to compete had been removed on his arrival at the emergency department and trashed, since they had to cut the garments off.

The van driver arrived and introduced himself.

"I'm Jace Pickens, and I'll get you home." The older man offered a smile and shook Jeb's hand. "They want you riding in the back in the wheelchair, so I'll let the professionals get you loaded."

"Who's gonna unload me on the other end?" Jeb sighed as he settled into the chair.

Steff Martin, the hospital social worker, hovered with exit paperwork Jeb had to sign. Once he'd initialed the appropriate places and inked his name, she stuck them into a folder. "We've got everything set up so don't worry. A local ambulance crew will settle you into your home, and your home health nurse will be there."

Nine and a half long hours later, the transport van rolled down Jeb's driveway in Missouri. His heart beat faster since he was here, but he couldn't enjoy his return. He had a headache, and his back hurt the worst it had in days. Riding so far seated in a wheelchair, strapped with a seatbelt, hadn't been comfortable. He didn't expect anyone he knew to greet him, but the ambulance crew included his cousin, Addison. A high school classmate, Dennis, another crew member, greeted Jeb before Jace Pickens lowered him to the ground using the van's motorized wheelchair lift.

"It's the return of the triumphant hero." Jeb forced a grin.

"Looks more like a broken cowboy to me." Dennis laughed as he slapped Jeb's palm in a high five. "Good to have you back."

Jeb inked his name on the insurance claim for the transport driver and thanked him, then steeled himself to be jolted.

After one look at the front porch steps, the

ambulance crew decided to bring him through the back porch and kitchen. Once inside, he shifted from wheelchair to a walker and hobbled with slow steps.

Jeb expected to use the downstairs bedroom, the one he kept for guests, but instead, a hospital bed loomed in the dining room. The table and chairs were pushed against one wall. Jeb leaned on his walker, more than a little winded, although he tried not to let it show. "I figured I'd be in the bedroom."

"Nah." Dennis shook his head and pointed toward a woman waiting in the open doorway leading to the front room. "We had detailed doctor's orders or, at least, she did."

The small-statured woman couldn't be more than five feet tall. Brown hair fell just past her shoulders, and her eyes were also brown. Her small heart-shaped face gazed at him, and her full lips were a lighter pink than her rose-colored scrubs.

She stepped forward. "Welcome home. I'm Shelby Thacker, RN, your home health nurse. Let's get you settled. I imagine you're tired after the long ride."

Her soft voice echoed melodiously in his ears as alto not soprano. Jeb usually preferred blondes, but something about the nurse appealed to him. Her hair appeared natural and not from a bottle. The fact she wore little, if any, makeup appealed to him. "I ain't sure you can wrangle me into bed." He flushed and felt the heat in both cheeks.

A fleeting smile lit her face. "I'm stronger than I look."

The familiar dining room, scene of more family dinners and celebrations than Jeb could count seemed strange. Granny's long maple dining table had been moved to the side of the room with the leaf removed. The matching sideboard remained where he remembered it but now it held medical supplies, not a silk floral arrangement and a Carnival glass bowl. The ladder-back chairs were stacked beside the table. A hospital bed, similar to the one he'd used in Tennessee, stood in the center of the room. The heavy navy drapes remained at the windows.

Addison lingered as the rest of the ambulance crew headed toward the rig. "Hey, Jeb, is there anything I can do before I go? Mom said she'll be over tomorrow to visit."

"Tell Aunt Jeannie I'll look forward to seeing her. Maybe she could bring me one of those oatmeal cakes with coconut frosting." The confection had been his favorite for years. His mom always baked one for his birthday, but after she lost her battle to cancer, his aunt had stepped up.

"I will. Glad you're home, cuz." Addison patted his arm.

"Me, too." Jeb stared at the familiar walls. Home. From what he could see of the front room, the furniture there hadn't changed from the 1970s-era floral brocade couch. Gramp's brown recliner, a gift from Jeb, sat in the same spot beside Granny's wooden Colonial-style rocking chair. *I wish it felt more like a homecoming than a dead-end. If I had anywhere else to go, I'd be there.* Jeb wasn't sure what to say to the nurse who waited, arms folded.

Their stalemate ended when she approached and tapped his arm.

Since his injury, he had been poked, prodded, and touched in countless ways. Contact had been clinical, but Shelby's grasp seemed different. Her fingers were gentle; yet a ticklish tingle went through him. Her nudge came closer to a caress than anything since he got injured.

"Let's get you comfortable." Shelby guided him toward the bed. "Do you want to change, or are you good with what you're wearing?"

Jeb glanced at his sweatpants and T-shirt. "This is fine." He clumped the walker close to the bed and let her maneuver him. Shelby tucked him into bed, on his right side with such speed he didn't feel any pain. Pillows supported his head with more tucked against his back. Jeb sighed. "That actually feels comfortable."

"I'm glad." Her capable hands pulled a quilt he remembered well over him. Granny had made it with scraps of his old shirts and some of Pop's.

"Do you want the TV on or some music?"

His old twenty-inch television rested on a cart, rolled in from the living room. "Not right now. I kinda like the quiet. The hospital was pretty noisy, you know?" Jeb relaxed more than he ever had in the hospital.

"I do. Can I get you anything else?" She fidgeted with her hands as she spoke and moved toward the sideboard. A small purse and set of keys rested there.

Jeb considered soda but decided against it. Right now, he would be content to rest and hopefully sleep. "I'll probably nap for a bit."

Shelby nodded. "That's good. You need one. If it's okay, I have to run back to town for something. I won't be gone long, I promise."

"Why?" Curiosity made him pry.

Her cheeks pinked. "I have to pick up something."

"Like what?" He liked her calm presence and hated for her to leave.

She hesitated, then sighed long and loud. "My kids. School gets out before long, and I have to be in the pickup line. I'll bring them here, but I promise I'll keep them in the kitchen. They're incredibly good children and quiet."

Kids. He hadn't expected little ones to hang around and wasn't sure if he liked the idea. Jeb didn't dislike kids; he just wasn't familiar. "How old and how many?" His nerves couldn't stand a crying infant, but then she had mentioned school.

"Two. Levi is eight and in the second grade. Lexi's six and goes to kindergarten." Shelby picked up her keys and slung the purse over one shoulder.

She had children so she must be married. Weary from the road trip, disappointment filled Jeb although he wasn't sure why. He'd liked thinking of her as a single woman. "Why doesn't your husband get them from school?"

Shelby's smile flipped into a frown. "I'm a widow. My husband died three years ago. I really need to go, or I'll be late."

Jeb tried to nod. "Go ahead. It's not like I'm going anywhere." He listened as she exited the house and started her car. He wasn't an expert mechanic, but the motor sounded strained, like it might need oil or have mechanical issues. Jeb doubted he would fall asleep, but he drifted off and didn't hear Shelby's return.

When he awakened, the surroundings seemed unfamiliar until Jeb remembered he had come home. The familiar blue-and-gold-striped wallpaper in the dining room matched the navy drapes. A delightful aroma wafted from the kitchen. Although he wasn't sure what might be cooking, Jeb felt hungry for the first time since he was hurt.

Soft whispers from the other room distracted him. Jeb couldn't make out the words, but he heard the voices. He shifted position, wanting to sit up, and winced. His muscles were stiff, and his back hurt enough he could use ibuprofen. Dr. Ahmed had weaned him away from the heavy-duty narcotics, and the over-the-counter pills helped. "Hey, Shelby." Jeb raised his voice, hoping she would hear him.

Still wearing scrubs, the nurse popped through the kitchen doorway in a hurry. "I'm here. What can I do?"

"I want to sit to eat. I'd really rather get up if I can. I'm tired of eating in bed like an invalid." A whine crept into his voice, and Jeb cleared his throat to remove it.

"No problem. I can help you if you don't mind the kitchen table. I can send the kids outside to play…"

Jeb waved one hand. "They can stay. I'm not some kind of old ogre. Whatever's cooking smells good."

Shelby maneuvered Jeb into a sitting position, then assisted him until he swung his legs toward the floor. She moved the walker within his reach.

"Thanks." Jeb grasped it and pulled himself upright. He groaned. "No pain, no gain, or that's what they tell me." He hitched the walker forward with effort. Shelby hovered until he reached the table and sank into a seat.

"What's your pain level?" She steadied his chair and moved it closer.

"Don't ask me again." The query irritated him, and he grimaced. "I got tired being asked the same question six times a day in the hospital. I'm hurting a little, but ibuprofen eases the pain. Supper will help even more. What are we having?"

Two wide-eyed kids, a boy, and a girl, stared from the opposite end of the table. Both had Shelby's dark hair and eyes.

"Salisbury steak, mashed potatoes, carrots, and brown gravy with mushrooms." Shelby turned to stir something in a saucepan on the stove. "I hope you like mushrooms."

"I do. In fact, you're fixing one of my favorite meals. It'd be perfect if we had fresh baked bread or hot rolls." Jeb licked his lips.

She tucked her hair behind her ears and faced him. "I've got rolls in the oven, but they're store-bought. I didn't have time to make any. Do you want sweet tea?"

"Sure, I'm thirsty." He took a deep swig when she delivered a glass. "How'd you happen to make some of my favorites?"

Shelby laughed. "Apparently, they asked you in the hospital what you liked to eat, what you don't, made a list, and then passed it on."

Jeb vaguely recalled a dietician who fired questions and made notations. At the time, he thought she wanted his preferences for hospital use. He hadn't been served anything he had mentioned so maybe not.

The boy huffed. "Mama, when do we eat? I'm hungry. I didn't like the school lunch today. It had beets."

"Levi, don't be rude. It's Mr. Hill's house so he says when I serve." Shelby reached into her purse and pulled out a package of crackers. "Here, this will keep you from starving. Jebediah, this is my son, Levi

Thacker. And the girl coloring a picture is my daughter, Lexi. Kids, this is Mr. Hill."

Until now, Shelby hadn't used his full name and she drew out every syllable. He shook his head. "It's just Jeb." Mr. Hill sounded like an old man. His grandpa had been known as Mr. Hill. "Call me Jeb. The kids can, too. I'm not very formal. I'm hungry, too, so whenever the rolls are done, I'm ready."

"Jeb." Shelby repeated his name and wrinkled her nose. "It suits you."

He laughed out loud for the first time since he busted his back. "So does Hillbilly Hotshot." From the way her eyes grew big and her lips parted, he guessed she hadn't heard his rodeo name. His life had just taken a one-eighty turn, and so far Jeb didn't really think it was for the better.

"What does it mean?" Shelby lifted one eyebrow.

"I rode as Jeb Hill, the Hillbilly Hotshot for the last fifteen years." He stared at the table; painfully aware those days were over. Either she might be slow or didn't understand.

Shelby stood near the stove, oven mitt on one hand. "Rode what?"

It dawned on Jeb she didn't know his history. "Look, honey, I am, well I *was*, a saddle bronc rider and a good one. I got this spinal fracture when a wild bronc tossed me at a rodeo. Could have been worse, I reckon. I was awfully scared I might not walk again." He paused and drew a deep breath. "Didn't they tell you anything about me?"

Shelby shook her head back and forth. "Just your name, what injury you had, and where you live. I thought you'd been in a car wreck."

Jeb guffawed. "No. Might have been easier if I had been."

Shelby pulled the tray of rolls from the oven, tossed them into a basket, and put them on the table with the butter. She quickly fixed four plates. His had a helping of everything including a sizeable helping of gravy. Hers had a smaller portion and the two other plates were child-sized for her kids. Each of them ended up with a hamburger steak and mashed potatoes, a few carrots, but no gravy.

Shelby clasped her hands together. "Do you want to ask the blessing?"

Caught unaware, Jeb nodded. He hadn't said grace since he lived in this same house with his mama and daddy, later with his grandparents who took over his care after his mom died and his dad took off. This had been Granny and Pop's house first. They had relocated to town but returned when needed. He spoke the remembered words, thanked God he could be home instead of in a facility, and dug into the food.

The first bite of Salisbury steak melted on his tongue, the best thing he'd eaten in a long time. The mashed potatoes were real, not from a box, the carrots were tender, and the rolls, despite being from the store, were flaky in his mouth. If he ate like this every day, he might get fat, but better still, he would heal. "Thank you for a fine meal, Shelby." He wondered if she planned to cook every day. He had no idea if she would be his sole nurse or if others would arrive to follow a schedule.

Lexi ducked her head as she blushed. "We're not done yet."

"We're not?" Jeb turned toward the little girl. Until

now, she hadn't said a word.

She grinned, revealing a gap where she'd lost a baby tooth. "No, there's still ice cream."

Jeb stacked his silverware onto his empty plate but kept the spoon. "Bring it on, then." He winked at Shelby and grinned.

So far, being home had turned out better than he'd ever dreamed. Maybe it wouldn't be a total nightmare after all.

Chapter Two

Shelby Thacker held her breath when Lexi told Mr. Hill, *Jeb,* about the ice cream. She released it, relieved when he wasn't angry. She needed this job more than anyone except her mom knew. With it, she could pay the bills and stay afloat. She reflected on her current situation and thanked God she had the job. So far, she liked Jeb Hill just fine, and he hadn't been as difficult as some patients often were.

Since Jimmy died in a roadside accident while on the job, her life had turned upside down. The kids had been four and two. With two paychecks, they had managed with Jimmy working for the highway department and Shelby as an overnight emergency room nurse at the local hospital in southwest Missouri. She kept the children during the day, although she got little sleep, and he was there at night.

After the funeral, she took time off, then became a home health nurse. Shelby managed to find a babysitter during the day, and once both kids were in school, she kept the same hours. To be near her mother, Shelby had moved back to her hometown, St. Joseph, Missouri, fifty miles north of the Kansas City metropolis. Once in a while, she had to take calls and venture out at all hours, but that's when Mom would step up.

Shelby's grandparents had once lived in the old frame house she called home on North Tenth. The place needed a new roof, which she couldn't afford, but it provided a mortgage-free place to raise her children. Her mom, also widowed, lived four blocks away on Grand Avenue. Despite the name, the narrow street was anything but.

Shelby's job entailed visiting different patients each day in their homes. Most were elderly and suffered from chronic illnesses ranging from cancer to Parkinson's. She lost few patients because hospice nurses took over when death became certain. Three patients had passed under Shelby's care. Sometimes that bothered her, but the job kept her home with the little ones most nights. She racked up the miles on her beat-up old car, so when her supervisor, Michelle, approached her with a six-to-eight-week one-patient job, Shelby took it and counted her blessings.

"If you're interested, I'll reassign your other cases because this is a single-duty job." Michelle explained. "It's a male patient, Jebediah Hill. He suffered a spinal fracture, not a broken back, but damage to his vertebrae, T-10, L2. The expectation is for full recovery in about eight weeks, but he can't manage at home alone. It's not far, about fifteen miles out of St. Joe and near Savannah on a farm. His insurance will kick in for the first couple of weeks, but Mr. Hill offered a generous bonus for the remainder. Do you want the job?"

"I do." Shelby accepted it without consideration. His name made her think the patient must be an older man. "Is he in the hospital now?"

Michelle nodded. "Yes, in Columbia, Tennessee. He'll be transported home on Friday. Arrival should be around two p.m. It's a nine-and-a-half-hour drive, so he'll be wiped out by the time he arrives. There's not really a back-up nurse so it's a twenty-four-seven position. I'll get the contract ready if you're sure."

On Friday, waiting at the farmhouse, Shelby's nerves went on high alert. Urban-raised, she had spent her married life in Monett, a small town in the Missouri Ozarks. She hoped this old guy wasn't too persnickety, and prayed he didn't mind kids. Her mom worked overtime, serving at school functions, this week and next, so unless Shelby hired a teenager to babysit, Levi and Lexi would be with her after school.

Her new patient arrived in a medical transport van, and she noticed gray shot through his black hair. *So, he is old.* Then she caught sight of his face, and her mouth dropped open. Mr. Hill wasn't old at all, despite the salt-and-pepper hair. His lean face tapered to a pointed chin, and he sported a slender hawk-style nose. His eyes were the deep-blue of the ocean or the sky in summer. *He isn't old, and he's very handsome.*

When he stood, using the walker, Shelby realized how tall he was. Still, she remained professional. She introduced herself, settled him into bed, and positioned his body for comfort. When he didn't object to the kids, she heaved a sigh of relief.

She chose the menu early from a notebook where she'd written down everything she received about his case, from his dietary preferences to the doctor's orders. Shelby had a section on his medications and his medical history, and flipping through it as she cooked, she realized she'd missed his birthdate. In case he had a birthday coming soon, she wanted to know so found the date in his records.

He would turn thirty-one in December, which

made him three years older. Nothing indicated his career, and she had guessed him to be an attorney or a college professor or an advertising man. When Jeb mentioned he'd been a saddle bronc rider, Shelby had been stunned. It wasn't a career she'd considered he might have. Once she knew, however, she understood and realized it matched his injury.

Now, after the meal, which he ate without complaint, Shelby parked the kids at the table. Levi had math homework and Lexi focused on her coloring book. She needed time to think. *I was wrong about almost everything.* She chuckled, then peeked at Jeb, who still sat in the kitchen. "Let me know when you're ready to lay down."

Focus on the job, Shelby, don't be a fan girl.

"I can wait until you finish, then I want to pop some pain relievers. I thought I'd sit in the recliner for a bit, but I've changed my mind. I probably will tomorrow, though."

"I'll be here as soon as I drop off the kids in the morning. If you need me earlier, I can come, but I'll still have to drive them to school first." She dried her hands after she put the last dish in the drainer.

"Isn't there a school bus?" He held up his tea glass for a refill and accepted some ibuprofen.

"I think so, but the driver wouldn't know he should stop for my kids. Besides, your house is probably on a Savannah route. Their school is in St. Joseph." Shelby retrieved hand lotion from her purse and rubbed some into her hands.

Jeb swallowed the pills and cleared his throat. "Is a night nurse coming or what?"

Shelby jerked. "I'm afraid there won't be. I'm the

primary nurse for your case, but if you need help at night, I can call and find out if someone is available. It'll cost more, though. I'm available around the clock. If I'm not here, you can call me and I'll come."

Jeb frowned. "No, don't get anyone else. I'll be all right."

She patted each child on the arm. "Stay in here until we're ready to go. Jeb, here's the walker." His blue eyes met hers.

"Okay." With the gait of the old man he wasn't, Jeb clumped to the bathroom, then to his makeshift bedroom.

Shelby helped him change from sweats into shorts, then arranged him in the same cozy position as earlier. Then she made sure he had a bedside urinal within reach, a bottle of water, and a pay-as-you-go cell phone programmed with her number. "If you need me, call. It doesn't matter what time." She smoothed the sheet, then the quilt over Jeb. Shelby resisted a sudden urge to kiss his forehead. "Good night."

"Good night, Shelby. Thank you." His body relaxed once he was prone.

Despite daylight savings time, dusk fell before Shelby rounded up her kids and headed to the car. Although she had locked the door behind her, she worried about leaving Jeb defenseless. *He's a grown man. He'll be fine.* With limited mobility, though, he might not be. She fretted all the way into town, stewed while she gave her children their evening bath, and remained anxious after she tucked them into bed.

In her bedroom, she hesitated when she grabbed her nightgown, then sighed, and called her mother. "Mom, it's Shelby." She sank onto the edge of her bed.

Mom always thought the worst. "What's wrong?"

"Nothing. I'm fine, and the kids are good. I just need to run out and check on my guy, uh, my patient. He can't get around by himself, and I'm worried. I need this job." Shelby closed her eyes with a prayer. Besides, she couldn't shake her concern about Jeb.

Delia Brown blew into the phone. "Do you want me to come over and stay with the littles?"

"I do. I won't be very long." Shelby released the breath she'd been holding. "Thank you."

"Take all the time you need, Shelby. I'll stay with the kids anytime you want. As long as I get to work on time, I'm good."

Shelby took the older two-lane highway, then exited onto the county road leading to Jeb's place. After cutting the headlights so they wouldn't sweep across the windows, she parked where the driveway ended between the barn and backdoor. With the key she had been issued, Shelby entered through the enclosed back porch. She took slow steps and moved with stealth so she wouldn't wake Jeb. If he proved to be asleep, then she would tiptoe out, coast down the drive, and head home. A floorboard creaked beneath her feet in the kitchen, and she paused.

"Who's there?" Jeb's voice was a low growl.

"Shelby." She walked into the dining room and turned on a lamp.

His sigh echoed through the quiet house. "I almost called you."

"What's the matter?" Shelby grabbed a dining room chair and placed it beside the bed, facing Jeb.

"Can't sleep. I'm jumpy. I thought I would fall asleep without any trouble. In the hospital, they woke me every couple of hours to push and prod and do stuff. Now it's too quiet." As he spoke, his eyes darted around the room.

"I understand why you're nervous." Shelby took his wrist between her fingers to check his pulse. As she expected, it raced.

He squinched his eyes shut and frowned. "Could be worse, I guess."

Jeb's vulnerability moved her. Shelby understood. Sometimes home wasn't what you hoped, and if you couldn't move well or much, anyone would be dismayed. "I wondered how you were doing and got a little worried, so I came back."

He offered a tiny smile. "I'm glad, Shelby. I didn't want to bother you at home, but I'm happy you're here."

It takes humility for a top rodeo rider to admit his emotion.

"You didn't." Shelby combed her fingers through her hair. She almost added his care was part of the job, but she didn't want to hurt Jeb or make him feel like just a patient. In her home health career, she had never experienced such an emotional tug. As a nurse, Shelby maintained a professional distance. She learned early in her career, especially in the emergency room, not to engage her emotions. Jeb Hill, however, was different.

"Where are Levi and Lexi?" Jeb tossed off the quilt.

"With my mom." Any other patient wouldn't ask or use the kids' names. "She lives close and didn't mind."

"Nice. My mom died when I was twelve." Jeb's voice fell to a whisper. "Cancer."

"I'm sorry. Where did you grow up?" If she didn't make small talk, she would doze. The day's fatigue had caught up, and she yawned.

"Right here. I graduated from Savannah High School and even went to classes at Missouri Western. But my rodeo career took off, and I didn't go back." Jeb's blue eyes glistened in the lamplight.

"Small world. I got my nursing degree at MoWest." For the first time in ages, Shelby thought about Jimmy. She graduated, married, and moved to South Missouri to his hometown within six months. She rose with restless energy and paced the room.

"Must have missed you by two or three years. Are you from St. Joe?" Jeb shifted his position and winced.

"Born and raised. I came back after my husband died and plan to stay. It's home." Shelby rose to fidget with cut-glass pieces on the sideboard. "We live in my grandma's old house. I inherited it or I might be living out of my car. Rent isn't in my budget."

Jeb quirked one eyebrow. "Surely not."

Shelby sat and spread her hands wide. "It's not impossible. Money is sometimes a struggle, even with my job." She didn't want to talk about her financial troubles, especially not with her new patient. "You should try to sleep. Rest is important when you're healing." The last thing she wanted to think about or discuss was her finances. This eight-week job with Jeb would make a difference, but her earnings never kept pace with inflation. Something always broke or quit working or the children needed stuff.

Elementary school parents needed unlimited funds. Almost daily, the kids came home with requests for snacks, field trip money, a book, or a T-shirt to tie-dye with the class. Both of Shelby's kids outgrew shoes and clothing at an alarming rate. Her older model car often sputtered and sometimes quit. When it required repairs, Shelby struggled to pay expensive shop bills.

"I'm worn out but not sleepy." As Jeb spoke, his eyelids fluttered.

"Maybe I should turn off the lamp." Shelby shaded her eyes from the glare. "I can turn on a smaller light in the living room."

Jeb shrugged, then winced. "How long will you be here?"

"I'm not sure." Shelby didn't want to drive home drowsy. "What were you thinking?"

"Could you stay all night?" His cheeks pinked as he asked. "I know it's a lot since you've got kids but…"

It wouldn't be the first time Shelby stayed overnight with a client, and she doubted it would be the last. Her mom had the kids covered so she nodded. "I will, Jeb. Mom can drop them at school in the morning."

He released a long breath. "Thank you, but I think it's Saturday, Shelby."

"You're right." She'd lost track and felt like an idiot. Shelby fluffed and rearranged his pillows. She adjusted his covers and Jeb's position. She sat beside him, idly talking, until he slept. Jeb snored lightly, and she smiled. Shelby retreated to the living room, removed her shoes, and kicked back in the recliner. Shelby tossed a shawl from the back of the couch over her shoulders and dozed.

She woke early and tiptoed to the car for a change of clothing. She always carried one, never knowing if a patient might vomit or otherwise soil her scrubs.

Although she would have liked a shower, Shelby settled for washing up in the sink, then donned navy-blue scrubs. She called home, talked to the kids, and assured them she would pick them up later.

A quick peek at Jeb revealed he still slept; one hand curled against his cheek. She positioned the walker within his reach. Shelby made coffee and pondered what to fix for his breakfast. After consulting his preferences from the notes she'd made from the information the hospital sent, she got out a mixing bowl and the ingredients to make pancakes. While the griddle heated, she fried bacon and sipped coffee. She poured the first pancakes.

Jeb entered the kitchen, hunched over the walker.

"Good morning. The coffee's hot and the food's almost ready." Shelby kept a close eye on the griddle, spatula in hand.

"Morning." He shifted from the walker into a chair. "I'd love a cup of coffee. What's for breakfast?"

"Pancakes and bacon." Shelby brought him a mug of black coffee, his preference.

He lifted the cup to his mouth and smiled. "Sounds great. These meals based on my favorite foods are like having a fairy godmother. I don't even have to make a request. You fix something I like."

"That's the plan." She laughed as she slid a plate with three perfect pancakes and three slices of bacon in front of Jeb. Shelby brought butter and maple syrup to the table. As soon as the next set of cakes was ready, she joined him. Shelby noticed he hadn't taken a bite. "You didn't have to wait."

Jeb stretched out his hands and took hers. "I thought we'd ask the blessing together."

Surprised, Shelby twined her fingers through his. A delicious shudder passed through her body sparked by his touch.

"Thanks for breakfast. It's delicious." He paused and met her gaze. "We need to talk, Shelby."

Her pancakes turned to rocks inside her stomach. Shelby appreciated the compliment, but his request to talk brought fear. If he fired her, then she would have to scramble to replace the lost income. "Okay."

"It's the last week of August, and they said I need help for eight weeks, right?" He forked a bite of pancake, then lifted it to his lips.

"Yes, for two, possibly three months." Shelby put down her utensil. She couldn't eat until she found out what he intended.

"You'll be here until the end of November, then." He crunched another slice of bacon, then washed it down with the rest of his coffee.

"I suppose so." Maybe he wasn't letting her go, after all.

"When does school start?" Jeb blotted his lips with a napkin.

Shelby frowned. "It already did. The first day was mid-month. Why?"

He finished his last bites of breakfast. "I wondered if you would bring the kids out and stay here. I'd feel better if you were under the same roof as me in case I need some help. There are four bedrooms upstairs, clean sheets in the linen closet, and blankets if you need any. Since you'll cook, you and your kids can share meals with me. What do you think about staying here as long as I need you?"

His request stunned Shelby. Her mind raced

through scenarios on Jeb's farm and in this house. On one hand, it would solve a few of her problems. He wanted a caregiver at night, and if she agreed, she'd be here. The kids would love playing in the large front yard, and Shelby was the first to admit the old neighborhood where they lived wasn't as safe as it used to be. Utilities and groceries would be on Jeb's dime, not hers. On the flip side, however, she would burn more gas driving farther to drop the kids at school. Her car used too much oil and wasn't reliable. It could strand her anywhere between here and town. The same held true, though, if she continued to commute to the farm.

Jeb waited for her reply, focused on Shelby. "So?"

"Maybe." Shelby released a long breath. Staying here might make some things easier but it could create new problems. "I don't know. Let me think about it." The farm offered a more wholesome environment for her kids. In the late-night wolf hours, Shelby often worried if she was a good parent. She hadn't planned to be a single mom but was. Her struggles to keep her children fed, clothed, and happy were real.

"Sure. If it helps, my truck will arrive later today. Rob Nugent, a friend of mine, is driving it from Tennessee, where I got hurt. You can drive it and save your vehicle." Jeb stacked his silverware onto his plate.

His offer appealed, but she questioned his motive. At the moment, Jeb's mobility remained limited, but at the end of eight weeks, he would be able to get around. Shelby chose her words with care, but she had to know. "I'll sleep upstairs, and you'll be down here, right? Because I'm not the kind of woman who gets into any hanky-panky. I need to say that right now."

Jeb's eyes widened. "I'm glad you did. I'm not the sort of man who wants to get intimate with a woman, not outside of marriage. I've avoided buckle bunnies all these years, so I'm not about to start chasing women now. And even when I can climb the stairs, I promise I won't sneak into your bedroom, honey."

His answer pleased her. Shelby reached across the table and took his hand. "Then yes, I'll move here temporarily with my kids. I didn't want to make you mad, but I had to ask."

"I totally get it. Why don't you trot home and get your kids while I wash up the dishes?" He wore a slight grin.

Jimmy never did kitchen chores. If he had offered, Shelby might have fainted. He didn't vac or sweep or dust or do laundry, either. "Are you serious? How?"

Jeb pulled himself up using the edge of the table and grasped the walker. "I can lean on this contraption. My hands aren't broken, and I ain't too good to wash a dish or pan."

A smile spread over her face. "All right. I'll get Levi and Lexi. We'll pack up our things to come stay. Will you be all right until I get back?"

He stood at the sink, adding dish soap to hot water before stirring it with one hand. "I believe so, Shelby."

She stepped out into the late summer morning. Birds trilled in a nearby tree, and she noticed wildflowers in bloom along the fence row. The country air smelled fresh and sweet. A tire swing dangled from a sturdy oak tree, and Shelby grinned.

This job had turned out to be a blessing, in more way than one. She turned on the radio and sang along to vintage country tunes all the way to town. A few misgivings crept into her mind, and Shelby prayed she had made the right choice. She had never moved in with a patient before and wasn't even sure if it was the best idea. *As long as Jeb doesn't get the wrong idea, I think it will be okay. Once he's healed, I'm gone to the next job. That's the way it has to be.*

Chapter Three

Once he'd washed the dishes, the griddle, and the skillet Shelby used to fry bacon, Jeb decided he'd clean himself up. He was well aware he wasn't ready for a shower, not without assistance, but he could scrub a little and put on fresh clothing. He studied his reflection in the mirror. He had more gray hairs than he recalled, and he made a face. His resemblance to his dad and to Pop could be seen, and he wondered if Addison had noticed yesterday. *I should call Dad.* The thought came and vanished. His father lived near Boise, Idaho, and Jeb seldom saw him. Sometimes he showed up to watch Jeb ride but it had been some time since he had.

Every once in a while, his father might call but he was usually drunk. He left Jeb behind not long after his wife, Jeb's mother, died and had seldom returned for more than a few days.

Still, since his old man followed his rodeo career, he would hear he'd been hurt. Jeb could be the better person and pick up the phone. He might summon the strength to make the call once he felt better. His back still twinged, so he gulped down ibuprofen, then tottered into the living room. Jeb settled into the recliner. When the pain med eased his hurt, he exhaled with relief.

His cell phone got smashed when he smacked into the arena, but Jeb tucked the pay-as-you-go model

Shelby provided into a pocket. He wore jeans, for the first time since the accident a week ago, paired with a snap button, faded-blue chambray shirt. He'd left them here last winter and would need to buy more. Jeb hadn't tried to put on his boots, but he wore socks so his toes wouldn't get cold.

Jeb almost forgot Aunt Jeannie planned to visit until he spotted a dark-green sedan traveling down the drive at slow speed. With the walker, he pulled himself upright and managed to meet her at the back door. "Hey, Auntie. Addy said you might bake a cake." He maneuvered so she could enter, a trickier move than he expected. *I guess this is what I have to look forward to, disability and difficulty.*

"I did. It's your favorite." Jeannie held up a plastic cake carrier. "You poor thing, you shouldn't be up. Do you want me to help you lie down?"

Bed was the last place he wanted to be. "No, I'm good. Just let me get out of your way, so you can come in." He traveled backward and made it to the kitchen without falling on his rump.

Jeannie trailed him with a frown. "Sit down so we can have cake. Do you want something to wash it down?" She glanced around the kitchen and pulled out a chair. "You should take a seat. You shouldn't be eating dessert now. It's lunchtime. Where's your home health aide anyway?"

"Shelby's a nurse. She ran into town, but she'll be back pretty quick." Jeb glanced out the window.

"Maybe I should hang around until she does. You're in no shape to be here alone." Jeannie walked to the counter where the coffeepot sat. "I'll make coffee before I go and cut you a piece of cake. If there's a can of soup or any deli meat, I'll fix you lunch, too."

Jeb swallowed a harsh protest. He loved his aunt, but she could be prickly. Right now, she reminded him how much his life had changed. If he hadn't been hurt, he'd still be on the circuit. On a Saturday, he would be competing tonight. "I'll take the coffee, but I'll wait on lunch. Got a buddy bringing my truck, and he should be here any time."

"You can't drive with a broken back!" She paused, placing coffee into the filter before placing it in the machine. She added water and flicked the switch.

"Aunt Jeannie, I didn't break my back. I've got a spinal fracture, but it's one vertebrae. I wouldn't be out of the hospital or limping around if I had." Jeb headed for the table, more than ready to sit.

"Well, still…" The woman fluttered her hands.

"I'll be driving in a few months so I might as well have the truck here." Jeb parked in a chair at the table. He hoped Shelby or Rob would arrive soon to run interference. As he savored his first sip of coffee, Jeb spotted his pickup as it exited the road and headed up the driveway.

The 1980s vintage, two-tone-blue model rolled to a halt. Rob climbed out and approached the house with his bowlegged cowboy walk. He didn't bother with knocking. "Jeb, I'm heading inside."

"Come on in!" Jeb bellowed with full force as he saw his aunt cringe. "I'm in the kitchen."

He stood using the table for support and hugged Rob. "Thanks, man, for driving the truck here."

"No problem, wheelhorse, no problem. Glad to do it. How are you? You look better than I expected. Thought you'd be laid up in bed." Rob removed his hat, pounded Jeb's shoulders, then sank into a chair. "I'd take a cup of coffee, if you've got it."

"You bet, there's plenty." Jeb lowered his body into a chair with effort.

Jeannie poured a cup and brought it over.

"Rob, this is my Aunt Jeannie, my mom's sis, and Auntie, this is my rodeo pal."

Rob extended his hand. "Rob Nugent."

Jeannie acknowledged him with a curt nod.

Rob shrugged. He shifted his focus from Jeannie back to Jeb. "Yeah, I worried how bad you got busted up when they carried you out of the arena. I would have come by to see you in the horse pistol, but I had to move on to the next rodeo."

Rob's funny name for hospital amused Jeb and he laughed. "I know the life well. How're you getting somewhere from here?"

A grin stretched Rob's lips. "I got a ride coming. She ought to be here any minute."

"She?" Jeb asked as a late-model silver pickup came into sight.

The driver wore a fancy cowboy hat trimmed in feathers. Long blonde hair escaped beneath it to her shoulders.

"Kentucky horse farm heiress, Arabella Andrews." Rob leaned forward and lowered his voice. "She's been following me on the circuit since last spring. She'll drive me back. Left my truck at her folks' spread."

"Is she a bunny?" Jeb had to ask.

Rob shook his head. "Nope. She's smitten with me. I gotta get going. It's Labor Day weekend, and we're heading down to Oklahoma for the PRCA Rodeo of Champions."

"At Elk City." It wasn't a question. Most years, Jeb had been there. Regret he wouldn't experience the annual event at the Beutler Brothers arena made his chest ache. He hated to lose the rodeo lifestyle and the thrill of competition. *Never gonna be in the arena again.*

"Yep. I'm not riding this year. We're just going for fun. Weren't you supposed to ride?" Rob stood and picked up his battered hat.

Jeb sighed. "I was. I'm already missing rodeo. Looks like I'm finished with it, more's the pity."

"Hallelujah!" Jeannie clapped her hands. "I've never approved of rodeo. I always hoped Jeb would get a real job."

Rob squinted and ignored Jeannie's outburst. "What do you mean? Ain't you bustin' broncs anymore?"

Jeb stared at his coffee cup. "Cain't, not after this. Docs said it'd be risky after this injury. I'd rather not end up a paraplegic." Jeb shuddered as he spoke. His greatest fear with his injury had been he'd be paralyzed. "Besides, I turn thirty-one in a few months. I'm getting old for it." Jeb hadn't quite adjusted to his future yet, but saying it aloud made it real. He didn't like it, though.

"Hush your mouth, son. I'm almost forty and still going strong." Rob scratched his head and put his hat back on.

The blonde tooted the horn three times.

Rob grinned. "She's impatient. I'd best go. Hang in there, Hillbilly Hotshot."

"Will do." Jeb shook hands with his buddy from his seat.

After the couple vanished down the road, Aunt Jeannie picked up her purse. "Unless you want me to fix something to eat, I need to go. I promised Aunt Tressa I'd come over. I made her gals dresses, but they needed to be hemmed."

Jeb rose and brushed a kiss across his aunt's cheek. "I appreciate the cake. I won't keep you. Shelby'll make lunch after she comes back from town."

"Tell her to take good care of you, Jebediah." Jeannie hugged him, then departed.

Alone with his thoughts, Jeb brooded. He replayed those last moments in the arena and wondered if he could have prevented his injury. Although he had no idea how, he wished he had. He'd be in Elk City now, not here.

More than an hour passed before Shelby arrived, her kids in tow. She carried a large bag. The delicious aroma of fried chicken wafted from it, and Jeb inhaled with delight.

"I brought home lunch. Chicken, mashed potatoes and gravy, corn on the cob, coleslaw, and biscuits. Are you hungry?" Shelby placed the containers on the counter.

"Starving. Aunt Jeannie brought over a cake." He pointed at the confection.

"I noticed. Is someone else here? I saw the truck." Shelby unpacked the bag with deft hands, then pulled paper plates from a kitchen shelf. She grabbed serving spoons and the butter. Shelby peeked through the window and relaxed when she spotted the kids playing near the house.

"It's mine. My friend brought it from Tennessee, but he's already gone. It's been parked down there at the arena." Jeb already missed driving and the freedom of going where he wanted.

Shelby nodded. "If you'd like, I can move it to wherever you want it parked."

"If you don't mind, pull it closer to the house." Jeb pushed the keys across the table. "Feel free to drive it instead of your car if you want. I won't be behind the wheel for a while."

She picked up the keychain and tucked it into a pocket. "Thanks. I still have to bring the rest of our suitcases and other stuff we'll need. It'll be easier with a truck. I can make one trip work."

"Sure, anytime, honey." Jeb nodded. "I'm ready to eat. Where's your kiddos?"

"They're playing in the yard." Shelby called them and reminded them to wash their hands. They came to the table as Jeb snared a drum and a thigh from the container.

Levi grabbed the other drumstick with a grin. "Legs are my favorite piece."

"Always was mine, too." Jeb resolved next time he'd let the boy have first choice. Jeb ate a good portion, pacing himself. He considered the cake but decided he lacked belly room. "Shelby, can we save the cake for supper?"

"It's your treat, so sure. Are you done with the chicken?" She gathered up the few leftovers to put in the fridge.

"I am." When he stood, his back spasmed hard, and he winced.

Shelby noticed as she finished clearing their trash. "It's about time for a pill. Do you want over-the-counter or prescription?"

"Ibuprofen's fine." Jeb had seen too many good cowboys get hooked on the high-powered pain meds. "I'm gonna crawl into bed for a nap, if you'll help." Her capable hands guided him to bed and started to position him prone. Jeb lifted his hands to protest. "I'd rather try propped against the pillows."

"All right but if it hurts, tell me." Shelby manipulated the bed and brought the mattress to a forty-five-degree angle. "I'm heading back to town for our stuff, but I'll be right back." She leaned close to fix the pillows under his head.

He caught a whiff of a sweet fragrance. Lavender, he thought, and liked it. "I'm not going anywhere."

Shelby chortled. "I hope to shout not."

For a half second, Jeb thought she was about to kiss his cheek.

She stroked it with three fingers. "You've got bristles. Remind me and I'll give you a shave later. Thanks again for letting me use the truck."

Jeb parted his lips to object to being shaved, then closed his mouth. Washing up at the bathroom sink had proved more difficult than he expected. Shaving would be worse. "*De nada.* Be careful."

Halfway across the room, Shelby turned. "Don't worry. I won't put a scratch on your vehicle."

"I don't care about the truck." He did but not so much. "I meant you and your kids stay safe."

A blush touched her cheeks, then faded. "I appreciate it. Rest well, Jeb."

He reclined and listened as she rounded up her kids and loaded them into the pickup. The familiar growl of the engine delighted Jeb, and he anticipated the day when he could drive again. Jeb drifted into an uneasy sleep, dreamed of the arena, and relived the brutal moment when he'd been hurt. He woke thirsty, hurting, and out of sorts.

Lexi tiptoed through the dining room, cradling a baby doll wrapped in pink blanket in her arms. The little girl whispered to her dolly. "Sh! Don't wake Jeb. He's hurt and needs his rest. Mama said. We have to be good."

Jeb shut his eyes and feigned sleep, doing his best to wear a sleep face when he ached to grin. He listened as Lexi's small feet pattered up the steps, still talking to her doll baby. Jeb tried to guess which room was her destination. In addition to the guest room downstairs, which he would use once he graduated from the hospital bed, the house had four more bedrooms on the second floor. Jeb's overlooked the front lawn as it sloped down to the road. Two more rooms were on the west side of the hall and the last bedroom was on the east. The old-fashioned bathroom at the opposite end of the corridor had both a clawfoot tub and a stall shower. From Lexi's footsteps, Jeb guessed she picked the east bedroom. During his childhood, it had served as his playroom. His grandmother had turned it into a guest room although he doubted anyone ever stayed there.

With precise moves, Jeb shifted position and swung his legs over the side of the mattress, reaching for the walker.

Levi slammed the back door and burst into the adjacent kitchen. "Mom, can I watch TV? I want to watch the cartoon about the race car driver." Unlike his sister, he made no effort to be quiet as he bolted through the dining room.

Shelby trailed behind her son. "Lower your voice.

You can't watch anything while Jeb's asleep because the only television downstairs is in here. Even when he wakes, whether or not you watch is up to him."

"Mom, please." Levi stretched 'mom' into three syllables.

Jeb chuckled. "It's fine, Levi. I'm awake. I always liked the same cartoon."

Shelby appeared, one hand on her son's shoulder. "If he woke you…"

"He didn't. There's another TV in my room upstairs. It's mounted on the wall and gets better reception, as well as streaming services. Levi, I don't mind if you watch your show in my bedroom, as long as you ask first." Jeb placed his hands on the walker and concentrated on standing.

The little boy's face brightened. "Awesome! Can I go up now, please?"

Jeb grinned. "Sure, it's the front bedroom, and the remote should be on the nightstand. Bring up the menu and take your pick. Can't get anything streaming downstairs, anyway."

"Thank you, Jeb." Levi escaped his mother's hand and headed for the stairs.

"Just until I serve supper, Levi," Shelby called after him. "Tell Lexi we'll eat at six."

Jeb pulled himself upright. "What time is it, anyway?"

"Four thirty." She steadied him as he positioned the walker. "Go easy, hotshot, and don't hurt yourself."

"Huh?" He didn't understand what she meant.

"You're trying to do too much. You only came home yesterday, Jeb. I'm here to help you, so let me." Shelby adjusted the height of the device. "Where do you want to go?"

"Bathroom, then kitchen." One slow step after another required effort, but he made it. The short trek sapped his strength more than Jeb wanted to admit, but he reached his chair at the dinette. Jeb reflected a week ago, he had been goofing around at the arena in Tennessee, joking and laughing. He anticipated his ride, figured he would make eight seconds with a high score or scratch. Afterward, he'd planned to devour a thick cowboy-cut ribeye steak.

If he hadn't suffered an injury, his next move would have been to hightail it to the nearest rodeo. Considering what happened, Jeb realized he had done better than expected. Most people would remain laid up, but he'd never been one to linger in bed, sick or well. He caught his breath and watched Shelby move about the kitchen.

Without asking, she poured a cup of coffee and placed it on the table.

"Thanks. What's for supper?" Jeb stirred a half teaspoon of sugar into the brew and sipped.

"Cheeseburger pie." Shelby stirred a chopped onion into a skillet to brown, then added ground beef. "I'll have to go grocery shopping Monday. You didn't have much food on hand."

"I'll pay." Jeb reached into his pocket for his wallet before he realized the trifold must be with his stuff from the hospital. He needed to track it down. They'd given him a bag with his possessions.

"Of course, you will. If you waited for me to buy groceries, you'd starve to death." She meant it. She lacked money for a big supermarket trip and faked a laugh.

Jeb didn't think she joked. He'd already figured money must be an issue for her.

"I found a chicken in your freezer, so I'll roast it tomorrow with potatoes and stuffing. Whatever else you want, let me know. I'm making a list."

Jeb thought of a dozen things but didn't reach for a pen. He sipped coffee, brewed strong the way he preferred, and watched Shelby work. She moved with swift grace, hands dexterous, concentrating on the task. He'd lived solo and lonely for so long he'd forgotten what having a woman in the house could add. He liked her presence, found her pretty, and appreciated her assistance. "I'm gonna need my wallet. I think it's probably in the bag the hospital gave me. Do you know where it might be?"

"I do." Shelby walked into the dining room and pulled it from the sideboard drawer. "I put it up so it wouldn't get lost."

Jeb counted the cash tucked inside, then thrust it and his debit card at Shelby. "You'll need this when you go shopping. I'll give you the PIN number, too."

She held the thin plastic between two fingers. "Are you sure? You haven't known me very long. What if I'm not trustworthy?"

He rose and, without the walker, tottered a few steps to where she stood. Jeb caught her chin with his right hand. "I have no doubt you are." His gaze met hers. "I've already trusted you with my life and house. Why wouldn't I?"

Shelby flushed. "You can, but, Jeb, you should know better than to trust a stranger."

"It's not anyone. It's you." He removed his grasp and managed to make it to the table.

"Thank you," she spoke in a soft voice. "Jeb, you're different than any patient I've ever had."

Over the simple but savory supper, Shelby and her children chattered while Jeb listened. He chimed in occasionally, but mostly he sat back and enjoyed the conversation.

Levi shared his admiration for racecars, with enthusiasm.

Memories of the vintage cartoon returned. If Jeb recalled right, the teenage character competed on the international racing scene. As a kid, he'd found the animated racing show exciting. Now Jeb thought it sounded too much like the circuit he'd ridden for fifteen years. *Probably just as grueling in reality.*

"Blake said there are race car models you can build," Levi announced with enthusiasm. "I want one."

"Finish your meal if you'd like cake." Shelby sidestepped the request.

Levi scooped the last bites of his meat pie into his mouth, then nodded. "I hope I get a model for Christmas, Mama."

Shelby frowned. "Christmas is a long time away, and you know we don't focus on presents. It's about the birth of Jesus, not getting gifts."

"I want a baby buggy for Molly and maybe one of those doll houses." Lexi stacked her empty plate on top of her brother's. "Right now, though, I want dessert."

Jeb had no idea why, but the talk of toys brought tension into the room.

Shelby squared her shoulders, fidgeted with her silverware, and stared at the table. "So do I. Let's cut the cake."

Jeb's mouth watered as he anticipated the sweet

flavor. The oatmeal confection with brown sugar, coconut, and pecan frosting tasted as wonderful as he remembered. Jeb devoured a slice, then prepared to ask for a second when he realized neither child had touched theirs. "Don't you like the cake?"

Levi wrinkled his nose. "It's got plastic on top. You can't eat plastic."

Shelby frowned at the boy. "Levi Wayne Thacker! It's coconut."

Jeb swallowed a chuckle. The kid had a point. "It's not plastic, though the coconut kind looks like it could be. This is one of my favorite cakes. I always had it for my birthday. I still do if I'm home. It's incredibly good. You might like it if you tried it."

"I don't like the way it looks." Lexi made a face.

"Granny told me you don't eat with your eyes. Once I listened, I realized I liked all kinds of foods I thought I hated." Jeb grinned.

Both kids stared at Jeb.

"Like what?" Levi crossed his arms over his chest.

"Guacamole dip. It's green, and when I was older than you guys, I told Granny it looked like snot." Jeb still remembered the fixed stare his grandmother shot in his direction. "Refried beans were another. I wouldn't touch a banana because I didn't like the shape or color. I could keep going."

"Tell me one more and maybe I'll try a bite." Levi unfolded his arms.

"Raisins." Jeb laughed as he said the word. "I thought they looked like dried, wrinkled-up bugs."

Lexi picked up her fork and took a tiny taste between pursed lips. Her expression changed as she chewed it, then she had another. Her eyes grew big. "It *is* good. It tastes sweet."

Levi took a bite and chewed it. He swallowed. "It's not bad. I'll eat my piece of cake."

Jeb savored each crumb of his second piece, smiling.

As she shook her head, Shelby grinned.

Perhaps dealing with kids wasn't so hard after all. Like the little ones taking a taste, Jeb had given it a chance, and so far, he liked the interaction. *Maybe these kids will keep my mind off everything I've lost.*

Chapter Four

Shelby remembered as babies, her littles ate everything she spooned into their mouths, from thin rice cereal to green goo from baby food jars and smashed potatoes. Then they developed their own palates and rejected much of what they once liked. One food at a time, she had convinced them to try new things, but it often proved to be an uphill battle.

She knew from the moment she saw the cake's topping neither of her kids would eat any, but she tried. Neither touched the coconut until Jeb got involved. Shelby almost asked him to mind his business since he wasn't a parent but didn't. Now, as Levi and Lexi gobbled cake, she realized she had been wise not to interfere.

For a man who admitted he hadn't been around children often, Jeb had a rapport with them. He related, either since he drew on his own childhood to bridge the gap or because his laid-back personality resonated. Her children liked the man, and so did Shelby, more than she should since he was her patient. *I have to be careful. I can't get emotionally involved with him.*

Bath time and bedtime took longer than usual in the new setting. Shelby tucked Levi and Lexi into unfamiliar beds but left the hall light on, so they could find their way to the bathroom, if necessary. She trudged downstairs to spend more time with Jeb.

He rested in his recliner and balanced a notebook in his lap. Jeb jotted down a list. His forehead was furrowed as he wrote. He hunched his shoulders with deep concentration.

Lamplight highlighted the silver strands in his hair, and he had good color but Shelby found his appearance wasn't as haggard as when he arrived. She sank into the rocking chair across the room. "We should rent an overbed table."

"What's that?" Jeb looked up.

"A rolling tray table like in the hospital. It's easy to raise or lower and fits over the bed.

"I don't need one." Jeb shook his head. "There's an old set of TV trays around here somewhere to do almost the same thing. I hope I'm out of the hospital bed soon, anyway."

Shelby dropped the overbed table notion. Arguing wasn't her job. "I'll see if I can find them tomorrow. You can ask Tuesday about the bed."

His expression shifted to a blank stare, then he blinked. "I almost forgot I have an appointment. I see the doctor at ten, right?"

She nodded. "Yes. He'll check how you're doing and then work out a physical therapy plan. You must decide if you want to go to a clinic or have a therapy nurse come here."

Jeb sighed, then put down the notebook to rub his face with both hands. "Can't you help me with therapy?"

"I wish, but I'm not trained in PT." Shelby slipped off her shoes. "We'd better make a list of things to ask the doctor. I also want to be sure we get you a back brace. I'm surprised they didn't send one."

"They tried. I said *no*. I didn't want to be trussed up like a prisoner at the county jail." Jeb scowled.

Shelby held in a laugh as she imagined him wearing an orange jumpsuit. "You need one, though, Jeb. You won't wear it more than an hour or two a day, but it'll help your back heal. I'll assist with choosing a less-restrictive one."

"All right. I want to graduate to a cane, too, from the walker." Jeb pulled himself up. "I'm headed for the bathroom and bed. I must be about as much a handful as your kids."

Shelby giggled. "They're not any trouble, and neither are you. I'm ready for bed myself. Tomorrow we all need to rest. Tuesday will be a busy day."

Most Sundays, Shelby took the children to church at the same large brick structure she attended as a child. This week, she opted to remain on the farm. One, Shelby didn't want to leave Jeb any longer than necessary, and two, both she and the children needed to adapt to their new surroundings. She had laundry, her own list to make and the one for Jeb's household.

Both kids brought home additional requests for school supplies, which would stretch her tiny budget. Although Monday would be Labor Day, Shelby had no plans except grocery shopping. If Tuesday weren't earmarked for Jeb's doctor visit, she would have waited.

Shelby made peanut butter chocolate chip muffins for breakfast and fried some bacon.

As soon as they finished eating, the kids begged to go outside.

"Can we explore?" Levi carried an old backpack. "I've got bottled water, some crackers, and a couple of cookies each."

She bit her lip and considered his request. Her first impulse was to say *no* because they weren't familiar with rural life. "All right. Stay close, though. If I can't see you, at least be within hollering range, okay?"

Her son grinned. "You bet. And I'll mind Lexi."

Levi and Lexi spent the morning exploring the farm, near the house, barn, and sloping front yard. Shelby peeked outside often. Levi's orange T-shirt and Lexi's pink dress were always visible.

"They're having fun," Jeb spoke from memory. "Don't fret so much."

"Guilty as charged but I can't help but worry." Shelby smiled. "I think of things like snakes or them falling in a ditch or running across a wild animal."

He laughed. "There might be a few snakes but they're harmless ringnecks. They'll be fine."

Although she wasn't as certain, she nodded. Jeb meant well but he wasn't a parent and didn't totally understand.

After shaving Jeb as promised, Shelby got busy in the kitchen while her patient relaxed with a book in the living room. She baked cornbread for the dressing, then mixed all the ingredients, and stuffed the five-pound chicken. Shelby peeled and cut potatoes into quarters, seasoned the bird, and put it in the oven. She made a tossed salad and opened a can of corn to serve on the side.

Music rang through the quiet house. Her first thought was Jeb had turned on a radio or a TV program, but the sound had an immediate quality. Shelby wiped her hands on a towel and followed the sound.

Jeb sat at the piano, head down, as his fingers

skimmed the keys with agile ease.

She crossed the hardwood floor to stand behind him and listened. The tune was an upbeat hymn dating to the 1970s. Shelby loved the song and waited until after the refrain, then she sang.

Jeb swiveled his head without missing a note or losing the beat and offered a grin. Their voices blended in the gospel favorite. After the song ended, Jeb shifted into the classic hymn, "Amazing Grace."

Shelby sang, but this time Jeb didn't. She wondered why not until he finished.

"Granny's favorite." He turned around on the bench and gazed at Shelby. Tears glistened in his eyes. "I can't sing it without flashing back to her funeral."

Shelby placed a hand on his right shoulder. "It's a beautiful hymn. I didn't know you had faith. Do you go to church?"

"Not very often and never when I'm out on the circuit." Jeb stared at the floor and scooted over. "I sometimes go when I'm home in the offseason. There's a little church not far down the road. It's my home church, where we went when I was a kid. I wouldn't mind going now or at least when I can get around. Seems like I have so much to be thankful about." *Like being able to walk and have a full recovery. Maybe if I do, God might fix it so I can ride again. I can hope.*

Shelby sat next to him on the piano bench. "I wouldn't mind coming along. I'd be there if you need help. I usually take the kids to church, but I didn't want to drive into town today. We're all tired. I wanted to give Levi and Lexi extra time to get settled. I also don't want to push my car."

"I told you to use the truck whenever you need it.

It's not just for when I'm riding shotgun. Your car isn't running well. I heard it when you took off yesterday." Jeb twined his fingers around hers.

She sighed. "I know. It uses too much oil, and the engine started knocking. I checked with a mechanic, and he said it could be anything–water pump, alternator, timing belt, compressor, or the crankshaft. All can be serious and expensive."

"You'd better get it fixed before it leaves you on foot, honey." Jeb released her hand.

"I would if I could afford it." Shelby poked her hair behind her ears. "I still owe on the car, too."

Jeb stilled. "If I'm not paying you enough money, I can up the amount."

Shelby ached to hug him. Instead, she rested her head against his shoulder for a moment. "It's not that, Jeb, but thanks." She balled her hands into fists because she hated talking about money. Shelby could appreciate his well-meant intentions but she hated to feel like he offered charity. To avoid being rude in rejecting his offer, she tried to explain. "I don't pay rent or have a mortgage because the house belonged to my grandparents, but the utilities are high. The house is old and has so many problems I can't get repaired right now. I really need a roof, but that's way out of reach. I dipped into what little savings I had to buy the kids new shoes for school and a new outfit. They need more school supplies when they go back on Tuesday. I still owe on my husband's hospital bill and a bunch of other stuff."

Unshed sobs gathered in her throat and made her chest hurt. Shelby wept as Jeb slid an arm around her shoulders. Her life lacked kindness or tenderness.

"Oh, Lord, don't cry." Jeb didn't deal well with women's tears. He never knew what he should say or do so the moment became awkward for him. "Is this why you didn't want the kids to talk about what they want for Christmas?" He pulled tissues from his pocket. "Money trouble?"

"Yes." Shelby blotted her eyes. "I'll be lucky if I can buy them one present each. Mom always buys things they need like winter coats or pajamas. I don't encourage the idea Santa will come because there won't be many gifts. I haven't even put up a Christmas tree since Jimmy died."

"Those kids need a tree and some presents under it. I can help." Jeb took her hand in his for a brief moment.

"No, no, it's okay. I don't want a handout or charity." Shelby shook her head. "This job already helps more than you could ever think. If not for it, I might have had to move in with my mom. Her house is small, and her job doesn't pay very much. I shouldn't unload my troubles to you." She stood and took a step away. "I need to check on dinner."

"Ain't no hurry, Shelby. Sit back a minute so your kids don't come in and see you've been crying." Jeb patted her shoulder.

"Okay." She returned to the bench and blew her nose.

"Can I ask you something? It's really not my business." He shifted closer and met her gaze.

Shelby shrugged. "Go ahead."

"What happened to your husband?" Jeb reached for the walker with his free hand and pulled it closer.

"Jimmy worked for the state highway department. Usually, he operated the road paver, but the day he suffered injuries, he had been picking up the orange cones on a finished stretch of highway. An elderly driver became distracted by a wasp in the car, swerved, and ran over him. He didn't die for a couple of days." Shelby paused to draw a breath. She twisted her hands together as she struggled to find words. Things hadn't been perfect in her marriage to Jimmy but his death still hurt. "It happened three years ago, the week before the Fourth of July. One more reason why I'm not into holidays."

Jeb leaned close, kissed her cheek, and nodded. "I'm sorry, Shelby."

Her face tingled where his lips touched; although she knew it had been a friendly, not romantic, gesture. "Me, too. It is what it is, though. I just keep on keeping on."

"What about his parents? Don't they help with the kids?"

"Jimmy's parents both died before we met." She pressed her lips together for a frown. "So, no."

The back door slammed with a reverberation strong enough to shake the house.

"Mom!" Levi shouted. "Lexi's hurt."

Shelby bolted from the bench and dashed to the kitchen, heart pounding. She imagined a broken arm, sprained ankle, or knock to the head, but her daughter entered behind her brother.

Blood ran from a skinned knee as Lexi sobbed. "Mama, I'm bleeding. Make it stop."

Relief made Shelby dizzy. "Sit down. I'll fix it."

Jeb stumbled into the kitchen. The walker clicked against the tile floor as he hurried. "Is she okay?"

"Just a skinned knee. Levi, bring the first aid kit

from the car, please. I don't have any adhesive bandages or anything." Shelby grabbed a clean dishcloth, wet it, and washed the scrape with a gentle touch.

"Everything you need is in the bathroom cabinet. It's closer. I've got bandages, peroxide, antibacterial cream…everything." Jeb halted beside the table but didn't sit.

Levi dashed to fetch the items.

Shelby knelt, blotting the wound as the bleeding slowed.

"Does she need stitches?" Levi patted his sister on the head.

The girl shied away.

"No, thank goodness." Shelby applied peroxide which fizzed and bubbled on the broken skin. She placed a bandage over it. "There. It's okay now, Lexie. Hush crying. We're about ready to eat."

"Hold me, Mama," Lexie wailed. She held her arms out.

"Give me a minute, sweetie." Shelby's heart ached for her daughter. The oven timer sounded. "I have to get dinner out of the oven first if we want to eat." Shelby put oven mitts on her hands and pulled the roaster from the oven.

Lexi rushed to Jeb. She lifted her arms upward.

Jeb hoisted the child without hesitation and held her close.

Lexi wrapped her arms around his neck, clinging like an opossum.

His expression shifted as Jeb turned pale, then staggered into the nearest chair. He had the little girl in his arms.

Shelby placed the roaster on the top of the stove and tossed down the mitts. "Be careful and don't hurt your back! You're not supposed to be lifting anything. Are you hurting?"

"I ain't, not much." His attempt to grin failed. "Lexi needed a hug."

"I planned to pick her up and hug her tight as soon as I pulled the chicken out." Shelby expelled a sigh as she took her daughter from his arms and cradled her. "Lexi, honey, I'm sorry."

"It's okay. You were busy so Jeb gave me hugs." The little girl smiled at Jeb.

"I saw." Shelby inhaled the fragrance of her daughter's baby shampoo. They grew up so quickly. "How's the knee now?"

"It stings." Lexi had a whine in her voice. "Can you kiss it and make it better?"

"Of course, I can." Shelby lowered the child to the floor and kissed the bandage. She turned to her son. "Levi, can you set the table?"

"Sure." The boy grabbed a stack of paper napkins, then reached into a drawer for silverware. As he placed a spoon, knife, and fork at each place, he squinted, his forehead furrowed as he tried to do the job right.

"Go wash up, kids." Shelby removed the stuffing from the bird and carved the chicken. She delivered the food to the table. "Are you all right, Jeb?"

"I'll do." Jeb hunched forward in the chair. "Let's eat."

Shelby frowned. Jeb appeared stiff from the way he sat, and she suspected he was in pain. She said nothing. She wouldn't want Lexi to feel bad or consider it her fault. Instead, she asked the blessing. Midway through the meal, Shelby's cell phone on the counter rang. "I'd better answer. Hello."

"Hi." Delia greeted. "I hope I'm not interrupting anything. I thought I might run out, grab the kids, and take them to get those things for school. I miss them being around the corner."

"We've only been gone a day, Mom, but sure. I'd appreciate it. We're eating, but we'll be finished before you arrive." Relief flooded Shelby. The kids would get the things they needed, and she didn't have to spend money. "I'll see you soon."

She returned to the table and picked up her fork. "Grandma's coming to take you to get the rest of your school stuff. As soon as you're finished eating, get ready to go."

"I'm done." Levi scraped the last bite of potatoes from his plate. "I want cake, though."

"You can have a piece with supper." Shelby eyed Jeb. "I can cut you a piece, Jeb."

His brow knitted in a tense line as he stacked his silverware on his empty plate. "I'll wait, too. I could use ibuprofen, though, and a refill on iced tea."

Shelby dosed him, then cleared the table. As she scrubbed the last pan, she saw her mother park near the house. "Come on inside, Mom," Shelby yelled through the open window.

Delia tooted the horn. "Send the kids out. I'll visit with you when I bring them back."

"Be good for your grandma." Shelby kissed each child on the forehead. She watched as they sprinted to the car and climbed inside. Once they'd gone, she approached the table and sat across from Jeb. "Are you all right? You look like you're in pain."

"I'm hurting a bit, but it's not bad. I do think I'll rest a while if you'll help me lay down." He grasped the walker and rose with a groan.

For the first time, Shelby wished he'd use the wheelchair with which he had arrived. It had been relegated to the back porch. If he'd injured his back more, he shouldn't be using the walker. She kept the notion to herself and positioned Jeb in bed on his side. "If it hurts too much, tell me. I can take you to the emergency room or call an ambulance."

"No way. Picking up Lexi didn't hurt me much. It's just sore." Jeb grimaced.

"Jeb, you need to be more careful. I had one patient who didn't do what he should have after back surgery. He refused to go through his exercises or walk or anything. He ended up in surgery again after two months, then needed a third one."

"Did he recover?" Jeb's gaze met hers.

"No, he ended up as a quadriplegic and spent the rest of his life in a nursing home." Shelby pushed a stray lock of hair away from Jeb's face. "It was sad. I wouldn't want to see the same happen to you."

"You and me, both, honey. Do you think a heating pad would help?" He shifted position and winced.

"Maybe, if there's one here." She hoped so. Her supplies didn't include one, and she'd rather not trek to town to buy one.

"I got one upstairs, in my bedroom. It should be in the second dresser drawer. Cain't do saddle bronc riding without getting stiff and sore." He bit his lip and moaned.

Shelby suspected he downplayed how much he hurt but didn't call him out. Shelby located the heating pad. Once she had it plugged in and in position, she dragged the rocking chair from the living room so she could sit with him. She needed to assess his condition and make sure if he needed medical attention, he got it. "Sleep if you can. I'll be right here." Shelby settled into the rocker.

"I'm not tired. It feels good to lie down, though." He shifted his head on the pillows to meet her gaze. "Do you want to grill burgers or hot dogs tomorrow for Labor Day? I've got a gas grill on the back porch under a cover. I think there's still a charcoal one in the barn."

"Maybe after I run to the store. We'll see." Shelby set the rocker moving in slow motion.

Eventually, Jeb slept.

Shelby managed the laundry, folded clothes, and put them away. She searched through closets and found the TV trays he'd mentioned. After choosing one without a wobble, she cleaned it and carried it to the living room. It wasn't tall enough to work in bed, but Jeb could use it with his recliner. Since supper would be leftover chicken served with biscuits and cream gravy, time hung heavy, and she had little to do. Shelby prowled the house and took a closer look at the photos hanging on the walls. Shelby recognized a younger Jeb in more than one. His features hadn't changed as much as matured.

Curious, she picked up a photo album and opened it. Numerous pictures filled the pages, but there were also rodeo clippings about Jeb. The earliest dated back to when he was a teen, then continued until about five years ago. Written comments were inked on the wide margins. Shelby squinted to make out the elaborate old-school handwriting. She read the captions aloud. "'My grandson,' 'Jebediah at the rodeo,' and 'the night he won a buckle'." His grandmother must have compiled the collection. Shelby smiled at the idea, and since the last photo was five years old, Shelby guessed it might have been when the woman died.

Shelby found a bookshelf crammed with older volumes. She read the authors' names, Grace Livingston Hill, John Steinbeck, Frank Yerby, and Edna Ferber. She noted classics like *Oliver Twist, Anne of Green Gables,* and *The Last of the Mohicans* had been shelved beside newer novels. Delighted to find reading material, she wondered what book Jeb had been reading earlier. The paperback rested on the lamp table beside the recliner, a bookmark placed between the pages. Shelby picked the novel up. The book was James Michener's *Centennial*.

She had read the title and liked it. Shelby wondered if Jeb chose the novel from boredom or if he might be an avid reader, diving into an old favorite. Earlier, looking for the TV trays, she'd found a bookcase with children's books old enough they must have been Jeb's. Shelby recognized familiar titles, but she didn't know many of the others.

Shelby could read to the kids again, a habit she'd fallen away from in the last year or two. As her job demanded more, she read less. Without a commute, she might pick up reading again, both to the children and for herself.

Imagining having book discussions with Jeb brought a smile as she settled into his recliner and opened the pages of a novel she'd never read.

This job had perks she'd never dreamed about, and she liked it. Living in someone else's house, though, seemed awkward, and she wondered how long the arrangement might last.

Chapter Five

Labor Day dawned cloudy, and by breakfast, heavy rain fell. Jeb woke early, his back sore, but overall, he felt better. He managed to sit and reached for the walker with stiff limbs. His house loomed quiet, and he didn't think anyone else had risen. Jeb made his way to the bathroom without an aide, but he used caution. He recalled what Shelby said about her client who ended up quadriplegic and decided not to push too hard. He didn't notice his truck wasn't outside until he made coffee and poured the first cup. *Where in tarnation could Shelby have gone so early?* Curious about her whereabouts and concerned, Jeb picked up the phone. "Where are you?"

"I'm at the store." Shelby named a discount retailer offering both groceries and goods. "Since it's raining, I decided to get it over with. How's your back?"

Jeb grunted. "Tolerable. Why didn't you tell me you were going?"

"You were asleep. I didn't think you'd wake until I got back. I left you a note on the fridge."

He hadn't looked, but when he did, he saw it. Jeb pulled the piece of lined notebook paper with ragged edges from the front of the harvest-gold refrigerator. Her looped cursive handwriting filled half the page with a simple message. "I've got it now." Jeb noticed she had drawn a heart after her name. A funny, warm happiness swelled within his chest, and he grinned. "If the kids wake up, should I feed them?"

"I'll pick up something in town, unless you'd rather do something else."

A bag of sausage biscuits or a box of donuts appealed. "Sure, that's fine. Use my card for it, too. Don't spend your money."

"Don't worry, I won't. Thanks." Shelby wouldn't because she couldn't. *Must be nice not to worry over every dollar.*

A few seconds passed and she gave a light laugh. "I'll be there soon."

"All righty." Jeb changed from flannel sleep pants into his jeans before Levi or Lexi came downstairs. Jeb settled into his recliner to wait. The kids rushed downstairs.

"Where's my mom?" Levi dashed to the kitchen and back. He glared at Jeb.

"She went to the supermarket." Jeb downed the last of his coffee. The kid acted like he'd made Shelby vanish. "I talked to her on the phone. She'll bring breakfast when she comes."

"Okay. Can we watch TV?" Levi paced the room.

"You won't be able to get much down here on the old set, and your mom won't be long. How about we head to the kitchen instead?" Jeb craved another cup of coffee.

"I guess." Levi shrugged. "C'mon, Lexi."

Jeb filled his mug and offered the children apple juice.

"I'd rather have orange." Levi wrinkled his nose.

"Apple's all there is until your mom gets here."

The rain slacked into light showers by the time

Shelby returned. Jeb considered stepping out to help carry the bags but didn't. He hadn't used the walker outside yet, and he didn't want to chance a fall.

Shelby entered with a bag of fast-food biscuits. "Lexi, put these on the table. I'll be right back with the groceries. Levi, come help me."

Jeb poured coffee for Shelby, and at Lexi's suggestion, he filled two tumblers with milk. He also brought a stack of napkins to the table.

Together, Shelby and Levi toted multiple sacks and dumped them on the counter. Shelby put the perishables away. She began placing the other goods in cupboards and on shelves.

"Sit down and eat. I'll help put stuff away after breakfast." Jeb eased into a chair.

"It won't take but a minute." Shelby lifted three cans of salmon and placed them on a rack filled with canned goods.

"Coffee'll get cold. There's no rush."

"You're right. I get in a hurry, sometimes." Shelby laughed and found a seat. She took her children's hands and grasped Jeb's.

They waited, staring at him. *They want me to say the blessing.* Jeb fumbled and found a few words. "Dear Lord, thank You for each of us around this table. I thank You for the companionship and fellowship. Thanks for the food. Let it nourish our bodies, and let us all be safe, healthy, and happy."

"And let Jeb heal," Levi added.

"Amen." Shelby grasped the sack and handed out the sausage, egg, and cheese biscuits. There was a biscuit each for the little ones and two each for her and Jeb. She dug deeper for hash browns and passed them around the table. "I hardly ever pick up fast food, especially not for breakfast, but it's raining so I thought it'd make a nice treat."

"It does." Jeb munched a bite of biscuit. He liked it although on the circuit, he relied far too much on fast food. "I guess we won't grill today with this weather."

"I doubt it." Shelby sipped coffee with an appreciative sigh. "I bought a bag of catfish fillets, so I thought I'd make those for supper instead, with fried taters and roasting ears."

His mouth watered. "I ain't had catfish in a long time. It sounds good. What about hush puppies?"

"I can make some if you want." Her lips twitched, then she smiled.

Jeb noticed for the first time she wasn't wearing scrubs. Faded blue jeans suited Shelby and so did the pale pink blouse decorated with deep-pink and yellow roses. She had tucked her hair up with a plastic clip, and he liked the view of her pretty features. "I do, so thanks." He planned to enjoy the meal she offered.

He lingered in the kitchen after Shelby put it to rights, pleased with her company. When he reached for the walker, she placed a hand on his shoulder.

"Wait. I'll get your vitals while you're sitting there." She picked up a spiral notebook from the counter and a pen. "Let me get my nurses' kit." Shelby rolled up his left sleeve and attached a blood pressure cuff, then pumped it up. She tucked the ends of a stethoscope into her ears and listened. She jotted down a number with a slight frown. "It's a little elevated, Jeb. Do you have high blood pressure?"

Jeb shrugged. "I'm not aware, no. But I don't get to the docs much usually. Should I worry?"

"I don't think so. What's your pain level?" Shelby clipped an oxygen monitor onto his finger. "Be honest, not macho."

"Five or six. It hurts more when I'm moving, though." Since yesterday, the occasional pain grew sharper with motion, but it wasn't unbearable.

"That's likely why the blood pressure's up. Your blood oxygen is great." Shelby wrote more digits in the notebook. "Let's check your temperature." She inserted a digital thermometer in his ear and leaned close.

Jeb inhaled her fragrance, some floral perfume and shampoo. Her warm breath wafted against his cheek. A line from an old Peggy Lee song about fever popped into Jeb's head. "It's probably ninety-nine, always is, always has been."

The device beeped, and she removed it. "Ninety-nine point five. If that's normal for you, it is. Ninety-eight point six is an average. Most people's body temperature isn't exactly ninety-eight point six." Shelby's slender fingers rested on his wrist as she took his pulse, then counted his breaths. "Pulse and respiration are both good."

"Do I pass?" Jeb resisted an urge to tug her hair.

"You're fine." Shelby put away her equipment and stroked back a stray strand of his hair.

Jeb peered at the notebook. "Do you keep track and turn those stats in or what?"

Shelby laughed. "I'll take it with us tomorrow to the doctor so he has a baseline. I keep track so I notice if there are any major changes in your condition."

He had almost forgotten about the upcoming doctor's appointment and the physical therapy planning session. "Right. I'd like to take a shower if I can before tomorrow."

"We'll see. At the moment, what do you want to do?" Shelby questioned.

Jeb considered his limited choices, watch television or a movie, read, play the piano, engage in a card game like solitaire, or stare at the walls. He definitely didn't want a nap, although he might later. He enjoyed talking to Shelby and to her kids, but he'd love some fresh air. "I'd like to sit on the front porch for a little bit." He loved listening to rain and seldom had a chance.

"Good idea. Let me check out the porch. Is there a swing or what?" Shelby closed the notebook and slid it beneath her purse on the counter.

"Some old-fashioned metal chairs and a glider." Jeb stood. He would need shoes to sit outside. "There are cushions for the glider in the guest room closet."

"I'll find them. I'll ask the kids if they'd like to go outside, too. I'll help you get to one of the chairs so you don't have to drag the walker." Shelby bustled out of the room.

Jeb drew a deep breath and made his way into the living room. He kept an old pair of sneakers beside his recliner. Putting them on took effort. But since he already wore socks, he managed to slide his feet into them—although he couldn't bend to tie them.

"Let me do it." Shelby dropped the floral cushions onto the couch and knelt. Once finished, she helped him to his feet.

With slow steps and her support, he walked several feet to the door. To steady him, Shelby put her arm around his waist until he sank into one of the metal seats. He gripped the chair arms and took a long breath of rain-scented morning.

"Are you okay?" She remained close, hands wide to catch him if he slid onto the floor.

"Yeah." Jeb relaxed his taut posture and managed a grin.

"I'm going to get the kids and those cushions. Don't try to get up, please."

He wasn't sure he could. "I won't."

Five minutes later, the two kids worked the glider back and forth in easy rhythm.

Shelby slid a pillow behind Jeb's back before she settled into the chair beside him. "If you want some more coffee or tea, let me know." She stretched out her hand across the small round table between them to touch his.

"I will." Jeb folded his fingers around hers. "I needed this." Rain drummed a steady cadence on the porch roof, and the sound soothed his spirits. The clean country air filled his lungs as contentment wrapped him like a favorite blanket. Jeb drank in the sight of the farm, the sloping lawn, the familiar gravel road, and the pastures where he hoped to run cattle again. This homeplace ranked as his favorite spot in the entire world, his touchstone, and his strength. Until he got hurt, he had forgotten how much he loved it here. Although he had spent some of each off season here, Jeb realized he had been away too long.

On any other Labor Day, he would have been in an arena, waiting his turn to ride a crazy horse. The smell of popcorn, peanuts, and barbecue from the concessions had filled his nose. So had tobacco wafting from the cowboys who smoked or chewed. Dust from the ring rose in clouds to dry out his nose and coat his throat. If it rained, the particular aroma of mud would replace it.

Jeb could almost catch the rangy smell of horses and bulls. Unanticipated regret welled up within. Although being home felt good, Jeb ached for rodeo. He would miss the lifestyle as well as the money. With his injuries, he couldn't ride professionally again. Since he'd been rodeoing since his late teens, he lacked other career skills and knew it. *What am I going to do to make ends meet? I have savings, yeah, but they won't last forever.*

I might go watch a rodeo or two, but I won't ride again. He'd been restless for a long time, drifting through life without direction or purpose. Jeb rode broncs because he had for years. He'd traveled because everyone did to compete. He'd roamed from one town to another and performed in venues large and small. Over the years, he'd had occasional girlfriends, a barrel racer, a woman he'd known since high school, and others. But none had ever connected with him on a deep, inner level. *Will I ever find a woman?*

His thoughts drifting, he tuned out until he realized Lexi sang the old song about ants marching two by two, echoing a tune Granny used to sing, "When Johnny Comes Marching Home." Her high, clear voice brought brightness to the dreary day. The little girl switched to the classic "Old McDonald Had A Farm." Jeb grinned and joined her.

Halfway through, he realized Lexi had changed the lyrics to 'Old MacJeb,' stretching his name out to two full syllables to fit the tune. She warbled, but his voice tapered off as he became too moved to sing. Until now, Jeb never grasped how precious children could be or how enjoyable.

"Jeb, we can go in if you're hurting." Shelby

squeezed his hand.

He blinked away tears. "I feel fairly good. Let's sing." From memory, he belted out songs he thought long forgotten, "Put On Your Old Gray Bonnet," "Froggie Went A-Courting," and "Down In The Valley." Although the tunes were new to both of Shelby's children, they learned quickly and soon sang along.

Despite the rain, temperatures remained in the mid-eighties.

When noon loomed, Shelby insisted they go inside, have lunch, and find something to occupy the afternoon.

"We could play a game," Levi cried. "I saw a stack of board games in my room. Jeb, can we play one?"

"Jeb might want a nap." Shelby offered her hands to help Jeb stand.

"I'd rather play a game or watch a movie." He hadn't enjoyed a game of Monopoly or Sorry in decades. "I've got a lot of DVDs." Once installed in the recliner, Jeb told the kids where to find the discs. They brought a stack over, debating what to watch.

Lexi spotted *The Wizard of Oz.* "I want to watch Dorothy!" She hugged the movie case to her chest.

"It's fine with me." Jeb smiled because the old film was a favorite.

"Can we eat in the front room? Please?" Levi glanced from his mom to Jeb.

Jeb didn't mind if Shelby wouldn't. "What is for lunch?"

"Grilled cheese sandwiches, potato chips, with a pickle spear. We'll have catfish this evening. It's your house, so it's your call." Shelby fiddled with her ponytail and twisted it up on the back of her head with a clip.

Grilled cheese ranked as Jeb's favorite rain or snow day favorite. "Let's watch the movie. I noticed you tracked down the TV trays."

"I did." Shelby bustled to the kitchen to prepare the food and delivered it. "I found enough for the kids to use, too."

At the kids' request, they dimmed the lights and watched the classic film in the darkness.

Jeb relished the simple sandwich as the story of Dorothy, the girl from a Kansas farm, took them all to the magical Land of Oz. The flying monkeys swooped out of the trees.

Lexi shivered, squealed, and scooted closer to the adults.

As Dorothy tapped her ruby red slippers together and repeated her mantra, "There's no place like home, there's no place like home," the words resonated with Jeb. He napped after the movie until supper, then devoured the crisp catfish. He enjoyed the hush puppies and could have eaten his weight in them. *This is what having a family would be like.* A pang of sadness touched Jeb's heart. As an adult, his only experience with such domestic downtime had been with his grandparents. Once he committed to a rodeo career, those days became few and far between.

After the meal, the evening wound down. Shelby supervised baths for her kids, then laid out their clothing and placed their backpacks in the kitchen. "It's eight o'clock and time for bed. We have an early start tomorrow." At the foot of the stairs, she kissed each child goodnight, then recited a prayer. "Now I lay me down to sleep, I pray the Lord my soul to keep. If I die before I wake, I pray the Lord my soul to take. Amen."

The words echoed in Jeb's head. A memory of kneeling down beside his bed with his mother popped into his mind. He didn't say the prayer aloud, but when they finished, he joined them in "amen." From his recliner, he smiled. "Good night, Levi. Good night, Lexi."

"Good night, Jeb!" They chanted in unison.

Before he retired, he convinced Shelby to help him wash up.

She insisted on administering a bed bath, unconcerned and unashamed. "I'm a nurse, Jeb. This is what I do."

He suspected she didn't normally provide sponge baths to otherwise healthy men in their thirties but didn't say anything. Afterward, he felt cleaner but tired and a little embarrassed. A shower would have required too much effort, but the bed bath had been disconcerting. Jeb had washed his own body since he was eight. Shelby's ministrations seemed almost intrusive.

"Good night, Jeb. If you need me, just holler." Shelby tucked the pillows into position.

"I don't know if I can yell loud enough you'll hear me upstairs." Jeb could, but he wanted to tease her a little.

Shelby brushed her lips across his forehead.

He wasn't sure it could be considered a kiss.

"I'll be on the couch, not upstairs, so I will hear you." She cupped her right hand against his cheek.

Jeb started to argue, to insist she sleep near her kids in a comfortable bed and not on the lumpy old couch, but he didn't. He liked the idea she'd be close, just in case.

In the morning, Shelby served a rushed breakfast with cereal and milk.

With her help, Jeb wore his good black jeans, a red-and-black snap-fronted Western shirt, and boots.

Lexi twirled around the kitchen in a plaid dress.

Levi dressed in jeans with a character T-shirt.

Although Shelby pulled the truck right up to the back door, climbing into the passenger seat proved harder than Jeb imagined. The kids rode in the middle, sandwiched between the adults. No one said much on the way into St. Joseph.

Shelby parked at their school, unloaded the children, handed them their backpacks, and sent them to join the other students. Shelby navigated through the morning rush traffic to a medical building where six physicians, including the orthopedic specialist Jeb came to see, practiced.

At the front entrance, she borrowed a wheelchair. It would make his trip to the elevator, then to Dr. Guiseman's office suite, easier. "He'll think I can't walk a lick." Jeb protested with a frown. Sometimes, she fussed more than he found professional. He liked Shelby. Jeb couldn't deny his attraction to Shelby, but he didn't like the nagging.

"No, he won't. This is easier than using the walker." Shelby propelled the chair with experienced skill.

"I'm not ready for this." Jeb looked around the huge waiting area after he checked in at the desk. "Let's go home. We can come back next week."

"Don't be silly." Her voice carried a brisk,

professional note. "You need a doctor to advise you how to recover. Are you nervous?"

Jeb didn't think he could be antsier if he dangled over a pit of rattlesnakes on a frayed rope. "My stomach's bothering me." He rubbed his upper abdomen.

Shelby turned him to face her. "Nerves. How's your back?"

He shrugged, which made it ache more. "Hurts although it's not too bad. What if he wants to stick me back in the hospital?"

"Why would he?" Shelby shook her head. "Don't be ridiculous."

Dr. Guiseman didn't. Instead, after a thorough examination, he pronounced Jeb to be healing well. He consulted Shelby as often as he did Jeb. "I'll see you again in two weeks. I recommend outpatient therapy. You'll progress faster with the available equipment than at home. I'll have my nurse call when you have an appointment. Make sure she has your number."

Jeb recited the old landline number. He hadn't replaced his cell phone yet and still used the pay-as-you-go mobile Shelby provided. "When can I drop the walker? I'd rather use a cane."

"That's up to Shelby, based on how well you get around. Be sure to pick up the back brace at the medical supply store. Shelby has the prescription for one. I'll write another for a cane, but it'll be Shelby's discretion when you start using it. I wouldn't give up the walker entirely yet." The doc looked over his glasses at Jeb. "Any other questions?"

"How long do I have to sleep in the hospital bed?" Jeb crossed his fingers, hoping the doc would say he could move into the guest room.

Dr. Guiseman spread his hands wide. "Right now, you need it. The end goal here is for you to regain full mobility, right? If you advance too fast, you'll delay your recovery, and you might cause permanent damage."

"All right." Jeb gave up. He would endure the medical equipment for now. "I have one more thing I want to ask–is there any remote chance I can return to rodeo? I know they said another injury might paralyze me but…"

"No." The doctor met his gaze. "You won't ever return to competition. I'm sorry to tell you what you'd rather not hear, but it's a fact."

Jeb's heart ached. "Thanks for being straight. I do appreciate it." *I won't ever best a bronc again. I ain't even asking if I might ride a horse. I don't want to hear the answer if it's "no."* He said nothing as he made his way to the truck. His mind reeled, and tears threatened to overflow. *I should just be glad I'm alive. I'll get used to this, someday.*

"You're quiet." Shelby commented as they left the medical center parking lot. "Jeb, are you okay?"

"Fine." He spat the single word like a bitter pill.

"Are you upset the doctor confirmed you won't continue with rodeo?"

Jeb folded his arms against his chest. He huffed air through his nose. "I don't want to talk about it, Shelby, if you don't mind."

Although she did, she didn't say another word until they departed the medical district.

"Do you care if I run by my house? I need to pick up things I forgot. I'll run in and get them."

"Sure." Jeb wanted to see her house anyway. He suspected it might be in worse shape than she admitted. His gut instinct proved right. Waiting while Shelby went inside, he studied the old structure. Two of the gutters were on the verge of falling off. The roof sagged. From the truck, Jeb saw the porch roof had collapsed in places.

The condition of her home sobered him and brought home the realization his inability to ride rodeo wasn't the worst thing in the world. If he could, Jeb would be here tomorrow, tools in hand to make repairs, and he would open his pocketbook to pay for any repairs. He doubted Shelby would go for it, though, so he said nothing. *She's touchy about money, and if I offer, she'll be annoyed.*

"Could we stop at a discount store?" Jeb asked after she emerged from her home.

"Sure, no problem." Shelby faked a smile. "I need to grab a few things."

Trekking through the aisles required extra effort, Jeb bought a baby monitor, two movies, and other items.

"What's with the device?" Shelby glanced at him when they reached the truck.

"It's for you, so you can sleep in a bed, but you'll hear me if I need you." Jeb eased into the truck with a groan.

Shelby clapped her hands together. "Sometimes, you're the sweetest man, Jeb Hill. Thank you."

Her delight pleased him, but he acted gruff. "It's no big deal."

It was, though, and so was Shelby. Her comfort mattered more than his, and Jeb could think of many things he'd like to buy her. Most would make her life easier, and all would please her.

In time, he hoped he could provide them. First, he had to recover. Then he had to adapt to his new reality.

Chapter Six

Next stop was the medical supply shop. Shelby assisted Jeb in choosing the right brace for his recovery. He wanted a plain design, but she insisted on a complicated thoracolumbar spinal brace.

"It looks uncomfortable." Jeb stared at the device, as if there were teeth that could bite. "Might as well put me in a full body cast."

Shelby smacked his arm with a playful gesture. "Don't say it—don't even think it. You wouldn't be able to move at all. You'll only wear the brace for an hour or two a day."

Jeb lifted one eyebrow. "For real?"

"Totally. And you have a nurse to help you get it on and off." She held her choice up for his inspection.

"Looks like I need one but okay, we'll get it." Jeb leaned on the walker and sighed. "I'm more interested in a cane so I can get mobile quicker."

The choice narrowed to a sturdy quad cane, which Shelby suggested, and a standard cane.

Jeb tried each in turn as he took forward steps.

"I like the quad cane, the one with feet." Shelby lifted it up to his view. "It's more stable."

He used it for half a dozen steps. "I agree. Are we finished in town?"

Shelby wished, but she had to pick up the kids this afternoon. If they returned to the farm now, she would need to make another round trip. "It's late enough we might as well have lunch, then pick up Levi and Lexi when school gets out unless you're too tired. If you are, then I can take you home." Jeb appeared weary to her trained nurse's eye. His eyes drooped, and he had fine lines around his mouth.

"I'll make it. Do you mind if I head for the truck, though?"

"Go ahead. I'll be out as soon as I take care of these items." She watched through the front glass as he made a slow, steady trek to his pickup. First, Shelby handed over the prescriptions, then displayed Jeb's insurance card, and used his debit card to pay the remaining balance. She loaded the items into the truck and climbed behind the wheel.

By the way Jeb hunched forward, she suspected he suffered pain. His eyes were shut, and she wondered if he'd fallen asleep until he blinked. "Hey, is the big trip to town taking too much out of you?" Shelby snapped her fingers to get his attention, but her concern was genuine.

Sometimes, she struggled to remember she was his hired nurse, not his girlfriend or even friend. Once he healed, she would move back into her old house and pick up her life. The very thought made her stomach tighten enough to hurt. Life in the farmhouse offered cozy comfort and much-needed relief from her daily grind.

Shelby admitted she'd miss Jeb if she didn't see him every day, but he wouldn't need her forever. *I refuse to get dependent on him, anyway. He's a client. Once he's better, I'll move on to another patient.* Her heart twinged at the thought, but it was true. *I shouldn't let the kids get emotionally attached.* The thought came too late because they already had.

"I'm a little worn out but okay. Back's hurting a bit, but it's the most I've moved around since I got hurt." Jeb straightened his posture and smiled. "Ibuprofen will take care of it. Where did you want to eat? I'll buy."

"I'm not picky. Whatever sounds good to you works." Shelby seldom had extra money to dine out so anything would be a treat.

"Barbecue." He didn't hesitate. "There's a place way out on Frederick Avenue with good brisket sandwiches and great smoked meats."

"Sure. I think I know the place although I've never been there." Shelby pulled out of the parking lot into traffic.

"Just one thing." Jeb cleared his throat before he spoke.

"What's that?" Shelby chanced a glance at him.

"I don't want to go in there hanging onto this walker like I'm ninety years old." Jeb stared through the windshield.

She failed to understand. "What are you saying?"

"Can we get it to go?" He leaned closer and touched her knee.

"Sure. Let me call in our order if you know what you want, and we can take it to Wyeth Hill to eat. It's my favorite view of the river." Shelby loved the spot, and it wasn't too far from the elementary school. Once they finished a late lunch, it would be close to the time to pick up her kids.

"Barbecued brisket sandwich with cole slaw and a root beer." He rattled off his order without hesitation.

"Tell me what's good. I like brisket, but I'm fond of smoked turkey, too." She switched lanes as she spoke, then pulled into a parking lot so she could call in the order.

"Get the turkey sandwich with a side. They have fries, okra, potato salad, baked beans, baked potato, and a side salad to choose from. Sauce is served separately." Jeb licked his lips. "I think you'll like it."

Shelby put in a carryout order for two sandwiches, two sides, and two sodas. "We can pick it up in fifteen minutes. Want ibuprofen now?"

"Yeah, I would." Jeb bit his lip. "I've got enough water to wash them down."

Shelby reached into her purse for the pain reliever. She shook out two tablets and handed them to Jeb. The bills she picked up at the house loomed. She'd rather not look at or deal with them now. One was a water shutoff notice. Shelby hadn't made the payment on time, and since she'd been at the farm, she'd forgotten. Jeb hadn't paid her yet, and she hated to ask when he would. Sometimes, a private pay assignment wasn't reimbursed by the client until the end of the job, but Shelby's bills couldn't wait months.

A van pulled into the slot beside them.

The couple exited their vehicle and Shelby turned to Jeb. "I hate to ask, but how often will I get paid? I didn't know if it would be weekly, monthly, or what."

"Whenever you want, honey. I can pay you the second we're home. I'd write you a check now, but I didn't bring the checkbook." He patted his pocket where his wallet resided. "I promised a bonus, too. I can pay it right now instead of later, when I'm okay. If you want to run by the bank, then I'll get cash."

She exhaled. "Thank you. A check's fine. I only asked because I picked up a stack of bills at my house and need to pay them."

Shelby could deposit a check on her way to drop off the kids at school. She could write the bills tonight and drop them in the mail.

"How often do you need a paycheck? I can give you one as often as you want." Jeb thumbed open his wallet. "If you need something now, then I've got it."

Shelby sighed. She had so many past-due bills, as well as the monthly ones, he could pay her every day and she still might never catch up. "Weekly works." She wanted what she earned, nothing more and definitely not any handouts. She went into the restaurant to pick up their order.

Fifteen minutes later, she parked the truck at Wyeth Hill, a scenic overlook above the Missouri River. From it, the vista stretched out over the river and into Kansas. "Have you ever been here?"

"I have, but it's been years. Let's grab one of the picnic tables under the shelter." He climbed out of the truck on his own. After three or four halting steps, Jeb halted. "Let me try out the cane."

Shelby carried the bags with their food. "Are you sure?"

"I am. I've used one before when I hurt my knee five years back. It's not far, Shelby."

She dug it out and handed it to him. "Just don't fall. I don't want to call an ambulance."

Jeb snorted. He worked his way to the covered shelter and sat at the first table. "I made it."

She put down the food and wished she had brought a plastic tablecloth. She'd had no idea they would eat at

Huston Wyatt Park. "Let's eat." Even on a picnic, she offered thanks and noticed Jeb said "amen" at the end without hesitation. The smoked turkey melted on her tongue, not dry but moist and tender. Shelby added barbecue sauce, and the combination with the meat proved delicious. She shared her fries with Jeb.

He offered some coleslaw in exchange. "Try a taste of the brisket." He pulled off a good-sized chunk and placed it on her tongue.

"Ohhh, that's marvelous." Shelby savored the smoky flavor.

Jeb blotted her lip with a napkin. "You've got a spot of sauce on your face." He leaned close.

The simple action brought tingles. For a moment, she thought he might kiss her. When he didn't, Shelby couldn't decide if she was relieved or disappointed.

After the meal, they admired the panorama from a bench perched on the edge of the hill. A sweeping view of the river was visible from the spot. The railroad bridge spanning the Missouri for decades proved visible, along with parts of downtown St. Joseph. In the far distance, the Pony Express highway bridge loomed. Below, a walking trail along the water was in view. On both sides of the river, a blend of trees and open spaces offered a beautiful panorama. Fluffy white clouds dotted the bright blue sky, and Shelby's heart filled with peace. Beauty like this had one source—the Lord of all creation. "When we lived in southern Missouri, I missed this place," she confided to Jeb.

"How long were you away?" He took a swig of root beer.

"Eight years. Jimmy came from down there, so we moved after the wedding. I met him during college, but after he died, I came back." Her throat turned dry, but she'd already finished her soda. Shelby reached for his and drank. "Three years since I've been home. It's like I never left."

Jeb stretched across the bench and took her hands in his. "Do the kids remember living somewhere else?"

Shelby sighed. "Not much. Levi was five when Jimmy died and Lexi only three. She doesn't remember Jimmy. Levi doesn't recall his dad very well."

"That has to be rough. I remember my mom, but I was twelve." Jeb shifted their linked hands.

Shelby relished the way his large hand wrapped around hers. His strong grip brought a sense of safety and care. "I'm sorry you lost her. My dad passed away right before Christmas not long after I got married. Jimmy didn't want to come back or take off work, so we didn't. With Jimmy's folks gone, my littles never have had a grandfather in their life. Jimmy said it didn't matter, but to me, it did." She shook free of his grasp, uncertain why she'd shared. Although she'd loved Jimmy, or thought she had when they wed, their relationship became rocky over the years. Shelby mourned him but didn't miss his tight control in her life.

Jeb put his arm around her shoulders. "I would have gotten you there, somehow."

His quiet voice eased a deeply buried hurt. She leaned against his shoulder, glad for the kind support. "Thank you. I believe you."

They spent another fifteen or twenty minutes in restful silence. Shelby relaxed and put her emotions away. She savored the pretty day and was content to idle in the park. On her own, she might have been late to pick up the kids.

"What time does school let out?" Jeb nudged her.

Shelby consulted her watch with a gasp. "In thirty-five minutes. We need to go soon."

He rose, using the cane for support, and walked to the truck with slow, halting steps. Jeb climbed into the seat unaided. "What do you have planned for supper?" He rested one hand on the dash as she drove down the narrow street away from the park.

"I don't know. Don't worry, I'll find something." She hadn't given the menu a thought. *I should have. Now, I'll have to scramble to figure out what to fix.*

"Why don't we pick up a couple of those take-and-bake pizzas? It's been a long day, and pizza would be easy. I bet the kids like it." Jeb put the cane between his knees as he got situated.

"They love it, and I'd appreciate it." She wouldn't have to rush back to the farmhouse to rustle something up from the cupboard or freezer. On impulse, Shelby stretched across the seat to kiss Jeb's cheek. As she did, he turned his head, and her lips touched his mouth instead. The friendly gesture became something more as she let her lips linger.

Jeb caught her chin with one hand and kissed her with full intent. "I've wanted to do that since the first day."

A sweet quiver rippled through Shelby as his mouth evoked a rush of tenderness and emotion she wasn't sure she was ready to explore. "Jeb. We shouldn't. I know I started it, and I'll admit I liked it. But I work for you, Jeb."

His fingers caressed her cheek before he faced forward. "You won't forever, honey. Let's get over to school. We'll pick up the pizza on our way out of town."

By the time they reached the farmhouse, Shelby dragged and had a nagging headache. Her children's chatter about their school didn't help, but she ignored it and, once home, popped aspirin. They were excited about the pizza, a rare treat for the Thacker family unless Shelby made it from scratch. If she did, it was usually for a birthday, or when she splurged on frozen pies.

If she was this weary, she knew Jeb must be twice as tired and offered to help him lay down. "I'll go to bed early, after supper, but it won't be much rest if I get back up for supper soon." He had switched back to using the walker once they were inside. "I'll probably want a high-powered pain pill tonight."

She frowned. "I hope you didn't overdo it today."

"I don't think so. Yeah, my back hurts, but it figures. I did more today than any time since I hit the dirt in the arena." He paused, remembering the taste of dust in his mouth and how much it hurt. "I'm heading to the front room. Once you get the pizza in the oven, why don't you set up the monitor?"

"I will." Shelby should have thought of it. "Would you rather eat in here again?" Normally, she didn't allow the kids to dine anywhere except in the kitchen or dining room, but this was different. It wasn't her house or her call. Lunch while watching the movie had set a precedent. Besides, eating supper in the front room would make it easier on Jeb.

"Okay." Jeb paused en route to his recliner. Shelby had moved the older television back into the living room at his request. "We don't need to watch anything, though. I'd rather just talk and hang out."

"Perfect." When given a choice, she preferred conversation over television.

The kids were settled at the kitchen table. Levi completed the math worksheet assigned as homework. Lexi colored with bright crayons.

Shelby slid the first of two pizzas into the oven and set a timer before returning to the living room. She placed a pillow behind Jeb's back and plugged in the monitor near the hospital bed. "Lexi, come in here while I take the base unit upstairs. We need to make sure it works."

Moments later, her daughter's voice emerged from the device. "Hello, hello, Mama. It's Lexi."

Shelby paused and glanced around the bedroom. She would sleep here for the first time tonight although her clothes and possessions were already in place. The spacious room already seemed more comfortable than hers at home. She turned on a small vintage hurricane lamp with a white shade painted with roses. The cozy space appealed as she sat on the edge of the bed.

"Did it work?" Lexi's voice echoed from the monitor again.

Shelby hurried back downstairs. "It did, Lex. Thanks for helping." She served dinner in the living room.

Jeb used the TV tray while the rest balanced their food on their knees.

For once, Shelby used paper plates simply for the convenience. "Tell me about your school day, Lexi first."

"I made Jeb a card. I'll get it out of my backpack before I go to bed." Lexi grinned. "Teacher read to us after last recess."

"How about you, Levi?" Shelby took a bite of pizza with pleasure. The combination of Italian sausage paired with black olives, mushrooms, and onions blended into a rich, pleasing flavor on her tongue. Anything she didn't have to prepare always tasted wonderful. "Did you have a good day?"

He wrinkled his nose and glowered. "Not really. They had those nachos for lunch again, and I got a stomachache. I missed part of class while I was at the nurse. That's why I had math homework. At afternoon recess, Jase Preston shoved me so I pushed him down, but I got in trouble. I had to sit out of any games."

Since he'd motored through three slices of pizza so far, Shelby figured he had recovered, but worry still flared. "I hope you feel better now."

Levi snatched a fourth piece, added to his plate, and took a large bite. "Yeah, the nurse gave me something for my tummy. It's fine."

Shelby wanted to point out she hoped it would still be after he crammed his belly full of pizza but didn't.

"I'd hate to think you had to force yourself to eat. Did you have to go to the principal's office?" Jeb chuckled as he picked up another slice of pizza.

"Yeah." Levi hung his head and stared at the floor.

"Did you get a write-up?" If so, Shelby would have to sign it and make sure he returned it. Last year, when reprimanded for spitting water all over the hallway, Levi had torn the disciplinary form into pieces and tossed it in the trash. Of course, the teacher found it, and he ended up in more trouble. "I hope I don't have to have another conference with Mrs. Dickens."

"It's in my backpack," Levi mumbled.

"Make sure it's on the table so I can sign it in the morning. Go upstairs, get your bath, and go to bed. You know better than to get into a scuffle at school. You're grounded from any school and church activities for two weeks."

"Aw, Mom." Levi leaped to his feet. "I want to do peewee football this year and the first practice is on Friday."

"You should have thought about that before you shoved Jase. You won't be there." Shelby ached to hug her son but didn't. She had to be the enforcer. Besides, he should have told her sooner. "Good night."

If looks could kill, she would have been slain on the floor. "G'night, Mom. Good night, Jeb." Levi paused in front of Jeb, who fist-bumped him.

"Night, kid. Sleep well."

Shelby sighed as her son bounded to the second floor. "I'm sorry about all that. You didn't count on putting up with my family drama."

"I don't mind, Shelby. It's life." Jeb put his empty plate on the tray and sat back. "I hope you're not mad. I didn't mean to jump into your business."

She gathered the used plates. "Not at all. I appreciated your support." Shelby sometimes doubted her prowess as a single parent. Jeb's intervention had helped. "Do you want another glass of tea?"

"About half, then I'll take the pain pill." He handed off his tumbler. "Thanks, Shelby."

Lexi brought a folded paper from her backpack and handed it to Jeb. "It's for you."

Shelby admired the homemade card. Lexi had drawn a man on the back of what had to be a bucking horse. Beneath it, the child had scrawled with her sprawling, sloppy handwriting. *Get better Jeb!*

Jeb opened the card and smiled as he read the message. *I hope you are better soon. I like you. I like your house, too. Love, Lexi.* "Thanks, baby girl. I'm gonna hang up it in here so I can look at it every day." He scooted the tray table out of the way and opened his arms.

Lexi dived into them for a hug. "Good night, Jeb." The little girl touched Jeb's cheek with one small hand.

"Night, Lexi."

Jeb's grin lit his face like a candle in a dark room.

Shelby watched, and her heart brimmed full. "I'll be up in a flash, Lexi. I'll help you with your bath and put you to bed."

With both kids upstairs, Shelby turned to Jeb. "I need to refill your tea and get your pill. I can get you settled before I go upstairs."

"I'd like that, Shelby." Jeb raised himself from the chair and tottered into the dining room.

At Jeb's request, she taped Lexi's card within view. She settled him into the hospital bed, noting he grimaced several times. The prescription pill would ease his hurt tonight. Shelby resolved to pay attention in the morning. Jeb shouldn't be hurting as much by then. After she dimmed the lights and checked to see if the monitor was still on. "Anything else before I go up?"

He shook his head. "Nah, I'm good. I'll holler if I need anything. Sweet dreams, honey."

"Good night, Jeb." She leaned close, brushed her fingers across his cheek, and, on impulse, kissed his lips. The connection brought tingles down her spine as she savored the softness of his warm mouth against hers.

Before he could speak or she was tempted for another, better kiss, Shelby hightailed it upstairs. She placed Lexi in the tub, checked on Levi, who either slept or pretended to be asleep, and tucked her daughter in bed after the bath. Shelby donned a favorite, well-worn nightgown, crawled into bed, and savored the comfort of the cozy space.

Before she slept, she said her prayers, which now included Jeb. She knew falling for her boss wasn't smart. Shelby had passed the point of no return so she would face the future, no matter what happened. In two months, she would be back in her own house, facing her bills, and struggling to parent. *I have to remember to live in the moment. I'm living a fantasy, and it won't last.*

Chapter Seven

By mid-September, Jeb had put away the walker and managed with the cane. Dr. Guiseman approved and encouraged him to continue physical therapy. Twice a week, Jeb did at least an hour, sometimes more, at a rehab clinic in town. Shelby took him to the appointments and continued to assist him at home. For now, he still slept in the hospital bed, but Jeb hoped to retire it soon.

On many of their daily trips into St. Joe, Shelby headed to her house. Shelby continued to receive mail there. "You could have it sent out to the farm," Jeb suggested.

Shelby shook her head. "I'd just have to change it back in another month or so. I'm in town every day, between taking the kids to school and for your therapy." Shelby rubbed her lips with one finger. On Thursday, after his session, she swung by her home. "If you want to come in, you can." Shelby offered a hand as he navigated from the truck to the sidewalk. "It's not much, so I'm warning you. It needs extensive work."

Judging by the exterior, Jeb was aware, but when he entered, he winced because the place proved rougher than he expected. The front door opened into a small entryway with a living room on the left. Minimal furniture, including a daybed, a vintage analog television resting on a battered coffee table, an armchair with stuffing sticking out of the seat, and a 1960s floor lamp were the sole furnishings. Three photos hung on the wall: an eight-by-ten of the kids, Shelby's wedding portrait, and a studio photo of an older couple.

"The daybed serves as our couch." Shelby tugged at her ponytail and tightened it. "I didn't bring any furniture back from southern Missouri. Most of it wasn't worth moving. My grandparents' stuff was sold at an auction. These are hand-me-downs from Mom or one of my aunts or junk shop specials."

Jeb noted a gaping hole in the ceiling where plaster had fallen, leaving open timbers in view from the floor above. In places, wallpaper peeled in faded curls. The same level of disrepair continued into an area with a desk and dining table. Someone had painted the kitchen a bright sunshine-yellow, but Jeb noticed the floor tiles were dull. Many were broken in spots. Water stains on the ceiling indicated leaks above. If the damage wasn't repaired, Shelby would have more problems to deal with in the near future.

"Wait here and I'll run upstairs for a couple of things." Shelby disappeared through a doorway in the dining area to a closed staircase.

Jeb walked around, noting more spots in need of repair. He peeked onto a back porch and saw the floor had fallen through, rendering the space unusable. He hadn't mounted his own stairs yet, so he didn't attempt to go to the second floor. He figured it had to be in the same, if not worse, disrepair. *I can't imagine Shelby and the kids living here. I don't want them to come back to this.*

He compiled a mental list of things needing immediate attention. If possible, he'd pay for all of it, but he suspected Shelby would object. She dismissed most of his offers and suggestions. The only thing she had relented on was Levi's chance at peewee football. Jeb insisted she talk with Levi's classroom teacher and the principal, and Shelby learned the other boy had acted first. Jace Preston owned a reputation as a bully, and after questioning Levi in detail, Shelby lifted the punishment.

Levi attended the first practice. During the tryouts the following Saturday, he made the team. Although the kid wanted to play quarterback, like his hero, Patrick Mahomes from the Kansas City pro team, Levi got tabbed as a wide receiver. Jeb bought Levi cleats and the gloves he needed as a tight end.

"Hey, Jeb." Shelby's voice echoed from upstairs. "Would you come up here a minute?"

"I'm on the way, honey." Jeb left his cane behind as he climbed one stair at a time, using the handrail for support. He paused midway to glance through a diamond-shaped window overlooking the backyard. Weeds grew waist high, and a heaped jumble of lumber indicated there might have been a shed at one time. He added another chore to his mental tally. "What's the matter?"

"Come see. I'm in the bathroom." Shelby stood, hands on hips, at the back of the narrow room at the top of the steps. "The floor is sinking, and I'm afraid it might be rotten around the commode."

Jeb entered the space for a better view, and his heart sank. The toilet rested two inches below the sagging floor. If someone, even a child, sat on the stool he feared the floor would drop lower, "Stand back, Shelby. You're right. It's been leaking, and water damage has rotted out the wood. The wax ring probably eroded over time, but it's gone."

"Can it be fixed?" She pressed her hands to her mouth.

Thank God, they haven't been living here. It would have crashed through by now. Jeb shuddered at the idea. "Yeah, but the floor will be to be ripped up and replaced with a new subfloor."

"I can't afford that!" Shelby sobbed. She leaned against an ancient stall shower. "Oh, Jeb, what will I do?"

He pulled her into his arms and cradled her close. They had kissed, but until now, Jeb hadn't held her in his embrace. "Honey, you have two options. Stay at my house until the floor is fixed and let me pay for the repairs or move. This house isn't livable, not the way it is, and it's sure not safe."

She cried so hard her tears wet his shirt, but when she calmed, Shelby shook her head. "I can't do either, Jeb. I love staying at your house. I won't be here forever, though. I have to find a new job after you recover. I'll likely have multiple patients again, too. I can't afford to move or pay for repairs, but I'll have to do one or the other."

"Hush." He stroked her hair with a gentle hand. "Let's don't worry about it right now. I'm still a long way from being back on my feet. Heck, I'll be lonely if I go back to living alone. Even when you get a new job, you're welcome to stay, because I've got plenty of space."

"I can't." Shelby pulled away and grabbed a roll of tissue to blot her face. "It wouldn't be right to take advantage of you, and continuing to live with you would send the wrong message to my children."

Jeb ached to keep her in his arms. He had become very fond of her, not as a nurse or as a friend but more. "I understand, sugar, but we're not doing anything wrong. What could you do about any of it today?"

Shelby drew a deep, shuddering breath. "I don't know. I guess nothing right now. Let's go. Levi has football practice after school. I thought while he's there, I'd take Lexi to pick up a couple of things at the dollar store."

"Sounds like a plan. What's on for supper?" Jeb's stomach growled. They'd eaten an early lunch at the farm.

"I've got a chicken in the slow cooker, and biscuits ready to pop into the oven." Shelby grimaced at the disaster before heading down the stairs. She folded her arms across her chest.

Jeb snapped a photo with the cell phone he'd recently acquired and followed after peering into the small bedrooms. Only two showed signs of occupation and he wondered if Shelby slept on the daybed downstairs.

Shelby retrieved an electric skillet from the kitchen and snagged a pile of bills from the mailbox on the porch. She grabbed a few other items as she headed outside.

Jeb caught up with her at the truck and climbed inside. "We've got forty-five minutes before you have to pick up the kids. Would you like a hot fudge sundae?"

She smiled for the first time since discovering the rotten floor. "Thanks, but not right now. I'm sorry I'm upset. It sometimes seems like the bad things won't stop happening, and I can't keep up. My job with you is the only good thing I've had come my way in so long."

"I understand, honey." Jeb adjusted his position in the seat and scooted closer. "I'm happy to help, however I can. Once I'm back up to speed, if you'd like, I can do most of the repairs myself. I might be a cowboy, but I do have other skills."

Shelby turned the key in the ignition. "I believe you, Jeb. I just can't be your charity case. I'd rather be…oh, never mind. I'm just daydreaming. How's your back? I wasn't thinking when I called you to come upstairs. I forgot you haven't mounted the steps at home yet."

I wonder what she started to say and what she wishes. Jeb shrugged off the question. "It's good. I doubt I'm ready to run up and down the steps six times a day, but at least, I can get up there if I want."

At the practice field, Jeb perched on bleachers and watched as Levi's team, the Wolverines, ran plays. They began with exercises and jogged around the perimeter. The coach divided the team and had them scrimmage until six o'clock.

Shelby returned with Lexi before practice ended and climbed into the stands beside Jeb. She sat on one side of him, with the little girl on the other.

He draped an arm around each of them. *My gals.* The thought blasted his brain out of nowhere, but it was the truth.

"Mama, Jeb, I got a joke. How does the ocean say hello?" Lexi laughed, even though she hadn't shared the answer yet. "It waves!" She giggled with a sweet merry sound.

Shelby smiled. "I needed to hear something funny.

Thanks, Lex."

"You sound happier." Jeb grinned at the child's pun, but he liked the smile on Shelby's face even more.

"I'm in a better mood, now. I'll figure the house repairs out, somehow." Shelby leaned against Jeb.

"*We* will, honey." Jeb delivered a light kiss on her lips. "I promise."

Lexi tittered. "You kissed Mama!"

"I did." Jeb noted Shelby's blush.

"Mama and Jeb sitting in a tree," Lexi chanted. "K-i-s-s-i-n-g."

Even Jeb knew the next line and so did Shelby. It mentioned love, marriage, and a baby carriage. He could accept love and possibly marriage. The idea of a baby carriage daunted him. Until now, he'd never been around children and hadn't ever thought he would have any.

"Hush, Lexi. Friends kiss, sometimes." Shelby leaned across Jeb and tapped her daughter's knee. "Your brother's almost finished with practice. When he's done, we'll head home."

Levi reeked of sweat, like any decent football player, so Shelby sent him upstairs on arrival to shower.

Jeb plopped into a kitchen chair and watched Shelby. She multitasked, as she placed biscuits into the oven, chicken on a platter, and stirred together instant potatoes in a pot with skillful ease. Jeb admired her grace. "I can carve the chicken." He reached for a knife and a long fork. As he detached the legs from the bird, then sliced the thighs and breasts, he removed the pully bone. Jeb offered it to Lexi, who tugged it with him. He schemed to end up with the smaller piece, Lexi the larger.

"I get to make a wish." The little girl shut her eyes and whispered something low.

Jeb caught the words, although he didn't think he was supposed to hear. Telling your wish negated it, if he remembered the lore from childhood. Lexi had whispered, "I wish for a Christmas tree and Christmas at Jeb's." If possible, Jeb would make sure both came true.

Levi joined them, and they dined on chicken, taters and gravy, and biscuits.

Shelby added leftover salad from the previous night for the adults. "Save room for dessert." She winked as she brought out a box of clearance cream-filled donuts with chocolate frosting. "There are six. We each can have one tonight, and one for each of the kids at breakfast."

Jeb accepted his cruller. Once again, she served a favorite. He wasn't sure if it was chance this time or not. "Tasty and a good bargain." He bit into his and savored the sweet taste.

Shelby offered him a thumbs-up in response.

"They had Christmas stuff out when we did the shopping!" Lexi's eyes sparkled like bright stars. "Christmas trees, decorations, and toys!"

"Man, I wish I'd been there." Levi wore a chocolate mustache as he polished off his donut. "I still want a race car model, but I want a football, too. And at least one Mahomes jersey. Everyone has one."

"I hope I get the doll buggy. And another doll and books. I saw pretty red velvet dresses with lace collars, too. Mama, can I get one? I could wear it in our holiday program." Lexi hadn't eaten much of her dessert as she jabbered.

Shelby laid down her untouched pastry and sighed. "Kids, you know I can't afford a bunch of presents, and we don't do a tree."

Considering the major issues evident at her house, Jeb thought Shelby dealt with the requests well. He considered offering to buy gifts but decided to wait. This wasn't the moment Shelby might be receptive.

"What I really want is a computer." Levi leaned in toward the table and eyed the remaining pastries. "I think every kid in my class has one but me. If I had one, I would use it to look up stuff for school. I could play games on it, too.

"Computers are expensive. I don't plan to buy one any time soon." Shelby cut her cream-filled donut in two. She hadn't taken a bite. "Do you guys want to split this?"

"But, Mama…" Levi's voice rose in a whine.

Jeb had a desktop model he hadn't even thought about since coming home. He'd been focused on his injury and recovery. "I've got a computer. It's in the guest bedroom where I have a desk. We can boot it up tomorrow. It's late, tonight." Jeb beamed and wished he'd thought about it sooner.

He would fire it up, Jeb resolved, and share it with the kids. Maybe he could download some age-appropriate games, too. Shelby didn't need to know they hadn't been already installed. Temptation to buy Levi and Lexi laptops loomed large, but Jeb figured they were too young. Besides, Shelby would likely refuse the offer, and he'd rather not argue.

"Really? Way cool!" Levi's grin returned. "Can we use it?"

"Sure, but only when your mama says it's okay."

Jeb winked.

"Thanks, Jeb." Levi fist-bumped him.

Shelby cleared her throat. "All right since it's already here, and Jeb doesn't mind sharing. It's time to get ready for bed. Levi, go ahead. You already showered. I'll be up with your sister in five minutes for her bath. Don't dawdle, either. Put your PJ's on."

The boy nodded and whirled up the stairs.

Lexi tugged Jeb's sleeve. "Will you read me a story?"

Jeb, who enjoyed reading, had never imagined he'd ever read aloud to anyone. "I can. Do you have books?"

"She has a few." Shelby rose and began cleaning the kitchen. "I saw more upstairs, and we brought a few of her favorites."

Those upstairs are mine. I forgot about them until now. Jeb recalled his old favorites, *Curious George, Where The Wild Things Are,* and *Robinson Crusoe.* The last one dated from his junior high years.

Lexi bobbed her head. "I have a library book from school in my backpack. Can we read it?"

"Sure." He gripped the table for support and reached for his cane. "Grab your book, Lexi. I'll meet you in the front room."

"Jeb, you don't have to read to her." Shelby filled the sink with water and added soap.

He frowned. "I don't mind at all." Jeb settled onto the couch and opened *The Poky Little Puppy.* He remembered the story from childhood. The child snuggled close so he opened the book and read. At first, he felt self-conscious, but Jeb soon filled his tone with enthusiasm. He enhanced the few lines of dialogue by changing his voice and used a soprano tone for the puppies' mother's voice.

"Can we read another?" Lexi clapped her hands.

"Bath time," Shelby announced. She had joined them midway through the tale. "Jeb, I'll come back down when I've tucked the kids in bed."

"I'll be here." Jeb moved to his recliner. He reached for the novel he'd been reading, one of Craig Johnson's *Longmire* books. He barely got into the storyline.

Shelby returned. "I want to talk to you." She slipped out of her shoes, curled into a corner of the couch, and rubbed her forehead.

"Got a headache?" Jeb frowned. He set the paperback aside.

"I do, a killer one. Stress always makes my head or stomach hurt." Shelby grimaced. "It'll pass."

"Can I get you something?" Jeb used his cane to stand. The effort sent spasms through his lower back, not as painful as earlier but it still hurt.

"No, I'm okay." Shelby waved her hand. "Come sit by me, though. I'd like it."

Jeb sank onto the couch cushions. "What's on your mind?"

"The house and the kids." Shelby blew air between her lips. "I know I can't move back home, not the way my house is. My mom doesn't have room. I really can't afford rent, so if you don't mind, we'll stay until I can get the bathroom floor fixed. Hopefully, it'll be before this job ends. I don't know what else to do."

His heart soared. He wouldn't mind if she stayed forever, although he wanted to change their circumstances. "Honey, I told you it's fine. You'll be here anyway 'til the end of October or into November, if I haven't fully recovered by then. There are plenty of things I still can't do."

Jeb continued to sleep in a hospital bed, by doctor's orders. He had yet to be released to get behind the wheel and drive. His long-range plans included running cattle on the place, but until he could do the work and chores, the option had to wait. He accepted Shelby's outstretched hand.

"Think about it, though, November, Thanksgiving, and the Christmas season. Even if we're here through November, I'll have to scramble to find someplace during the holidays if the floor's safe by then." She paused and sighed. "I've got other problems, too. The last time I tried to start my car, it didn't. It just ground until the battery ran down. I think the starter's gone out."

She hadn't told him, and it rankled. Jeb frowned. "You should have mentioned it."

"I didn't want to burden you. I can't drive your truck forever, Jeb, or expect you to pay my bills. You've bought too many things for the kids now. I worry I'll get you as broke as I am." Shelby lowered her head as she spoke. A single tear escaped down her left cheek.

He realized she had no idea about his financial situation or how deep his feelings ran. Jeb could buy her a vehicle, tomorrow, if she wanted. He would pay off all her overdue bills, if it would make her happy, and remove some stress. "That's not likely, honey. I'm not wealthy, but I'm okay moneywise. I own this place outright, because I inherited it from my family. Even when my folks lived here, it was Granny and Pop's place. They left me a bit of money, although it's not a fortune. I've rodeoed for fifteen years. I might not have become national champion, but I've ranked high. I've won substantial purses. We're talking in the thousands of bucks. I've saved most of the cash I've won. I wouldn't offer my help, if I couldn't afford it." *Can I, though? Without rodeo, there won't be money coming in, even if I do make this farm successful.* He'd never worried about money before, but for the first time, he did.

"I know you'll have huge medical bills. I'm still paying off Jimmy's, and he died after he got to the hospital over three years ago." Shelby straightened out her feet and moved closer. "You have to think about your obligations, Jeb."

"No, I don't." He wasn't concerned about what he owed the hospital. "Shelby, most rodeo folks don't have insurance, and an injury like mine crushes their financial future. I have, or had, a great sponsor—one of the biggest boot manufacturers in the US. They paid for my medical insurance all these years. The policy covers almost everything. They have deep pockets." Jeb rubbed his chin. Until now, he never realized what a blessing the provided insurance had been. Like the rest of his professional life, it would no longer be a factor after this. *I'll have to pony up for insurance now 'cause I have to have it. I'm not performing, but I might get in a wreck or fall out of the barn loft or something,*

Shelby scrubbed away the tear and smiled. "That's good to know. Jeb, I've worried so much about your medical bills." Her fingers strayed to caress his cheek.

Jeb pulled her onto his lap. If the move hurt his back, it did. Right now, he needed Shelby in his arms more. "You ought not worry over me. I doubt I'm worth the fuss."

She rested her left arm on his chest and looped the other around his neck. "You are. Jeb, you're the kindest, sweetest man I think I've ever known. I care about you, not just as a patient. I like to think we're at least friends."

Friends? Jeb's heart belonged to this woman, and he knew it. "I kinda hope we're more than that, Shelby." To demonstrate, he delivered a slow, tender kiss on her lips. His mouth lingered over hers. He intended to show her his emotions. Jeb hoped she felt the same. Shelby caught his face between her hands and gave back the kiss. Joy surged through him, powerful and filled with promise. His dreams might just come true. If Shelby's hopes did, too, it would be all the more a blessing. More than one roadblock stood in the way of a future. His injuries, her house, the children, and her reluctance to accept help loomed large. God would have to sort it out, because Jeb had no idea where to begin.

Chapter Eight

Their relationship shifted when Jeb held Shelby on his lap and kissed her. Shelby couldn't deny it and wouldn't. She wanted Jeb in her life for keeps, but she didn't dare hope or trust. Right now, he remained vulnerable. In the past, other patients had mistaken her professional care for emotional attachment. It hadn't been the case, then, but it proved true with Jeb. More than once, she stopped short in her daily tasks and savored the illusion they were a family. They weren't, but she dreamed they could be. *Time will tell. I pray Jeb's emotions run as deep as mine.*

On Friday, she strapped Jeb into the back brace he disliked. He'd nicknamed it Mr. Misery. "You can take it off after I get back from taking the kids to school." Shelby tugged on a strap to make sure the brace would be secure.

"Thank the Lord." He hitched his shoulders and frowned. Jeb sat at the kitchen table, drinking his third cup of coffee. Shelby's kids had already passed through, backpacks in hand.

"Be careful, honey." Jeb puckered his lips for a kiss.

"Always." She leaned close, then picked up her purse and his keys as she dashed outside. Most days, Jeb rode shotgun, but he hadn't wanted to leave wearing the brace.

Levi asked a question as they waited in the long drop-off line at the school. "Can we get pizza for supper?"

"No, I'm making spaghetti and meat sauce." Shelby glanced in the rearview mirror and tucked a stray hair behind one ear. She might be spending Jeb's money for groceries, but she remained budget-conscious.

"Half the kids at school get it every Friday night. Why can't we?" Levi opened the door, ready to step out.

"Jeb likes home cooking," Shelby stated, which was true. Her frugal nature wouldn't let her buy pizza every week. "I love you both. Have a good day."

At the farmhouse, she found Jeb hunched over a desktop computer in the guest bedroom. The desk sat beneath a window overlooking the side yard and a large pasture beyond. Shelby had the same view from her bedroom window. "Hey." She placed her hands on his shoulders, careful not to shift the brace. "How's it going?"

Jeb turned. "It'll be great once I shed Mr. Misery. I'll have everything up and running long before Levi gets home. I'd like to move the desk into the dining room, but right now, my back can't handle it."

"Why not leave it here?" Shelby peered over his shoulder. His bank account page appeared on the screen, and she stifled a gasp at the amount. He'd told the truth when he said he had enough money to help. It still didn't mean she would or should take it, though. *At least, he doesn't have to worry over every penny the way I do.*

Jeb leaned back and grimaced. "It would be better

in the other room, so we can keep an eye on Levi. I trust the kid, but there's too much serious stuff on the web. I wouldn't want him to stumble across things he's not old enough to explore." Jeb switched screens to a rodeo site. "I need to take this durned brace off. Once it's off, I'm calling a couple of my cousins to help move the desk."

Shelby nodded. Jeb had an excellent point. "You're right. Cyberspace isn't always safe. Stand up and I'll get the brace undone. Thanks, Jeb." *I thank him too often. He's probably tired of it.* She slid the straps away from his shoulders. Shelby unfastened the hook-and-loop clasps holding the device in place. "Better?"

Jeb rolled his shoulders as he shrugged the thing away. "Much." He reached for his phone to make the call. "I hope I can round them up to come help."

"I can try, if you don't." She would rather not. Laundry waited, and she planned to make cookies before lunch. "Are you coming to Levi's game tomorrow?"

"I wouldn't miss it." Jeb grinned.

Shelby laughed. "Good. He'd be disappointed if you did."

Five dozen chocolate chip cookies cooled as Shelby started lunch. Earlier in the week, she had served meatloaf. The leftovers would make thick, tasty sandwiches. She found a bag of corn chips in the cabinet to serve on the side. Shelby poured two glasses of iced tea and called Jeb to the table. "Looks like your cousins arrived. Should I make them sandwiches, too?" Shelby rose as a battered, older pickup arrived. They hadn't said grace or taken a bite yet.

Jeb stepped to the window, then sighed. "It's not

Zach and Bear."

A gray-haired man wearing a worn cowboy hat exited the truck and headed toward the house. "Then who is it?" Shelby reached for another plate so she could invite the new arrival to join them.

"My father." Jeb clenched his hands into fists. "He lives in Idaho, and I haven't seen him for a long time.

"Your dad? You've never mentioned him." Shelby glanced at Jeb. "Why's he here? Oh, I bet he heard you were injured."

"Could be, but I doubt he came because of me." Jeb narrowed his eyes and spread his hands wide. "I'm guessing he wants money. He's a moocher. He begged all he could from Pop and Granny when they were still alive." He sighed and flexed his fists. "Now he's after me. Joe wouldn't be here for any other reason. I'll get rid of him. He's not worth the bread he eats."

His careless condemnation upset Shelby. Her chest tightened as he faced her with an expression uglier than any she had seen him wear. "Jeb!"

Jeb ran one hand over his hair. "It's the truth. He lit out from here six months after my mom died without a thought or care for his son. Far as I know, he never sent any money to provide for me. My grandparents left the farm to me, because he would have sold it and drank away the money." He spat the words like bitter pills. His voice carried a sharp edge like a well-honed knife. Jeb smacked his open left palm with his right fist.

Shelby gaped at Jeb. She'd never known him to be so vehement or angry. "He drinks?"

"He's an unrepentant alcoholic." Jeb scowled. "He's a deadbeat and a loser. I guess like a bad penny, he always turns up."

His vehemence shocked Shelby. She was glad the children were at school so they didn't hear Jeb's rant. Shelby waited for the man to knock. He didn't.

He paused to scrape his feet on the mat. He stepped inside.

"Ever think about knocking?" Jeb folded his arms over his chest and glared as his father stepped into the kitchen. "You got about a minute to speak your piece and get out."

The tall man with weathered features resembled Jeb. Like his son, this man had height and was lean. On closer scrutiny, Shelby noticed the red, watery eyes and broken capillaries marring his otherwise handsome face.

He swept a worn hat off his head. "Jeb, I ain't gonna knock, not in my own house. Son, how are you? I came because I heard about your dustup in the arena. Got worried and thought you might still be in the hospital. I did try to call but couldn't get you on your cell. Glad to see you're up and about." The older man clutched his headgear against his chest.

"I'd believe you were worried when pigs fly." He took another step forward without the cane. "You know good and well it's my house. Anyway, has been since Granny and Pop died. I'm on the mend, as you can see. What do you really want?" Jeb barked the words with the force of an attack dog. He advanced a step. Shelby now stood behind him.

"Why, Jeb, don't be like that." Jeb's father hung the battered hat on a hook near the back door. "Won't you introduce me to this young lady? Did you get hitched and not tell me?" The man grinned, revealing a few broken and missing teeth.

"I wouldn't tell you, not even if..." Jeb broke off in mid-sentence as he raised his fist and shook it at his father. He stopped because he didn't know what he might blurt if he didn't. His father's unexpected arrival rattled his nerves.

Shelby feared he might strike his father, so she stepped around Jeb to prevent the possibility. "I'm Shelby Thacker."

"Josiah Hill." The man extended his hand to shake. "I go by Joe or Joey."

If it weren't for Jeb's hostile behavior, Shelby would offer Mr. Hill a cup of coffee or glass of tea, but she didn't. She waited and wondered what the back story might be.

Jeb clutched his stomach and frowned. "Cut to the chase. How much do you need?"

Josiah hesitated, then heaved a sigh. "Two grand, son. Got a couple of outstanding driving under the influence tickets I gotta pay, and I could use a little to tide me over until my next unemployment comes."

Shelby expected Jeb to find his checkbook.

But instead, he went to the freezer. He reached deep inside and brought out a blue bank bag. Jeb unzipped it, counted out twenty $100 bills, and handed the stack to his father.

Josiah counted it, then stuck it into the front pocket of his jeans. "I appreciate it, Jebediah, even if you begrudge giving it to me. You're stingy as Ma was. That's a fact."

"Granny had the most generous heart of anyone I've known." Jeb raised his voice for the first time. After a moment, he bowed his head. "Do you have enough to get to Boise?"

"I ain't going back. Too far. I got a line on a job working with horses less than fifty miles away, over in Kansas. I'm heading there. I know you won't but call me once in a while. Same cell number, and I know the landline number here. I hope you recover soon and get back to rodeo." Joe failed to meet his son's gaze as he grabbed his hat.

"I'm out for good this time." Jeb hadn't used the cane or walker to reach the kitchen. His legs quivered. "This injury finished me with rodeo, so I'm settling down."

Josiah nodded, but his expression wilted. "I'm right sorry to hear, Jeb. I'll get on my way, then. I won't write, but I might phone, if I take a notion. Call me, Son, anytime." He backtracked to his truck and never glanced back.

Jeb stood as hard and still as a granite monument until the truck bumped down the drive. Once out of sight, he sank into a chair at the table. "I'm sorry you had to see that, Shelby."

She took a seat across from Jeb. "I hate your dad's like that." Shelby had a ball of ice in her tummy. She'd never seen Jeb so vehement.

Jeb shrugged. "He is, though. From what my grandparents said, he wasn't always. When I was a kid, I remember some good times, but when he took off, he erased all those memories. He's just a sorry excuse for a man now. The only time I've seen him in years is when he shows up at a rodeo or needs cash. Wouldn't be so bad if he came to see me compete, but he always has his hand out for money. If I let him, then he'll run through everything I have."

Shelby's heart plummeted. *Does Jeb think I'm a*

moocher, too? A gold digger out to get money and take help? I'm the farthest thing from it. She resolved not to take any more financial assistance. She would accept her paycheck, but nothing more. Stung, with her feelings hurt, she made no reply. She bowed her head, spoke the blessing, and tried to eat. The cold meatloaf sandwich she craved earlier stuck in her throat, and she couldn't finish.

Jeb ate even less. "I lost my appetite. Don't judge me by him, please." He dumped his uneaten food into the trash and placed his plate in the sink. "I don't want you to think less of me. I might look like him, but I take after Pop. Granny taught me to be a better man."

"I'm not." What little she'd eaten soured her stomach. "I've never seen you so mad." *I haven't known Jeb long. There's things I haven't seen or don't know.*

"He brings out the worst in me, and I know it. I shouldn't get angry, but I do." Jeb rose and pressed a fist against his abdomen. "I've got a bad case of indigestion. I'm going to the recliner for a bit."

"Sure." Shelby picked up the bank bag. "I'll put this back in the freezer. I had no idea you kept cash in there."

"It's my rat hole money. Pop kept a stash there, so I always have. You can dip into it, though, anytime you want." Jeb took a couple of tottering steps.

"I'll pass, thanks." The words flew from her mouth before she thought. Although Jeb had been generous, he must have a hangup about freeloaders. *He could turn on me and be hateful. Maybe begrudge me the money he's spent. If we were ever together, it might be an issue.* Her tummy remained unsettled after the unpleasant encounter with Josiah Hill so she downed a dose of antacid. She didn't join him, either, but hung out in the kitchen and flipped through some old cookbooks she'd found.

His cousins, Zach, and a huge man Jeb called Bear arrived right before Shelby headed out to pick up the kids.

Jeb, using the cane, let them inside and introduced both men.

She acknowledged them with a nod but didn't linger to chat. On the way into town, she stopped at the supermarket to buy something to cook. Shelby picked out a large ribeye steak for Jeb, salad fixings, and baking potatoes. She purchased ground beef to make hamburgers for her and the kids.

His cousins were gone by the time Shelby returned. The desk and computer were in the dining room. The hospital bed had been shifted closer to the living room, and a pair of the dining room chairs sat beside the desk.

"Cool!" Levi dashed to the computer as he entered the room. "Can I use it?"

"Of course." Jeb grinned. "Let me go over the ground rules. Your mom or I need to be close when you're on the computer. No surfing to any weird sites. I put parental controls in place so you shouldn't be able to, but just in case, ask first." Jeb displayed his first smile since his dad departed. "Drag over a chair."

"What about me?" Lexi pushed past her brother to stand on Jeb's far side.

"You, too. There's more than one chair. Pick one and you'll get a turn, too." Jeb wheeled the desk chair out of the way as Levi scooted one of the ladder-back chairs into place.

"I'll go fix supper." Shelby retreated to the kitchen. Although Jeb now acted as if nothing unusual had happened, she hadn't forgotten his father's visit or the harsh things Jed said. Shelby wasn't a moocher, and she wanted to make sure Jeb realized it.

When they gathered for the evening meal, Jeb eyed his plate, then the others. "What's the deal?"

"I thought you might like a nice ribeye for a change." Shelby folded her hands to pray. Although she shut her eyes, she peeked to see Jeb's reaction.

He frowned and mumbled the blessing. "At every other meal, we've eaten the same things." He hadn't touched his silverware. "So, why do I have a steak, and the rest of y'all don't?"

Shelby felt heat in her cheeks as she flushed. "I figured you deserved a good steak, but meat is expensive. So, I bought hamburger for me and the littles."

"I'd like a steak." Levi stared at Jeb's plate. "I don't think I ever had one, but it looks good."

"I was raised to think everyone eats steak, or we all have burgers." Jeb glowered. "I don't get why you did this, Shelby. Is there another burger?"

She nodded. She had no idea what Jeb intended to do. "I ended up with one extra patty."

Jeb picked up his steak knife and cut the ribeye into fourths. He kept one portion and placed the other pieces on their plates. He halved the baked potato. "I'll take the extra burger, if you don't mind. Who wants a baked potato instead of potato chips?"

"Jeb, don't make a big deal." Shelby moved to return the shared steak to his plate. His actions flustered her, and shame rose in her heart. Maybe she'd grandstanded a little too much, but she'd been trying to make a point.

"I'm not. Bring me the burger, or I'll fetch it myself. I'll eat half the spud, if you want the other." Jeb stated in a mild tone. "I don't need salad tonight so it can go back in the fridge for tomorrow. Let's dig in."

Conversation during the meal remained muted. The kids picked up on the adults' dour mood and said little.

After the meal, Jeb cleared his throat. "Why don't you guys go play on the computer? You'll find several kids' games. If you need help, holler. I'll be right here with your mom."

If he wanted to talk about this, he'd have to start the discussion. Shelby bustled through cleanup in silence. Once finished with the chores, she took a seat at the table across from Jeb and squirted hand lotion into her palm. Shelby rubbed it into her skin, and the light lemon fragrance wafted through the kitchen.

"Tell me why, Shelby." Jeb met her gaze. His voice rang in the silence, although he sounded sad, not angry.

She knew exactly what he meant and flushed. "Why what?"

Jeb's blue eyes darkened into sapphires. "Why this nonsense of serving me steak and cooking burgers for you and your kids? I ought to be insulted. I'm not a man who'll begrudge anyone food. Like I said, in this house, we either all have steak, or we don't."

Humility didn't set well on her stomach. Shelby lashed out with everything she felt. "I saw what you think about charity today. I don't want you to think I'm like your dad. I don't have a hand out for what I can get from you."

"That's not what I think about you, honey." Jeb raked one hand through his hair. "Dad's been taking, not giving, for almost as long as I can remember."

Shelby huffed a huge breath. "I thought you meant it when you offered to help me or you bought things for the kids, like Levi's cleats and his gloves for football. Now, I don't know."

Jeb's eyes widened, and his mouth turned down in a frown. "I did mean it, and I do, Shelby. I'd like to help more if you would allow it. My dad's a taker, and you're a giver."

"I'm your hired nurse." She hurled the words like thrown stones. "I don't know why you want to offer, but I can't take anything more. I shouldn't have accepted the things I did."

"You're mad." Jeb stretched a hand across the table to take hers.

But she pulled away.

"Don't be angry. You're not just my nurse or an employee. I kinda thought we'd become friends, and I'm hoping we might become more."

A wild, crazy hope tempered her fury. "I *am* your nurse right now. I like the possibility of something deeper, but I don't know. I can't let you or anyone play games with my kids. They're already too close to you. When this job ends, they'll be upset." So would she, but Shelby held back. "Jeb, I can't be a charity case. I have some pride."

"Of course you do, honey. You're amazing, Shelby. Your kids are awesome. I want to help any way I can. Money doesn't mean much to me. You're not like my father. He just takes, takes, and takes. You give me more than I even know how to explain." Tears burned in his eyes.

She wanted to believe him. "Money matters more when you don't have any. I would hate for you to think I'm like your father. If you did, it would hurt me worse than a knife in my chest."

"I don't and I won't. You're nothing like him. Are we okay? Tell me we are so I can relax." He cocked his head.

We sounded like they were in a relationship. "Yes," she breathed. "I'm sorry, Jeb."

"Nothing to apologize about." His frown faded as he sighed.

"I didn't mean to be rude. From here on out, we'll eat the same. I promise." Shelby outlined a cross on her chest.

"I'm glad. Shelby, you mean a lot to me." Jeb stroked her fingers with a gentle touch.

Her ruffled feathers smoothed, and her heart quit aching. "It's okay. Jeb, I lo…" Shelby quit before confessing she loved him. She did, more than she wanted to admit, but she wasn't ready to tell him.

"Let's go see what Levi and Lexi are up to on the computer." Jeb found his feet and hobbled into the dining room. On the way, he linked his hands with hers.

Harmony between them had been restored. On Saturday morning, Shelby and Jeb sat together in the stands at Levi's game. The match took place on one of the local high school fields, complete with announcers in the press box and tiny cheerleaders on the sidelines.

Lexi bounced from one seat to another. "Grandma's here!"

Shelby waved so her mom could spot their location. "Mom, our team, the Wolverines are ahead.

Levi wears #15."

Delia made her way through the crowd and sank onto the metal bleacher below them. "Just like Mahomes. I bet Levi likes the coincidence."

"He does. Mom, I want you to meet Jeb Hill, my patient, and also a friend." Shelby held her breath for a moment before she made the introduction. Her mom could be protective and sometimes prickly. Until now, despite having picked up and dropped off the kids several times, her mom hadn't met her patient. "Jeb, this is my mother, Delia Brown."

"I'm glad to meet you, Mrs. Brown." Jeb dropped his cane and stood.

Levi, the wide receiver, caught the ball from the quarterback and ran. The kid passed it back, and the team made another touchdown.

"Go, Wolverines."

"I've heard a lot about you." Delia clapped her hands from her seat to celebrate the score. "Shelby's glad to have the job. She tells me my grandkids like you."

Jeb sat and grinned. "I'm fond of the kids, and we get along pretty well."

"Looks like you're mobile." Delia pursed her lips and stared at Jeb. "How much longer will you need my daughter's professional services?"

"Another month, probably two." Jeb never lost focus on the field action despite the inquiry.

"Mom, don't pry." Shelby tapped Delia's shoulder. "Watch the game."

Although Shelby lacked any athletic skill, and physical education had been her least favorite subject in school, she took pride in her son's prowess. Levi moved well, and his running speed proved beneficial for his team.

The Wolverines won, and as the cheering boys left the field, more than one of the kids' parents provided soft drinks and snacks.

Shelby hadn't expected parents would provide treats. She had no experience with team sports.

"Way to go." Jeb smacked his hand against Levi's in a high five when the kid met them at the bleachers after the game.

Levi grinned "Thanks, Jeb. Hi, Mom, hi, Grandma. Hey, can we eat out? Most kids are."

Shelby parted her lips to say *no*.

"That's out of the question, Levi." Delia hugged Levi. "You know very well your mama doesn't have money for extras like that. Come on over to my house. I bought a new jar of peanut butter. I'll fix sandwiches. I can make popcorn, too."

Levi's grin faded. "I guess, Grandma."

"I thought we were getting chicken tenders." Lexi jumped from one bleacher to another. "Jeb said we could."

"Did you?" Shelby adjusted her purse higher on her shoulder. She fixed her gaze on him.

"Yeah, I did." Jeb nodded. "Back when I played sports, we always grabbed a meal after the games. I wasn't going to step on anyone's toes, and I planned to ask." Jeb supported himself to stand with the cane and waited.

Shelby glanced from her kids to Jeb and then to her mom. "Let's go, then."

"Well, I never," Delia spoke in a loud voice, audible enough to make other spectators turn in their direction. "I don't really think it's appropriate."

Shelby stiffened her back. "Mom, it's fine."

"Mrs. Brown, come with us." Jeb exited the bleachers with extreme care.

Shelby smothered a smile at her mom's shocked expression.

"Well, I hadn't thought…I mean, I don't know." Delia fanned her face with her right hand.

"Please, Grandma, come, too!" Lexi clung to her grandmother's hand.

Shelby crossed her fingers and waited for the answer. She'd like to go, and her kids were counting on it.

"All right." Delia exhaled after a long pause. She crossed her arms over her chest. "I'm keeping an eye on you, Jeb Hill, and if you're up to no good, I'll warn my family to steer clear." She glared at Jeb. "Tell me where we're headed. The kids can ride with me."

Jeb named a popular casual dining restaurant. "We'll meet you there."

Jeb one, Mom zero. Shelby stifled a giggle and took Jeb's arm. "It must be hard, navigating across the playing field with the cane. Let me help. I apologize for my mom. She has good intentions."

He laughed. "She's looking out for you and the kids. I get it, I really do. Compared to your introduction to my dad, meeting your mom went very well, don't you think?"

Shelby did. Any doubts over money or Jeb's intentions vanished for the moment. "Definitely. Let's catch up before we get separated in traffic."

Jeb paused and caught her chin. "Sure, but I think we can find the restaurant, even if we lose track of each other on the road. Give me a kiss first, honey."

Her heart beat like a drum in the football homecoming parade as she pressed her lips to his. This Hillbilly Hotshot had found his way into her heart. *I let him in so please, God, don't let it be a horrible mistake.*

Chapter Nine

On the first Sunday in October, Jeb returned to his childhood church. His mom's funeral had taken place here, and so had his grandparents', but the good memories outweighed the sad. Jeb remembered Sunday School classes and sharing a pew with his folks. He'd been baptized in the fount behind the altar. Years had passed since he'd come on a regular basis, although Jeb had occasionally attended when he was home during the off-season.

Although he carried the cane, Jeb did his best not to depend on it. He wore his best pair of boots, a gray Western-cut sport jacket once belonging to Pop, a white-on-white Western shirt, and a string tie. He added a gray felt cowboy hat he'd had for years. Jeb had kept it for dressy and never wore it in the arena.

"You look handsome." Shelby smoothed down the shoulders of the jacket with her hands. "Did you dress up much when you were bustin' broncs?"

"Never. These are Sunday clothes." He enjoyed her touch. "You look pretty in a dress."

Until today, he hadn't seen her in anything but scrubs or the occasional pair of jeans with a T-shirt or blouse. Shelby wore a floral print dress with pink, yellow, and brown flowers against a navy background. The skirt swirled mid-calf with a ruffled hem, and the dress cinched her small waist with a belt. Instead of comfortable loafers or tennis shoes, she sported dark-blue pumps.

"Thank you." She blushed at the compliment. "We're ready whenever you are."

Lexi's dress combined a light-purple top with a royal-purple skirt covered with appliqued butterflies. She danced through the kitchen on the way outside.

Levi wore brown jeans and a snap-button Western shirt blending brown and blues.

"They're wearing their Easter outfits," Shelby confided. "Mom always gets them something new."

Faith Church sat beneath tall trees. Falling leaves held the first faint hint of autumn color. The white frame structure boasted a gravel parking lot and a dozen steps to enter. Jeb left his cane in the truck and allowed Shelby to escort him. "I don't want to lose my balance." He enjoyed having her on his arm. She might be his nurse, but she'd become very dear. None of the usual terms fit. He didn't want to call her girlfriend and sound like a teenager. Friend wasn't quite right either. *She's my lady.*

"I'll make sure you don't." Shelby increased her support.

They mounted the steps together, the children in front, and entered the sanctuary. The simple church dated to the mid-twentieth century. Inside the front doors, a cradle roll painted on the wall still bore Jeb's name. He touched it, almost awestruck, surprised it hadn't been painted over. They sat in a pew midway back on the left-hand side, and he thought they must look like a family. The idea pleased him very much. On his solo visits, Jeb always felt awkward as he sat alone on the end of a pew.

Although he hadn't expected to know many people, not after years and infrequent visits, the pianist at the front put her hands over her mouth, then called his name.

She stepped down from the raised platform.

The woman moved down the aisle with admirable speed for a woman who had to be ninety years old. "Good morning, Miss Bessie." Jeb stood to greet her.

The small woman, with white hair permed into tight curls, hugged him tight. "I'm so glad to see you, young man. I'd heard you were back because you got hurt. How are you?"

"I'm on the mend." He smiled, touched by her concern. "You're pretty as ever, Miss Bessie."

"Oh, pshaw, you're a charmer, always were." The old woman patted his arm and wore a wide smile. "I look like an old haint on my good days, and like something out of a nightmare on the bad ones. Is this your family?" She focused her gaze on his companions.

He wished he could say it was. "Miss Bessie, this is my lady friend, Shelby Thacker, and her two children, Levi and Lexi. Shelby's a widow and a nurse. She's helping me get back on my feet. Shelby, this is Miss Bessie Parker, one of my grandmother's oldest friends. I've known her all my life. She taught me in Sunday School."

Shelby shook the older woman's hand. "I'm pleased to meet you, ma'am."

"Likewise. I can't stay in the aisle. These days, I play the piano for services. They can't find anybody else, or I'd retire." Bessie planted her hands deep in the pockets of her dress.

Lexi peeked around her mama. "Jeb plays piano."

Jeb thought he might sink into the floor with embarrassment. Except for the few recent times he'd fooled with the piano at the house, he hadn't made music in years.

Miss Bessie clapped her hands together. "Oh, maybe you could take over."

"I'm pretty rusty." A flush warmed his cheeks. Jeb doubted he could play with Miss Bessie's skill.

"Maybe after Jeb's fully recovered. He's not there yet."

Shelby dived in and saved him.

The old woman beamed. "Practice and brush up your piano playing just in case."

Church uplifted Jeb's spirits. He belted out the hymns. He was glad they were traditional instead of modern. He liked using the aged hymnals in the pews. Jeb's Bible hadn't seen frequent use in recent years, but he found comfort in the Scriptures the preacher used for his sermon. The message, based on Mark, Chapter Five "Be not afraid, only believe" resonated with Jeb.

His life plan had been vague before he took a hard spill in the arena. Jeb had figured on riding rodeo until he got too old to continue. After that, he planned to come back to the farm to raise cattle or rough stock. Jeb had drifted for too long, and although he sometimes had dreamed of a wife and family, he never pursued marriage. The rodeo circuit hadn't been the best environment to find a good woman—not the kind he would want to marry. He'd met one or two, but none Jeb wanted for a lifetime. Before Jeb's injury, he'd been fearless, despite numerous bumps and knocks over the years. Nothing changed his attitude until the serious spinal fracture. Now, everything scared him.

Jeb worried he'd fall and hurt himself again or worse. He fussed about Shelby and fretted that her occasional headaches could be a sign of illness. Levi and Lexi brought new concerns. Jeb didn't want to see them hurt or sick. He'd never realized what a joy children were or understood what being a daddy meant. Josiah had failed to set a good example—although Jeb had been blessed with the finest grandfather a boy could have. He ached to become Levi and Lexi's dad so he could provide and nurture. Whether or not it might happen depended on Shelby.

Believe. The pastor's message resonated. In the pew, Jeb hoped God had a plan in place. For the first time in years, Jeb sought the Lord. He prayed early in the morning before he rose and at night after he'd gone to bed. The rented hospital bed had been returned to the medical supply company, and the dining room put to rights. For now, he slept in the guest bedroom, and he continued to use the baby monitor. Each day he wore Mr. Misery, the brace, for at least an hour, but he still didn't like it. He wasn't even sure if it did any good. Jeb turned his focus back to the service and his companions.

After a rousing rendition of "What A Friend We Have In Jesus," the service ended, and they filed out.

Brother Burnett, the pastor, stood near the entrance and shook hands. He pumped Jeb's with extra enthusiasm. "Good to have you home son. I hear you're on the way back to good health. I've been praying and will continue."

"Thank you." Jeb grinned. "I'm happy to be back." And he was, he realized, despite the upheaval he'd undergone to be back on the farm. He would have introduced Shelby, but the kids dashed into the parking lot, and she chased after them. At the truck, Jeb offered to buy lunch. "I was thinking about one of the buffets." He figured any decent spread would offer something everyone would enjoy.

"Asian or American?" Shelby backed out of the parking slot.

"Whichever you want. Will the kids eat Asian?" Jeb's tastebuds tingled at the idea of enjoying his favorite dishes including Kung Pao shrimp, beef pepper steak, and General Tso's chicken.

"They like chicken nuggets without sweet and sour or cashew sauce. Levi will eat his fill of any kind of shrimp, and Lexi loves crab rangoons. She'll eat rice, too." Shelby paused the truck at a crossroads. "Should I head for town? I can make something at home."

"Let me treat everyone. It's been hectic, and I figure you're tired." Jeb shook his head. He craved Asian, and he resented Shelby playing her frugal card. He could afford the meal and wanted to enjoy the treat.

Levi gave him a thumbs-up.

"I am. Town it is, then." Shelby pointed the truck for the main highway leading to St. Joseph.

I guess I need to chill out about money. It's just hard to break old habits, though.

Savory aromas wafted through the restaurant, and each selected their favorites from several serving stations. Everyone finished their meal with a dish of soft-serve ice cream. Jeb spooned the last bite of vanilla into his mouth. "I'm full and ready for a nap once we get home."

"I need to stop at a discount store first. We're out

of laundry soap, tissues, coffee, bread, and sugar. It won't take long." Shelby shifted her focus to Jeb as she ate her last spoonful of chocolate.

He held back a sigh. They'd be in town every day, between dropping off the kids, his physical therapy, and Levi's practice. On request, his PT had been shifted from Tuesday and Thursday to Monday and Wednesday, so it wouldn't conflict with football. If he could choose, they would shop another day. It wasn't worth disputing, though. "I'm okay with it." He patted his full stomach. Naptime could wait.

A worry line divided her forehead. "If you're worn out, you can wait while I run inside."

"I'd like do a little shopping, too." Jeb wanted to browse. He hadn't visited many stores since he came home. For the first time in years, he wanted to gawk at the Halloween displays, check out the costumes and candy, and glance over the Christmas decorations. To be safe, he used the cane to navigate.

At the store, Shelby grabbed a shopping cart from the rack and took a list out of her purse.

The kids whispered together. Levi became the spokesman. "Can we go with Jeb?"

Shelby shrugged. "If it's okay with him, sure. Behave."

"We will." Levi rolled his eyes. As soon as his mom vanished out of sight, he tugged Jeb's jacket. "Can we go look at Halloween stuff?"

The aisles brimmed with merchandise for the fall holiday. Among the straw scarecrows, bright pumpkins, and cute costumes, Jeb recoiled at grotesque devil masks, zombie costumes, winged demons, glow-in-the-dark skulls, creepy dolls, and evil vampire attire. In late

October, he usually had been traveling from one competition to the next. He had failed to realize Halloween had become huge or shifted from fun to almost sinister.

"I don't like the scary stuff." Lexi shivered and moved closer to Jeb.

"Neither do I." Jeb had thought he might get each child a costume, and although he saw some without evil qualities, he decided they could make their own. "I never had store-bought costumes. My mom would put together something. One year I was a farmer, then a cowboy, then a robot."

"I want to be a princess." Lexi turned away from the frightening selection.

"You could, and Levi might be a football player. What do you think?" Jeb imagined possible results and liked the idea.

The boy's eyes lit up. "Awesome!"

Jeb should consult Shelby, although he expected her to balk at his offer to buy Halloween items. "Let's see what we can find. I have one or two ideas." Jeb led them away from the aisle, his mind filled with the One Hundred And First Psalm, "I will set no wicked thing before mine eyes."

In the boys' clothing section, Jeb found a Mahomes red-and-yellow jersey complete with his number, 15. "Your youth football pants will work with this. We'll pick up a cheap football in sporting goods. You can carry it as a prop."

Levi's fist pumped the air. "Yeah! Thanks, Jeb. We don't do much trick-or-treating. I can wear the shirt to school, too."

"I heard the pastor announce a harvest party at

church. I figured we could attend." Jeb grinned. "If your mom doesn't care."

"If I don't mind what?" Shelby rolled her cart to a halt beside them. She glanced into Jeb's heaping basket. "What's all this stuff?"

"Costumes. All the Halloween merchandise with devils and demons made me uncomfortable. This is an alternative." Jeb lifted the jersey from the cart to display. "I told them it's my treat. Levi can be a football player, and Lexi a princess."

"Jeb, you don't need to do this." Shelby rested her right hand on her hip.

"I want to, sugar." Jeb met her gaze and smiled. "Please don't fuss. I'd like them to have fun, the way I did."

"But we won't be in town to go trick-or-treating. I usually take them to a couple trunk-or-treat events. I go by Mom's so she can see them dressed up." Shelby picked up the football and balanced it between her hands. "Maybe I should pay for this stuff."

"Let me, please, unless you don't believe in trick-or-treating." Jeb cupped her cheek with his left hand and gripped the cane with the other.

"All right." Shelby covered his hand with her fingers. "I'll let you help, this time. I don't mind them dressing up. My rule is they can't pick anything scary, so a football player is fine."

"Yeah!" Levi slapped Jeb's palm in a high five.

"What about me?" Lexi worked her way between to stand between Jeb and Shelby. "Can I be a princess?"

"You bet!" Jeb adjusted the cane for better support.

"I can take her to find what she needs. Can you pick up a pumpkin to carve? Levi can help choose one."

Shelby rubbed her forehead.

"Let's do it together." Jeb took over her cart and combined the contents with his. "I'll push. Does your head hurt?

"A little but I'm just tired." Her shoulders sagged. "Let's get finished so we can head home." Shelby found a cream-colored, full-length dress for Lexi. The garment featured a lacy overskirt and sheer sleeves.

With new dress shoes and a lacy shawl, the girl would transform into a beautiful princess. Jeb found a cubic zirconia tiara in the jewelry department and bought it along with some glitzy clip-on earrings. Before checking out, he and Levi chose the largest pumpkin in the store. By then, he was more than ready to leave. Although he'd enjoyed shopping with kids more than he ever imagined he might. Their smiles brought happiness, and he wondered if being a dad would be like this. Still, his back hurt, and Jeb wanted the nap he'd mentioned. After he'd slept, he idled away the rest of the day.

Shelby made a light supper of soup and sandwiches. No one, including Jeb, had much appetite after the midday meal. Jeb read to the kids from his childhood set of *The Bible Story.* Afterward, he fist-bumped Levi and kissed Lexi's cheek before their mom led them upstairs for bathtime and bed.

Once she settled the kids, Shelby came downstairs. "They like their costumes, and I love they're homemade. If they dress up at school, their outfits will be fine."

If? "Don't kids wear costumes at school on Halloween? We always did." Jeb placed a bookmark in the paperback he'd been reading. He remained on the couch, where he'd read to the kids.

"It's all fall parties now, and in December, it's winter break, never Christmas." Shelby sighed and took a seat on the couch. "Everything is so woke. I don't know about Halloween this year. Neither teacher has sent anything home yet."

"There's the thing at church." The harvest party had been announced that morning, and Jeb wanted to go. He twined his fingers through hers. "Will you be my date for it at Faith Church?"

"I will." She smiled, then frowned. "It sounds like so much fun. But I don't know if we should call it a date. I still work for you." Shelby bit her lip with enough force to leave teeth marks.

"I could always fire you, if dating turns out to be a problem." Jeb loomed in close for a kiss.

Shelby laughed. "Don't do that. I need the money!"

"I wouldn't, honey." He actually would, in a heartbeat, if the job prevented a relationship. "Hey, you don't have to wear scrubs every day. I don't mind, and I won't think you're any less professional."

"Okay, sure, if you'll do one thing for me." Shelby tilted her head.

"What is it?" He grinned.

"Practice the piano, so you can help Miss Bessie. She's so sweet, but she must be ancient. She deserves a break." Shelby stroked the back of his hand and caressed his long fingers.

"She's in her nineties, at least." Jeb released a relieved sigh. He'd thought she might ask something difficult. "Yeah, I will. I don't know how good I'll be, but I'm willing to try."

For the rest of October, Jeb worked hard at his PT

sessions. Sometimes, he rode an exercise bike, at the therapist's suggestion, and did exercises. When he had an idle moment at home, Jeb played the piano.

Sometimes, the kids and Shelby sang along.

Jeb called his sponsor to inform them he couldn't ride anymore. Since the boot company footed his medical bills, they had expected the call. Free from obligation for the first time in his adult life, Jeb struggled to adjust. He focused on healing, but he also thought a lot about Shelby's house. Jeb would pay for repairs, but he believed it wasn't worth saving. *She should sell the house as is. It's not safe, and it'll cost a fortune to bring it up to speed.*

The Friday before Halloween, Dr. Guiseman cleared him to climb stairs, which would allow him to sleep in his own bedroom.

"Don't overdo. Your body is healing on schedule, but I'd like to get X-rays to determine the extent. I'll schedule them for next week. How about Wednesday?" The doctor made notations on his pad as he completed the exam.

"It works." Relief he could sleep in his own bed warred against concern what X-rays might show.

"How's the pain?" Dr. Guiseman ran his fingers up and down Jeb's spine.

"It's almost gone. I can tell if I'm pushing my limits, because it hurts like someone stuck a knife in my back." Jeb hadn't mentioned his occasional suffering to Shelby.

"You haven't said anything. That's the kind of thing you tell your nurse."

Jeb shrugged. "It doesn't happen much."

"Still, I wish you'd mentioned it." Shelby

glowered.

"Avoid overdoing when you can. I wouldn't recommend going upstairs more than once or twice a day until we get those X-rays. Keep up the PT, and wear your brace daily. No driving yet, and no horseback riding. I'll see you in two weeks." Dr. Guiseman nodded as he exited the cubicle.

On the way home, Shelby took a side trip to Corby Pond, located along the parkways meandering through the city. She parked and sat in silence for a long moment.

"What's on your mind?" He'd fished here as a boy. Since then, updates to the pond had included fishing docks and a solid edge around the water.

She rested her chin on the steering wheel. "How often has your back hurt so bad?"

Busted. "Just two or three times. It's not a big deal."

"It could be if you mess up your back. I care about you, Jeb, and I'd hate for you to end up having more surgery. Recovering from it would set you back." Shelby wiggled the wheel back and forth, as far as it would go.

"I know, honey, and I don't want to go back to the hospital" He would balk at surgery unless it became a necessity. "I plan to enjoy the holidays, now I have someone to spend them with." Jeb caught her fidgeting hands and held them fast. Her words sobered him, and now he'd worry, but one thing encouraged him. She cared. "How much?"

"What?" Shelby tossed back her hair and pulled her fingers free.

"You said you care, so I asked how much." Jeb

held his breath, waiting for her reply.

"Jeb, I love you, just like in 'Forever And Ever, Amen.' "

Her whispered words echoed an old country song they both liked. Shelby's declaration touched his soul like rain refreshed the earth after a drought. His heart brimmed full of emotion, and he thought he might weep with joy. Friday afternoon overlooking a manmade pond wasn't the most romantic time or spot. The cab of a pickup truck might not be the best place to kiss his woman, but Jeb shifted position and locked his mouth on hers. "I love you, too, honey."

He still had concerns about his future and how he would fund it, solo or with Shelby. Jeb had no notion where they would go from here, but the journey had begun, for good or ill. The chance brought happiness, but it also scared the fire out of Jeb.

Chapter Ten

Although Halloween fell during the week, the harvest event at church would take place Friday night. There would be a chili supper in the fellowship hall followed by an old-fashioned party. Events would include a cakewalk, musical chairs, bobbing for apples, and a scavenger hunt geared to youth. Adults could participate, too. Each child in attendance would receive a bag of treats, including everything from miniature candy bars to popcorn balls. Although costumes weren't required, at the last possible minute Jeb decided he would dress up.

Buried deep in the guest room closet, he'd found garments belonging to his grandparents—a double-breasted black pinstripe suit of Pop's and a demure full-skirted black dress with a white collar and belt his grandmother must have worn. He knew the suit would fit, and if Shelby was willing, the dress might work for her. Over coffee, Jeb pitched the idea. "What do you think? Should we go as a vintage couple? The clothes date to at least the 1960s."

"I haven't dressed up since I was a little girl, but I will, this one time." She brought the coffeepot over to refill his cup. "How's your back?" Since Jed had admitted to the doctor he'd experienced some pain episodes, Shelby became relentless. It was her job to ask, and besides, she did care.

"Good." Jeb hadn't told her the complete truth, downplaying the incidents to two or three. If he counted, he might have suffered five or six times. Jeb planned to take things as easy as possible during the day in anticipation of the harvest party. He hoped to enjoy it, not suffer.

"Do you want pancakes or waffles?" Shelby opened the cupboards as she spoke.

"Waffles, unless they're frozen." Jeb watched as she dug out the waffle iron.

"Never in my world. Bacon or sausage?"

Shelby took the green mixing bowl his grandmother always used from the cabinet.

She added the ingredients and stirred.

"Just waffles are fine, honey. Where are the kids?" He hadn't heard a peep out of them since coming downstairs. "Did they already eat?"

Shelby laughed. "Yes, they had a bowl of cereal earlier. No school today for fall break. They're playing outside before the weather turns. It's supposed to get colder, with lows in the twenties by tomorrow night. I thought we should go by my house tomorrow and make sure everything's winterized. If we have to move back, I can't deal with frozen pipes on top of everything else."

Jeb's heart plummeted. The plumbing was the least of his concerns about Shelby's house. The sunken floor, issues with the upstairs toilet, the back porch, and the roof were far more threatening. He wasn't a roofer, but he could spot warning signs. The way it sagged concerned him. "Honey, the house isn't in any shape for you to live in right now."

"I don't know how much longer you'll need me. I

can't stay here forever." Her smile vanished as she spread batter over the heated waffle iron.

If it were up to Jeb, she could and would. "There's so much I can't do yet, like drive. Besides, I'd be awfully lonely rattling around this place alone." He made a mock shudder. Although Jed joked, he was serious.

"I understand, and it's not that I want to leave." Shelby put a waffle at his place, then brought butter and syrup.

"Then what is it?" He reached for his knife and cut the waffle into fourths.

"I want to see what happens in the long run, together. I don't want our relationship to be based on the fact I don't have a place to live, except here. How can we tell if it's right to be together if I'm already in the same house?" With one eye on the steaming waffle iron, Shelby sat across from him.

"I know it is." Jeb had no doubts. "I love you, and you love me. What else do we need?"

"It's a start, but there's a lot more to consider." Shelby leaped up, removed a browned waffle, then sat. She folded her hands for the blessing.

"Thank you, God, for this food, this day, and this time together." Jeb buttered his waffle and took a bite. "What else is there?"

"Right now, I'm your nurse, a live-in position. Once it ends, living together becomes something else altogether. I don't want evil-minded tongues wagging. The children don't need to hear such things." Shelby poured syrup on her plate. "I don't want people to say we're living in sin."

A bite caught halfway down his throat, and he

coughed to free it. "We're not, and we won't, Shelby."

"I know but…" She paused. "Besides, Jeb, Christmas is coming."

Six weeks loomed before the holiday. Thanksgiving came first. "I don't understand what Christmas has to do with us."

Shelby sighed and grimaced. "You know, it's not my favorite holiday. I love the birth of our Savior, but not the commercial stuff. I can't afford Christmas. It's better for you if I act like Scrooge in my own house. I don't want to ruin your celebration." She cut her waffle into pieces and forked one into her mouth.

His heart ached. His woman could be stubborn. Christmas happened to be one thing Shelby had a strong opinion about. Letting him pay for things was another. "There's no way you could ever ruin my holiday unless you're not part of it. I don't plan to go crazy, just celebrate." Jeb glanced at Shelby as he finished his waffle.

"You already bought Levi a Mahomes jersey and Lexi a fancy party dress, two of the things on their wish list." Shelby narrowed her eyes and glared. "Oh, a tiara and a football, too."

"Those are part of their Halloween costumes, not presents." Jeb already had more on his list for Christmas. He'd made plans to cut down a Christmas tree, decorate it, and revive the annual traditions from his family. "It's barely November."

"Thanksgiving will be here in a few weeks, though, and the holiday season will start." Shelby stirred pieces of waffle in a puddle of syrup.

Levi walked through the back door with slow steps, Lexi behind him. His cheeks were flushed and eyes bright. "Don't the holidays start with Halloween?"

Jeb grinned. "Not in my book. I say Thanksgiving myself. Pop wouldn't even agree with that. To him, the holidays were Christmas and New Year's."

"Halloween is over, after the harvest party tonight." Shelby finished half of her waffle and put the plate aside. "I like to have Thanksgiving as its own day, with a focus on giving thanks, feasting with family, and enjoying everything."

"Sounds perfect." Jeb resolved he'd buy all the groceries for the holiday repast. "I'm looking forward to it. Are you kids ready for tonight?"

"I'm not." Levi groaned and held his midsection. "I've got a bad tummy ache."

"How long has your stomach been hurting?" Shelby frowned as a worry line appeared in the middle of her forehead.

"Since after breakfast." Levi winced and rubbed his abdomen.

"Didn't it bother you playing outside?" Jeb eyed the kid.

"Yeah, it did." He placed both hands over his belly and made a face. "Mama, my tummy really hurts. That's why we came inside."

"Come here." Shelby beckoned him to the table. "Show me where."

Levi pointed to an area between his chest and bellybutton.

"How much candy did you eat this morning?" Jeb noticed the kids' plastic buckets weren't as full as before. Between a fall party at school on Thursday plus visits to several trunk-or-treat events last night, the pails had brimmed full.

"Some." Levi stared at the floor. "Well, maybe a lot."

Shelby picked up the two containers with their Halloween spoils from the counter and peered inside. "Over half of yours is gone, Levi. No wonder your stomach hurts. Lexi, did you eat candy, too?"

"She ate as much as I did!" Levi shot a glance at his sister. "She got a tummy ache first."

"Lexi, is that right?" Shelby frowned and scrutinized the child.

Lexi clutched her stomach and bent double. "My tummy is mad because I ate too much, and it hurts so bad."

After dosing both kids with pink medicine, Shelby insisted they go upstairs to lie down. "I'll check on you at lunchtime. You'll be having chicken noodle soup. It's easy on upset tum-tums." Once they'd gone, she sighed. "I hate when they're sick. I never know if it's serious, or if I should take them to the doctor. Every time their stomachs hurt, I worry about appendicitis or something worse. I went to school with a boy who had stomachaches, and it turned out he had cancer."

"Honey, they've got classic Halloween bellyaches. That's all." Jeb patted Shelby's hand. "They'll be fine."

"You're right. I hope they've learned a lesson. Now we can't go tonight, and I looked forward to it all week." Shelby stacked her plate and Jeb's.

"Why can't we?" Jeb downed the last of his coffee.

"I won't reward them for gluttony." She placed their dirty dishes in the sink. "They're too young to leave alone, and I'd worry about their stomachaches if I did."

Disappointment rankled. Jeb shook his head.

"Could your mom come out and watch them so we can still go?"

"Maybe. I hate to ask, though. She works all week, and she's tired. Do you really want to go?" Shelby's gloomy expression lightened as she placed the dishes in the sink.

"Yes, I do. It would be our first date without the kids. I'd enjoy spending time as just the two of us." He crossed his fingers and hoped Shelby would agree.

"I don't want to miss the party. I can't remember the last time I did anything but work or shop without Levi and Lexi." She rested her hands on his shoulders from behind. "Still want to dress up?"

"You bet. Who knows? We might even win a prize." Jeb yearned for an actual date. "I can call and ask your mom, if you want."

Shelby laughed. "Thanks. I'll do it. I think she likes you, but she'll be more likely to agree if I ask."

****

Delia arrived at five with two animated movies and a tub of chicken salad. "I hope they're feeling better. I thought sandwiches wouldn't bother their tummies."

Shelby hugged her mom. "They're both fine, except they're pouting, because we're going without them."

"They have to have consequences for their actions. They deserved their bellyaches. I feel sorry for them, but they have to learn not to overdo. Where on earth did you find the outfit?" Delia stroked the vintage dress. "It looks authentic."

"It is. It belonged to Jeb's grandmother. It's her hat, too." Shelby patted her headgear with a smile.

To compliment the dress, Jeb had unearthed a

black velvet pillbox hat with a jaunty bow in back and a net veil.

Shelby had pulled back her hair with a claw clip and the hat rested on top of her head, held in place with a hatpin.

Jeb grinned. He wore Pop's old suit and a fedora he'd found. "You're beautiful, Shelby."

"You look like you stepped out of the 1950s. You could be movie stars." Delia clapped her hands together. "Ricky and Lucy couldn't look any better."

"Granny loved their show. She watched "I Love Lucy" reruns right up till she died." Jeb crooked his arm for Shelby. "Ready to go?"

"I am." She picked up a vintage purse and waved to the children in the living room. "Bye, kids, behave for your grandma."

Halfway to the truck, giddy as teenagers on prom night, they clasped hands and ran.

Jeb stopped. "Shelby?"

She halted as she opened the truck door. "What is it?"

"This." He bent beneath the rim of his fedora to kiss Shelby. "I love you, honey. Let's have fun."

****

At Faith Church, they had an instant picture taken for five dollars. Jeb cherished it and vowed to keep it forever.

Miss Bessie wore a sunbonnet and old-fashioned, wire-framed glasses halfway down her nose. She carried a familiar children's book with a black-and-white checkerboard cover.

"I'm Mother Goose." She held up the storybook for emphasis. "I'll read to the little ones, though, so it's not just a costume. You two are adorable. I vow I remember your grandparents wearing those very clothes. You look wonderful!"

Jeb laughed. She would recall if anyone did. "Thanks."

"Where's the kiddoes?" Bessie glanced around.

"They stayed home with my mom, recovering from a candy overdose." Shelby rubbed her stomach.

Jeb bowed his head during the pastor's grace, then dived into his bowl of chili with gusto. He savored the spicy flavor of fall and crumbled corn chips into his.

Shelby opted for saltines. After the meal ended and the evening transitioned to games, she participated in the cake walk and came away with a two-layer, yellow bakery cake with fudge frosting. "I'll serve it on Sunday with dinner."

Watching the youth scramble for apples in a big tub and search for odd items in the scavenger hunt made Jeb wish the kids had come. They would have had a blast, but he agreed they needed to be disciplined for their actions. He and Shelby held hands all evening, and anyone who hadn't realized they had become a couple did now.

Although no prizes were handed out for costumes, they received compliments. At the end of the evening, Jeb wasn't inclined to rush home, so he suggested a slow drive along the backroads. He headed into Savannah to show Shelby the schools he had attended, the place where his grandparents bought them ice cream cones in the summer, and other landmarks. On the way back to the farmhouse, he visited a public access point on the Hundred And Two River.

"It's not the Missouri, but it's still impressive." He

observed the water as memories hit. He recalled old fishing trips and time spent with family, including his dad. Jeb shoved the thought away, so he wouldn't ruin the moment.

A full hunter's moon cast a bright glow over the slow-moving waterway. Recent rains had stripped away the remaining fall foliage from the trees lining the bank, but it remained a beautiful scene.

"I like this place." Shelby slid across the seat and rested her head on his shoulder. "I've had fun tonight. I'm sorry my kids missed it, but I'm happy we had time alone."

"So am I." Jeb smooched Shelby. "We need to do this more often, honey. Maybe plan some date nights."

"Sure. I don't know if we can manage it every week, but let's try for twice a month."

Her voice whispered sweetly against his ear, and her breath blew warm against his skin.

The weather had turned, and tonight temps would drop into the twenties. Jeb dreaded winter, but he liked the thought of cozy evenings inside the warm farmhouse. "Shelby, promise me something, would you?" The words escaped his lips before he thought.

"What's that?" She cocked her head in his direction.

"Spend Thanksgiving with me. I want to host dinner for all of us, your mom, maybe Aunt Jeannie's bunch, and maybe a few of my rodeo friends, if they're anywhere close. Let's have a traditional holiday with the biggest turkey we can find, homemade dressing, candied sweet potatoes, bread straight out of the oven, green beans, noodles…"

"And pumpkin pie." Shelby finished his sentence.

"Maybe a cake."

"Absolutely, yes." He hadn't experienced Thanksgiving at home in years. Jeb had gone to one of his aunts' houses more than once, but it hadn't been the same.

"All right, I promise. You carve the turkey, though." Shelby tapped his hand as she spoke.

"You bet. Would it be too much to ask you to share Christmas, too?" He held his breath, anticipating a refusal. Jeb already had a rebuttal ready if she did.

Shelby's tensed her muscles as she slid back behind the steering wheel. "Maybe, I don't know. I want to, but I'm afraid."

Jeb's heart ached. Her withdrawal reduced him to feeling like a kid who lost his favorite toy to a bully. "What are you scared of?"

"Failure. What if we don't work out?" Her voice broke as she asked the question.

"I think we will. " 'Love never fails.' " He quoted First Corinthians, and he believed it.

"Christmas frightens me. People wish for things. Their dreams seldom come true." Her hands drummed against the wheel.

"We'll take it slow, one step at a time. Anything you're not comfortable with, we don't have to do." Jeb crossed his fingers in the dark. "How about it?"

Shelby drew a deep breath and released it slowly. "I'll try. Okay?"

He marked her progress. Jeb decided he would continue to hope until Shelby loved Christmas as much as he did. "All right. Let's go home, put your kids to bed, and get some sleep."

Delia put a finger to her lips when they arrived.

"They're both tucked into bed sound asleep. No more tummy troubles, and they behaved like angels."

"Thank goodness." Shelby sat to remove her heels. "I appreciate you coming out, Mom. We couldn't have gone without your help."

"Anytime. I enjoyed it. Did you kids have fun?" Delia donned her jacket and picked up her purse.

"We had a blast. I'd like to take Shelby out more often if you wouldn't mind babysitting." Jeb sank into his recliner.

"I don't." Delia wore a big smile. "I love being with my grandkids, and Shelby needs a break."

Jeb and Shelby lingered downstairs for a little while. He downed a couple of ibuprofen tablets, although his back hadn't done more than twinge. He savored the harmony between them and hated to part ways. Upstairs, Jeb pulled her into his arms for a long kiss. "Good night, sugar. I'll see you in the morning. I love you, Shelby."

She gave back the kiss without restraint. "I do love you, Jeb Hill. Sleep tight." With a fleeting caress to his face, Shelby entered her room and shut the door.

Jeb did the same, but he didn't sleep right away. He didn't watch television or read. Instead, he stood at the windows overlooking the front yard and let his thoughts drift. He knew how he wanted to decorate the house for Christmas, what corner of the farm would yield the perfect tree, what to give the children, and now, he decided what he would buy for Shelby.

First, though, they needed to shop for turkey and all the fixings. With his heart full and spirit easy, Jeb lay down and hoped for sleep.

He had Shelby committed to sharing Thanksgiving.

Surely, she would follow through on Christmas, too. If she didn't, it wouldn't break his heart, but Jeb would be sad. *One step at a time, Lord, one step at a time. Let the coming days be smooth with no trouble ahead.*

Chapter Eleven

After weeks of wearing ordinary garments, donning scrubs again seemed strange. Shelby wore them to Jeb's scheduled doctor's visit to keep up appearances. She doubted the doctor knew she currently lived in Jeb's house. Her employer didn't, and wouldn't, if she could help it. Her attire probably wouldn't seem professional. There wasn't anything wrong with it, per se, but a crisp nursing appearance was preferred. In the near future, the job with Jeb would end, so she had to think about what might come next.

After reviewing Jeb's X-rays, Dr. Guiseman pronounced the fracture to be on track to heal and cut Jeb's physical therapy sessions to once a week. "You're doing much better than expected."

Shelby smiled. She'd worked hard to keep Jeb on track, insisting on his therapy and encouraging daily exercises. *I'm glad to see my efforts paid off!*

"How soon can I drive?" Jeb questioned the doc at the end of the visit. "What about riding a horse? I want to buy cattle to run on my place, and a good horse would be handy."

The doctor slid his glasses down his nose and peered over them. "I might release you to drive by the end of the month. It depends on if you continue to heal at the same pace. Horseback riding's another story. Remember, your spinal fracture was a burst fracture, meaning vertebrae shattered. If you're talking about rodeo, it's not happening, ever. I thought they made it clear at the hospital. I know I did when you asked before."

"I'm aware." Jeb's smile vanished. "I won't ever bust saddle broncs again, and I mostly don't mind. I want to stay on my farm and settle down. I just want a horse I can ride out to check the herd, once I have one."

"By the end of the year then, if your progress continues. If you ride, however, you must use extreme caution. I would suggest a mild-mannered horse. One wrong toss could paralyze you for life." The doctor paused to share a rare grin. "Frankly, I'm amazed at your progress. I'm pleased, of course, but I'm astounded you're doing this well. Complete bed rest for the first few weeks was recommended, but you used the walker to get around."

"The medical orders I received didn't state bed rest." Shelby frowned, worried her reputation might be at stake. "I would have insisted on it."

"It's water under the bridge now. Jeb's well on the way to recovery. Come back in two weeks. No, wait—that puts it on the day before Thanksgiving. My office will be closed. Three weeks, then. Keep up the excellent work." With the compliment, the doctor dismissed them.

On the way out of the office, Jeb shrugged into his fleece-lined denim jacket. "I'm glad he said three weeks. I can use the break."

"The next appointment will be close to your birthday. Isn't it December third?" Shelby remembered from the initial paperwork. Although she hadn't circled it on the calendar, she'd made a mental note. Her plans included baking an oatmeal cake with coconut frosting, cooking a special dinner, or taking Jeb out for a meal. Shelby planned to dip into her exceedingly small savings to buy a gift. Neither of the kids thought a present would be necessary, but Shelby did. She hadn't decided what to buy, but she had one or two ideas.

Jeb grinned. "That's right. When's yours?"

"April twelfth. It was Easter the year I was born." Shelby waited for the usual jokes about bunnies and baskets, but Jeb didn't make any.

"What a beautiful day to come into the world." Jeb took her hand as they walked out of the medical building. "All the rejoicing over Christ rising from the dead, and a pretty baby girl was born."

A rush of love filled her heart. She'd never met a man like Jeb Hill. He thought differently than most, and Shelby liked that.

"Where to now? I thought I'd buy you lunch." Jeb headed for the passenger side of his truck.

"I'd like a meal, but can we go by my house first? I need to get the kids' winter coats and their warmer clothes. It's supposed to turn really cold by the weekend and stay frigid." Shelby started the truck and turned it toward her home.

"No problem. We can grab a bite after." Jeb fiddled with the radio until music filled the truck.

As they approached her house, a cold sense of dread shimmied down Shelby's spine. Something felt wrong in a way she couldn't figure out. Midway down the block, she realized the house appeared odd. On closer inspection, she realized the roof slanted at a strange angle. Inner alarm bells rang a wild warning. Shelby bailed from the truck to stand on the sidewalk.

She ignored Jeb's questions. She stared at the house, then shrieked.

"What's the matter?" Jeb left the pickup and joined Shelby.

Shelby pointed upward because she lacked the words to describe the horror. A huge chunk of the roof had caved in, leaving a gaping hole on the left side of the old house. Beneath the empty space, the wall below had buckled.

"Oh, snap."

Jeb's voice rang in her ears as he put an arm around her shoulders.

"Shelby, I'm so sorry."

All Shelby could think about was how much her children needed their coats and winter clothing. She shoved Jeb away and dashed up the steps onto the porch. Hands shaking, she unlocked the door and stepped inside.

"Wait," Jeb shouted.

Shelby ignored him as she stared at the destruction. The kitchen was filled with waist-high debris. Conditions in the living room were the same. Dust floated in the air and filled her throat until she coughed. With slow steps, Shelby headed for the staircase and put a foot on the first step.

"Shelby, stay back." Jeb caught up. "Don't go any farther. It's not safe, honey. Come out of the house."

She had a single-minded purpose. Once she had what she'd come to retrieve, she would leave. Maybe then Shelby would feel emotion. Right now, she experienced detachment, a fugue state where she acted but couldn't think.

Once upstairs, Shelby found their winter coats and

dug out sweatshirts, long-sleeved flannel shirts, fleece pants, Lexi's warm nightgown, and Levi's PJ's, along with knit hats. She crammed everything but the coats into a canvas laundry bag. She descended the stairs with her load.

"Come on, let's go." Jeb waited at the bottom. "Give me the clothes."

"I need to get the pictures off the wall." Shelby dumped everything into his arms. In the living room, she plucked her wedding portrait, her grandparents' photo, and the kids' pictures from the wall. As she did, a shower of rubbish cascaded from the ceiling.

Jeb grabbed her arm and pulled her out of the house. He dragged her off the porch and to the sidewalk. "Good Lord, Shelby, you scared the fire out of me."

Before she could reply, a loud rumble echoed, and another section of the roof fell. Shelby screamed.

Jeb tossed the garment bag into the truck bed. He wrapped his arms around her. "You could have been in there." His voice choked out the words. "Shelby, honey, what were you thinking? You could be hurt or dead."

Reality hit. Her legs threatened to buckle, and she quivered from head to toe. When the last section of the roof fell in, she dropped the framed photos. The glass shattered and littered the sidewalk. "I just wanted their warm clothes." Her voice trembled in a harsh whisper. "I didn't think."

"I was afraid I might lose you, Shelby. It would break me if I did. I couldn't stand it." His arms tightened around her like a python. "Thank the Lord, oh, thank God. Are you hurt?"

"I don't think so." She shook her head, numb to the

bone. "Oh, Jeb."

His lips kissed her forehead. "I love you, Shelby. Are you sure you're okay?"

"I'm not hurt." She wasn't all right, though. Her house, the only home she had, lay in rubble. "Is your back all right?"

"It's good." He flinched.

"Jeb, are you sure?" Shelby wanted to take him back to the doctor's for another checkup or to the hospital for X-rays. She rushed into a dangerous situation without a thought how it might affect Jeb or her children. If she'd been killed, what would have happened to Levi and Lexi?

Mom would have taken them or Jeb unless he got hurt, too. Losing me would have damaged them, though, forever. They would have been orphans. Tears threatened, but Shelby swallowed them. If she started crying, she doubted she could stop.

"I am." Jeb tightened his arm around Shelby's shoulders.

A police cruiser, lights flashing, rolled up and stopped. Two officers stepped out, and the older one approached. "Is this your house?"

"It's mine." Shelby stepped forward from the shelter of Jeb's arm.

"What happened here?" The officer spoke with authority.

Shelby's mind couldn't focus to frame an answer.

"I'm Sergeant Sanderson. Who can tell me what happened here?"

Jeb stepped forward with a sigh. "The roof fell in, one section at a time. Part of it had already collapsed before we arrived." He moved closer as he spoke. "Her house was in poor condition. We recently found an issue with the upstairs bathroom floor sinking. I knew the roof wasn't in great shape, but I didn't expect it would collapse."

"Is this your current residence, and is anyone inside?" Sanderson asked.

"No and no." Jeb gritted his teeth.

"Ma'am, does this individual have the right to speak for you?" Sergeant Sanderson made notations on a pad.

Shelby nodded. "Yes, yes, he does. His name is Jeb Hill, if you need it."

"Is he your husband? Your name, please." The other officer, whose name badge read, *Jones*, spoke for the first time.

"No. I'm Shelby Thacker. I'm a nurse, and I've been on duty at Mr. Hill's residence near Savannah since late August. I've been staying there. No one was here." Shelby pushed hair back out of her face. "I came by to pick up my children's winter things and found this mess."

"Are you the sole owner or is there a mortgage holder?" the first policeman queried.

"I am, and no. My grandparents left it to me." Her eyes burned with tears, and she fought the urge to rub them.

"You have sixty days to get the debris removed. The house, in the current state, is a public danger." Officer Sanderson stated. "I'm going to use crime scene tape to secure it, and we'll add the address to our patrols. They'll keep an eye on it. I'm sorry to inform you it wouldn't be safe to enter, so you can't retrieve anything else. Did you have homeowners' insurance?"

"I do." Shelby sent a silent prayer of gratitude because she had brought the premium current with her first paycheck from Jeb. "I doubt it will pay much, though."

"I'll help her with removal and turning in a claim to her insurance company." Jeb remained at her side. He provided his contact information along with hers.

The officers were satisfied with the details and departed.

Shelby shivered in her hooded nylon rain jacket. "Let's go, Jeb. I can't look at it anymore, or I'll cry."

"It's okay if you do, sugar." He hugged her and planted a kiss on her lips. "You're freezing, and I'm hungry. Let's get lunch before it's too late."

Although uncertain if she could eat a bite, Shelby nodded. Jeb directed her to a twenty-four-hour chain specializing in waffles. She ordered a chocolate chip waffle, usually a favorite, but shook her head when Jeb asked if she wanted bacon or sausage on the side. "I don't." She put one hand over her tummy. "I don't know how much I can eat as it is."

Jeb motored through his waffle, a side order of bacon, and two eggs over easy.

Shelby ate less than half her portion. Memories of the old house haunted her mind. The snapshots of her life segued one into another, as she remembered making sugar cookies for Christmas with her grandmother, eating holiday dinners with family, having kinfolk clustered around the table, and drinking her very first cup of coffee at the age of nine. Shelby flashed back to sitting on the tall, red kitchen stool and watching Granma cook. She remembered the day her grandfather laid new linoleum. She'd danced in circles on it, as she twirled and swirled the way Lexi often did. *I learned to make biscuits in the kitchen and how to frost a cake.*

In the living room, or *front* room as her grandmother always called it, her grandparents had watched television together. Granma read to her there and rocked her when she was very small. Granpa had passed away in the living room, falling asleep in his chair, and never waking again. She recalled the day she and her kids had moved into the place. Levi's eyes had gone wide as he glanced around the old house. It was the opposite of their ranch-style home in south Missouri. Lexi had sucked her thumb and said nothing.

Three years of painting and patching to make the old house a home vanished now as if they hadn't happened. Although Shelby had never put up a Christmas tree, her grandparents always did, usually, a tall, graceful Douglas Fir centered in the front window. Back then, as a child, not yet jaded or beaten down by life, Shelby had been awed. Decorated with simple ornaments and decked in lights, their tree had been a thing of beauty. For the first time, Shelby realized she might have robbed her children of a lovely tradition and a pretty expression of faith.

"Shelby," Jeb spoke her name three times.

"What is it?" She glanced up from the waffle she couldn't finish.

"Honey, it's time to pick up the kids. Do you want a to-go box for your food?" Jeb stroked her fingers. "You barely touched it."

"No, thanks. I'm not hungry." She slid out of the booth and stood.

Waiting in the truck outside the school, Jeb rolled

down his window. "Tomorrow, we'll start your insurance claim, and I'll make calls to ask about demolition. If you want, we can grab take-and-bake pizzas on the way home." Jeb flipped open his phone to order.

"I don't want pizza. I can find something from the freezer or cabinet." Shelby massaged her forehead. Her head hurt.

"I'll make supper. You've had a terrible day." Jeb put his left hand over hers.

His sweet support touched Shelby, but she couldn't shake off overwhelming despair. Just before the children came out of the building, her cell rang. "Hi, Mom." Shelby forced a happier note in her voice. "What's up?"

"Are you all right? I came by your house on my way home from work."

Shelby shut her eyes. She'd meant to call her mother and hadn't. "I'm fine, just upset. Part of the roof had already fallen when we got there. I managed to grab the kids' winter clothes and some pictures. There were still things inside, though."

"Don't worry about it. We can always buy anything else they need." Delia paused and sighed. "I'm sure Jeb will help. Is he with you?"

Delia's early suspicions about the Hillbilly Hotshot had turned to admiration. "Of course, he's right here." She cleared her throat and swallowed a sob. "The house is compromised, Mom, and there's no fixing it." Shelby wiped away tears. Admitting the reality hurt.

"Shelby Jo! You shouldn't have gone inside. You could have been killed." Delia raised her voice by a decibel.

"That's what Jeb said. He pulled me out of the house and away when the second section fell." Despite her dark mood, Shelby smiled. Jeb had proven to be her hero. "Levi and Lexi will be here in a minute. We're in the pickup line now."

"Oh, my goodness. At least, you left all your photo albums and keepsakes at my place. Call me later, and we'll talk. Kiss the kids for me." Delia hung up.

"That was my mom." Shelby took the napkin Jeb pulled out of the glovebox and blotted her eyes.

"I figured." Jeb handed her more tissues. "Here come the kids."

Shelby burst into tears. She laid her head down against the steering wheel and sobbed.

Jeb stepped out so the children could climb into the cab. He settled back into place once they had.

"Mama, what's wrong?" Levi grabbed Shelby's arm and shook it.

"I had a really bad day. Everything's all right." Shelby lifted her face and scrubbed away tears.

"Just tell us what happened." Levi glared at Shelby.

Lexi's bottom lip quivered. "Jeb, why is Mama sad?"

"You'd better tell them, honey." Jeb caressed her cheek, despite the two kids between them. "They're gonna find out sooner or later."

Shelby covered her face with both hands. "Would you please explain, Jeb?" She figured he wouldn't. Jimmy would have refused. If something such as this happened before she'd met Jeb, Shelby would have struggled with telling the kids. As a single mom, she had a few weaknesses, and telling hard truths ranked first among them.

His sigh echoed through the truck. "Something awful and unexpected happened. Remember your house? It was old and worn out. Today, part of the roof fell."

"Like Humpty Dumpty?" Lexi's eyes widened, and her voice quavered.

"Are we homeless?" Levi brushed a tear from his cheek.

"God never takes away something without providing a replacement." Jeb met Shelby's gaze without blinking. "You've got a place to live at the farmhouse, as long as you need or want."

"Okay." Levi sighed. He leaned his head against Jeb's left arm for a moment. "Thanks."

"And, yeah, like Humpty Dumpty." Jeb focused on Lexi. He patted her cheek. "The house can't be put back together again. It's sad, but you know what? We need to thank God, because this could've happened when all three of you were at home." Jeb's voice cracked. He drew a deep breath. "Your brave mama got your clothes and coats. They'll need washing, but you have them."

Shelby nodded as a heavy silence filled the truck. "Jeb's right. We can replace the other stuff."

"What about my stuffed bears?" Lexi tugged on Shelby's sleeve.

"And my racetrack." Levi poked Jeb's shoulder.

"Gone." Shelby sighed. She thought of so many other things they had lost. Her grandmother's ancient sewing machine, the little maple rocking chair from Shelby's childhood, her grandpa's fishing gear, and the box of fragile glass Christmas ornaments handed down for three generations. Tears poured down her face, and both children cried, too. Lexi sobbed but Levi wept without a sound.

"Some things you valued are gone," Jeb spoke into the awkward stillness. "People mean more than things. No earthly possession is worth getting hurt or dying over. 'Lay not up for yourselves treasures on earth…' "

"Matthew Chapter six, Verse twenty-one." Shelby recognized the quote and ended it with the words she recalled. " 'For where your treasure is, there will be your heart also.' "

Jeb held out his hands.

Shelby grasped his left.

The children clung to his right. "You're my treasure, all of you. I love you, and so does God. This may seem like a terrible thing, and it is, but sometimes God blesses us when things seem like the worst. Let's go home."

A faint glimmer of hope crept into a corner of Shelby's heart. " 'Rejoice in the Lord always, again I say rejoice,' " she sang. Her children picked up the hymn based on Philippians Four, Four and so did Jeb.

The music carried them home. After the first song, Shelby sang others, her voice and faith returning with power. God loved them, and she knew beyond any doubt Jeb did, too.

She would deal with the loss of her home later. She had no idea how, but she would. No other options existed. Like always, she would get through it, no matter how dark things appeared.

Chapter Twelve

Although exhausted emotionally and physically by the day's unexpected turn of events, Jeb rallied to make supper.

Shelby protested. "I can fix something to eat." She sat at the kitchen table with a cup of tea. "Can you even cook?"

Jeb glanced over from the fridge. He was searching for something he could turn into a quick meal. "I can make a decent hamburger, fry bologna, make a grilled cheese sandwich, or warm up anything canned or frozen." Jeb pulled out a package of beef hot dogs, shredded cheese, and a can of biscuits. "I'm capable."

The items sparked the memory of something Granny used to toss together for a quick meal. Remembering brought a laugh, the first since the disaster at Shelby's house.

"What are you making?" Shelby peered at Jeb.

"Dogs in blankets." Jeb used his boyhood name term for fun.

"*Dogs?*" Shelby raised her eyebrows. "You must mean pigs in blankets."

Jeb popped open the canned biscuits and used his fingers to mash each one flat. "Well, Granny used that name, true, but I always thought since it's hot dogs, why not dogs or pups in blankets. I kinda like pups even better. Pups in blankets."

Shelby's lips lifted with a slight grin. "You're silly, but I like it."

To make her smile, Jeb would stand on his head in the corner, juggle kitchen utensils, or perform a soft shoe dance. "Finest convenience cooking in the state. I think I'll open a can of pork and beans for a side dish." His effort might not be a five-star menu, but the simple fare would keep them fed. "I might whip up some chocolate pudding, too."

Lexi and Levi enjoyed the dogs in blankets. Levi ate the beans, but Lexi turned up her button nose.

So Jeb offered her a handful of potato chips, instead.

Lexi munched them.

Jeb watched Shelby, relieved when she ate her pup in a blanket and half of another. Her lack of appetite at lunch had concerned him.

She joined in the conversation, although neither she nor the children mentioned the house.

"Why don't you go up and take a long, hot bath while I clean up?" Jeb cleared their dishes from the table. "It's been a hard day, and we'll have a lot to do this week."

"Oh, I like your idea. I could use a good soak." Shelby stretched as she rose from the table. "Kids, for once, I'll let you skip a bath or shower, so we can all go to bed early."

"Aw, Mama. I've got homework," Levi protested. "I have to do it before bedtime."

Shelby slumped. "So much for my long soak."

Jeb shook his head. "There's no reason you can't have it. Levi, park at the dining room table. Lexi, grab your coloring book. Soon as I finish in the kitchen, I'll be in there."

Thank you. Shelby mouthed the words, then brushed a kiss across his lips.

Levi's homework proved to be a spelling list, so Jeb drilled him until the kid could spell every word without any mistakes. Each had a Thanksgiving theme, which reminded Jeb the holiday would be next Thursday. Turkey, gravy, butter, dinner, family, rolls, green beans, pumpkin, and cake were on the list.

"Are we having a real Thanksgiving dinner, Jeb?" Levi put his spelling words away in his backpack.

"Turkey and all the trimmings, you bet. What do you usually have?" Jeb's curiosity prompted the question.

"Most years, Grandma makes a turkey with a box of stuffing and a pumpkin pie from the store. Mama always said if they didn't hand out free turkeys at work, we wouldn't have a bird. One year we had turkey legs." Levi stowed his pack, and his sister's, beneath their coats in the kitchen. He returned to the dining room. "Is Grandma coming on Thanksgiving?"

"You bet." Jeb made a mental note to ask, although he couldn't imagine Delia would refuse. "We'll have the best dinner ever."

Jeb took over bedtime duties so Shelby could savor her "me" time. He supervised the kids from the hallway, as they changed into their pj's Lexi managed her nightgown without assistance. He read a fairy tale about a princess to the little girl and shared "The Steadfast Tin Soldier" with Levi.

"It's sad he ended up melted." Levi yawned. "I liked the story, though."

If Jeb had remembered the ending, he would have

read a different tale. "Lights out, Levi." He encountered Shelby in the hallway. She wore a worn robe over a threadbare flannel gown. "Kids are down."

"Thank you. I'm going to bed unless you want me to stay up. I think I'll sleep now, though." She wrapped her arms around Jeb's neck and kissed his lips.

Jeb held her close for a moment. "You will. Say a prayer first, and I will, too. I'll see you in the morning, honey."

"Good night, Jeb. I love you." She vanished into her room and shut the door.

Jeb savored her sweet words. *I should go to bed, too. It'll be another long day tomorrow.* He didn't, though. Jeb traipsed back downstairs and made a holiday shopping list. By the time he finished, the list ended up longer than he expected, but he didn't care. He and Shelby needed to shop for Thanksgiving on Saturday. He made a mental note to call Shelby's mom and to check with his closest rodeo friends to see if they were within driving distance. Aunt Jeannie always hosted dinner at her house, but he would extend an invitation, anyway.

For the first time since he'd returned to the farm, Jeb slept in his own room. After the collapse of Shelby's house, he didn't enjoy the experience as much as he had hoped. His mind refused to shut off. He replayed the terrible moment when the rest of Shelby's roof collapsed. Once in bed, Jeb couldn't stop thinking about the holidays. He liked Thanksgiving, but Christmas had always been the highlight of the season. To celebrate the way he wanted, Jeb needed to kick into high gear by next week. Although he didn't make another list, Jeb noted the things he wanted to do.

Putting up a Christmas tree ranked high. He had his eye on a short-leaf pine tree on the far side of the farm. If it had grown too much, they could always cut a cedar or buy a tree in town. He wouldn't settle for an artificial version.

Although an increasing number of people decorated their Christmas tree the day after Thanksgiving, Jeb's tradition was to put it up the second weekend in December. He resolved to find Granny's holiday decorations. He had no idea what might remain. Jeb would buy new lights and ornaments, if needed. He also needed to start gift shopping, because he didn't want to be the lonely guy, wandering through stores on December twenty-fourth and picking through the leftover items.

By Friday, Jeb had arranged for a demolition crew to remove the rubble of Shelby's house. Shelby, with his help, had turned in a claim for insurance. Since the house had been old, dating to the World War I era, and in poor shape, the payout wouldn't be much. Shelby planned to use the money to pay off the remaining hospital bill from her late husband and consider replacing her worn car. By Jeb's calculations, Shelby wasn't likely to gain much, if anything. Down the road, she would need to decide if she wanted to sell the vacant lot, but it wasn't urgent.

On Friday afternoon, he and Shelby hiked to look at the tree he had in mind. It had grown since he last saw it. It towered more than ten feet tall, which was too large, even for the farmhouse's soaring ceilings. Jeb searched for a smaller pine, but he didn't see any. Each proved either too tall or bushy. He pointed out a pretty cedar tree.

But Shelby shook her head. "I don't want a cedar tree, Jeb. They look prickly." She touched a branch, frowned, and pulled her fingers back.

"They smell so good, though." Jeb loved the rich cedar aroma. "Are you sure?"

"Positive. I told you we don't even need a tree. I haven't put one up since I moved back. If you want to decorate a little, then I'm good, but I don't really want a Christmas tree." Shelby buried her hands in her pockets and hunkered against the cold.

"I do, though." Jeb would have a tree. He hadn't put one up in the years he had been here, off-season in the house, but he wanted one now. His heart craved an old-fashioned holiday filled with love and laugher.

Shelby turned toward the house. "We can look for one when we go grocery shopping in town. An artificial tree would be the best bargain. You'd use it more than once. We need to leave. It's close to time to pick up the kids."

"I won't have a fake tree, honey. I guess we can look for a fresh tree on a lot or find a Christmas tree farm." Jeb trailed after Shelby. He'd tried to convince her to transfer the kids to school in Savannah. A bus would pick them up at the end of the driveway every day and bring them home after school. So far, she resisted and insisted the farm wasn't her permanent address.

On Saturday morning, they dropped Levi and Lexi at Delia's house. She had agreed to watch them. The kids would spend the night.

Jeb hadn't been inside Delia's small home until now. Shelby's mom lived in three rooms, tucked into one side of an older duplex on Grand Avenue. The street was anything but. A large bedroom overlooked the street. They entered through the kitchen, which led to the living room. A bathroom opened off the kitchen. Although cramped, Delia made the space cozy with throw pillows, pictures on the wall, and knickknacks on every available surface. The kids would bunk in sleeping bags on the living room floor.

"I've got pizza planned for supper. I have a couple of movies, too. We'll have fun. Are you picking them up in the morning?" Delia took the kids' shared overnight case from Shelby.

"I am, so they won't miss church." Shelby handed her mom Jeb's phone number, in case Shelby couldn't be reached by cell.

"Why don't you let me take them to services with me?" Delia winked. "You and Jeb can go to church together. I'll bring them back to the farm in time for dinner. It'll save you the trip."

"All right." She kissed her mom's cheek. "Plan to stay and eat with us. I've got a roast I'll put in the slow cooker, and there will be plenty."

"Sounds good. Now, go on, get your shopping done." Delia shooed Shelby with her hands.

"Be good, okay?" Shelby wagged a finger at her children.

"I will." Levi waved.

Lexi pouted. "I want huggers!"

Shelby embraced both kids.

So did Jeb.

They departed in high spirits. Their first stop was the single mall in St. Joseph. Jeb remembered it well, although he hadn't set foot inside in years. He liked to browse, but he soon realized Shelby shopped like a woman on a mission.

Shelby bought each child a quality pair of athletic shoes. She found a pretty, patterned sweater for Lexi at one of the department stores, and two sports team T-shirts at another for Levi. Shelby picked out a warm robe on clearance for her mom.

Jeb, after learning Delia's preference, bought perfume.

He spotted a jewelry retailer at the mall. His main Christmas plan for Shelby involved a ring and a question, but he planned to surprise her. He wanted to ask her ring size but didn't because it might give away his intention. The lack of a toy store at the mall disappointed Jeb. They headed off to a discount department store on the North Belt Highway. Jeb found the racecar model Levi wanted and a doll baby buggy for Lexi. He also purchased a set of plastic play dishes for her and a miniature car set complete with a garage for Levi. He also chose a bicycle for each child. Lexi's was pink, trimmed with purple, and Levi's bike was powder-blue.

"Bikes are too expensive! Where are they going to ride them?" Shelby rolled her eyes.

"Up and down the driveway or around the barnyard for starters." Jeb didn't mention the road, but he didn't see why they couldn't pedal there with supervision. Traffic remained light on the rural thoroughfare.

"Neither of them knows how to ride." She shook her head, laughing. "They'll fall off."

"I'll teach them. And I'll buy helmets, I promise." Jeb crossed his heart and smiled.

"All right, but that's more than enough presents." Shelby pushed the shopping cart away from the toy department.

Jeb trailed behind, rolling the bikes.

With their goods secured in the truck, their next stop was another discount retailer for groceries. Jeb insisted, however, on visiting the toy aisles. He picked up a set of dominoes, a checkerboard, and two other board games.

Shelby admitted neither of her kids had a Christmas stocking to hang.

So, Jeb made a trip through the holiday area. Jeb picked out a large stocking for each of them. He also grabbed two strings of Christmas lights, wrapping paper, and tape.

"Can we shop for groceries now?" Shelby giggled. "I thought I said no more gifts. Besides, they might run out of turkeys."

Jeb took command of the cart. "Doubtful, but I get the hint, honey." He picked out a plump twenty-three-pound tom, the largest in the freezer case. He also grabbed onions, celery, potatoes, oranges, apples, and sweet potatoes in the produce section.

"How long is your list?" Shelby snatched the paper. "Goodness, Jeb, what's the head count at the table? This is enough to feed twenty people."

"The more the merrier." He planned on a crowd. "I'll help in the kitchen, don't worry."

"You certainly will." Shelby play-punched his shoulder.

His last stop was the seasonal candy aisles, where Jeb picked up boxes of candy canes, chocolates, hard candy, and more. "We need all this for the stockings, and some of the candy canes will go on the tree."

"If we have one." Shelby sighed as they made their

way through the crowded store to checkout.

"We will. After we get out of here, do you want lunch?" Jeb's stomach rumbled. Their quick breakfast of cereal hadn't lasted.

"What about all this stuff?" Shelby waved her hand.

"It's cold outside, so it'll keep." Jeb pulled out his wallet and paid, doing his best to keep Shelby from seeing the total.

An employee delivered the bikes to his truck.

As they traveled the length of the busy Belt Highway, Jeb pointed out possible lunch spots. "Steak or seafood?"

"A burger or chicken sandwich is fine." Shelby leaned closer.

"I'm hungry. I could devour a good steak, but if you want something else, then I'm good. Do you like sirloin or ribeye or a T-bone?" Jeb almost drooled, thinking of a thick slab of beef.

"Sure, although it's not something I've had often." Shelby laughed. "Let's go eat steak."

Jeb drove across town to a location near the former stockyards. They walked into Nellie's, a local café specializing in steak since the 1920s. Jeb chose a strip steak with fries, and she ordered steak with grilled shrimp with a side salad. He savored every bite of the tender beef, which was cooked to order. They split a slice of cheesecake with strawberries before they headed for home.

"I'm stuffed." Shelby patted her stomach. "I doubt I'll want any supper."

"By the time we tote everything inside, I'll work up an appetite." His claim was bravado because he couldn't eat another bite.

"Can you carry this stuff? I don't want you to hurt your back." Shelby scratched her nose.

"None of it's very heavy. We'll hide the bikes, and the rest can go in the guest room for now." He knew a perfect spot in the back of the barn, an old tool room, beside the room once used by the hired man. As far as Jeb knew, the kids didn't know it existed.

"What about the turkey?" Shelby quirked one eyebrow.

"I can carry it, unless you want to." At this stage, he doubted one turkey, no matter how big, would tax his back. "We can start thawing it in the fridge."

Jeb stowed the bikes and hid the candy along with the gifts in the guest room closet. He was far from finished shopping. Jeb had ordered some books for the kids online, and he still had to buy Shelby's presents. Jeb couldn't wait for the doc to clear him for driving. Once he could, Jeb planned a solo excursion.

He needed to invite the guests. Jeb called Aunt Jeannie to touch base, but as he'd expected, she had a holiday meal planned at her house. For the first time since coming home injured, he phoned Aunt Tressa, his mom's other sister. "Hey, Auntie, it's Jeb."

"Oh, Jebediah! I wondered if you'd call. I meant to come over to visit, but I haven't had a chance, not with the girls."

Tressa had four daughters, three still in their teens. Younger than his mom and Jeannie, Tressa had married when Jeb was already an adult.

"How are you?"

"On the mend." He drew breath to ask her if she wanted to come over to the holiday.

"If you're wondering about Thanksgiving, we're all going to Uncle Ted's folks down in Excelsior Springs. Now, if you don't have anywhere to go, you could come with us. I'm sure they wouldn't mind, or Jeannie could have you over."

Tressa tended to babble once she started talking. "I'm having dinner here at the farmhouse, but thanks. I called to see if you might want to come but sounds like you've got plans. What about Cousin Addy?" Addison worked on the ambulance crew and had been part of the group to meet him when he returned.

"Oh, call her! I know she works on the holiday, but she could come out after. I'm sure she would appreciate it." Tressa's voice rose.

"I will. Thanks. Come over anytime, Aunt Tressa." Jeb ended the call and phoned his cousin.

Addison confirmed she would come.

So Jeb checked in with his rodeo pals. As he anticipated, most were home for the off-season, and all had plans.

Two of them, cousins Davy and Waylon, known as The Big D and the Flying W, said they might swing by to visit. "Not on Turkey Day, though. My mama's putting on a spread the size of Texas." Waylon brayed with laughter.

Jeb chuckled, too.

On Sunday morning, Jeb and Shelby attended church. Most people asked about the kids, relieved to hear they were visiting their grandmother rather than sick.

Miss Bessie accepted his Thanksgiving invitation.

Jeb promised someone would pick her up for dinner. He invited Homer Anderson, an elderly man and lifelong bachelor, who also attended Faith Church.

Homer accepted without hesitation. "I'll be there, Jeb, and thank you."

Jeb did a head count. He, Shelby, and the kids made four. Delia and Addison brought the count to six, Miss Bessie and Homer totaled eight. *We'll need to use the leaf to extend the dining room table. It'll seat up to ten, and we can use kitchen chairs, if necessary.*

While in town, Jeb spotted a large Christmas tree lot. As long as he didn't wait too long, he figured he could find a good tree there. He'd refused to even look at the artificial trees at any of the locations they had visited.

With Thanksgiving just four days ahead, Jeb thought he and Shelby had everything in order. The ingredients of a fine feast were in the kitchen, he'd made a good start on Christmas shopping, and the holiday season loomed ahead, full of promise and possibility.

As hard as he tried, Jeb couldn't think of anything that might change their Thanksgiving plans.

Chapter Thirteen

On the day before Thanksgiving, Shelby got busy in the kitchen. Although the feast wouldn't be until tomorrow, she could do prep work today. She'd baked two pies, which cooled on the kitchen counter, and she had a pumpkin crisp cake in the oven. The house smelled delicious as cinnamon and other spices wafted through the air.

Jeb worked beside her with his sleeves rolled up to his elbows. He peeled and sliced the sweet potatoes.

Shelby cooked them. Tomorrow, she would candy them with brown sugar and butter. Later, they would prepare the huge turkey ready for roasting.

Yesterday, she had baked a large pan of cornbread for the dressing. Four loaves of white bread had been drying all week. In between other tasks, she and Jeb broke it into small pieces. Shelby decided not to stuff the turkey, but to bake the dressing separately using a large tabletop electric oven.

Two loaves of bread rose on the back of the stove beside a tray of homemade hot rolls. Jeb poured his third cup of coffee and sat to tear the remaining bread. "I'm hungry already." He glanced up as he broke small pieces from the dry slices.

"We'll stop for a sandwich soon. I need to finish off the bologna. After tomorrow, I'll need every inch of fridge space for the leftovers." Shelby pulled the cake from the oven. "The kids will want lunch, too."

"They're too quiet. I should check on them." Jeb pushed his chair back.

Shelby laughed. "They're fine. Let them run off excess energy." She had asked them to dust the dining room and living room for the holiday. Once finished, she suggested they rake leaves in the yard. Every few minutes, she glanced through the window. Shelby heard their glad whooping and grinned.

"All right." Jeb settled back at the table.

Shelby, in nurse mode, checked his vital signs every morning. Jeb had stopped using the cane. She hadn't worn scrubs since his last doctor's visit and wouldn't while she remained with Jeb. Her boss at the home health care agency, Michelle, had called twice, but Shelby didn't pick up. She knew what Michelle wanted. Her boss needed to know if Shelby's current assignment would end on November thirtieth. If so, she would line up a new job.

Although Jeb couldn't drive yet, he anticipated he would get the go-ahead at his next appointment. He no longer required twenty-four-hour nursing care. Either the job would end, or Shelby might make a home visit once or twice a week.

Michelle didn't know Shelby had moved into the farmhouse or that she didn't have a home any longer. If it weren't for the fact Shelby had fallen in love with Jeb, she would have hustled to find a place to live. He didn't want her to leave, and she wanted to stay, but somehow, Shelby doubted Michelle would understand. Sometimes, Shelby still didn't.

"Hey." Jeb tapped Shelby's arm. "You look serious. What are you thinking about?"

"My boss has been calling. She probably has a new assignment in mind since it's almost the end of the month." Shelby sighed and sat across from Jeb. "I have to talk to her, soon."

His smile faded. "What would a new assignment entail?"

"I'd travel to visit two or three patients a day. I'd be home in the evening unless I get called out. Sometimes, I do." Shelby frowned. She didn't want to work for someone else, but she had little choice.

"I still need you." His face clouded, and his lips jutted in a pout. "I don't want you to go."

She grasped his hands in hers. "I'd rather not, but it's the way I earn a living. It's my job."

"Maybe it's time for a new one." Jeb stared at the table as he spoke.

What if it is? I'm a nurse. I'm sure I can find an opening somewhere. "It could be." The possibility excited and terrified Shelby. She tightened her fingers around his. "I'll wait until after Thanksgiving before I call Michelle. I'll figure something out by then."

"I hope so, honey." Jeb released a long breath.

They shredded bread together until every piece became the correct size. Shelby crumbled the cornbread into the pan, then paused. "Someone's coming up the drive."

The distinct sound of tires on gravel crunched loudly.

Levi ran inside, his sister in tow. "Mama, someone's here."

Jeb grabbed his jacket. "I'll go see."

Shelby glanced through the window and gasped. She recognized the worn-out truck parking near the back door. Jeb's father had returned. "I'll go with you."

Before they made it outside, Joe Hill knocked. He hadn't before.

Jeb tensed. "What do you want?" Jeb answered the door with a gruff voice.

"Let me in, Son. I need to talk to you." Josiah Hill stood on the doorstep with his cap in his hands.

Jeb hesitated.

So Shelby quoted the Bible. " 'Whatsoever ye do to the least of my brethren…' "

" 'Ye do also to me.' " Jeb finished the sentence. "All right, honey, I get the point." He opened the door, then stepped back. "Come in. We'll go to the dining room. Kitchen's in a mess getting ready for tomorrow."

Josiah nodded. He carried a white envelope in one hand. Once there, he sank into a chair.

"Do you want some coffee or a soda?" Shelby ignored the tension and tried to be a gracious hostess. "Kids, go upstairs."

"A cup of black coffee would be nice. Thanks." Josiah put down his hat and laid the envelope on the table. "Jeb, I came home to make amends. Here's the money I got from you. It's all there, but three hundred dollars. I used it to buy gas, eats, and a cheap motel."

Jeb stared at the envelope but didn't touch it. "Did you lose the job you had?"

"No, I quit." The older man shook his head. "Quit the job and stopped drinking. I haven't touched booze since I left here."

Shelby studied Josiah Hill as she returned with his coffee. His hair had been combed, and his eyes were clear. His skin lacked the ruddy tones she had noticed the first time she met him. She inhaled deeply, but instead of the sour stench of alcohol and unwashed body odor, Shelby smelled soap.

"Are you serious?" Jeb failed to keep his voice from shaking. "Will you swear on Mama's memory it's the truth?"

"I will." Josiah bowed his head. "I'll swear it over her grave if you want. I've quit drinking, and I want to come home."

Jeb took a seat.

Shelby moved behind him. She rested her hands on his shoulders. Beneath her touch, he trembled but appeared outwardly calm.

"Tell me what you mean." Jeb lifted a hand to touch Shelby's. "You left after Mama died. I was twelve years old. I needed my daddy. It's been nineteen years. I've hardly heard from you. Fact is, I hadn't seen you for ages until you showed up last month. You say you want to come home, but how do you see it's even a possibility?"

"That'll be up to you, Son." Josiah picked up his coffee and sipped. "I know it's a big thing to ask. I could stay here in the house…"

"That's not happening, not yet." Jeb scowled as he scooted back from the table.

"There's the room for a hired hand in the barn. I'd stay there." Josiah finished his coffee and drew a deep breath. "If you don't have place for me in your heart, or in this place, then I reckon I'd understand. I failed you, and I know it. I'll go on down the road, and maybe find a mission or shelter in St. Joe to take me until I get on my feet. I already got a job." He shoved the envelope of money toward his son.

Jeb's shoulders hitched.

Shelby thought he might be crying. Although she couldn't see his face, she ached to weep. *Lord, let him make the right choice. Let him forgive his father.*

Levi poked his head around the corner.

Shelby waved him back. "Go back upstairs. I'll call you when it's time for lunch."

"Mama…" Levi's protest died.

Shelby pointed toward the stairs, "Now!" Shelby's voice cracked like a whip, and her kids obeyed. Until she knew how this scenario would end, and how Jeb would react, they shouldn't be here.

"Where?" Jeb cleared his throat. "A job where?"

"Custodian, at a long-term care facility in St. Joe. It ain't the best work, but I can still use a broom and mop. It's a start." Josiah stared at his son, eyes glittering with tears.

Jeb buried his face in both hands. After a long pause, he sighed and met his father's gaze. "That room in the barn ain't in great shape, Dad. It's filthy, and we'd have to clean it up."

"I could do it. I wouldn't ask for a thing, except rags, some cleanser, and a bucket." Josiah's lips trembled.

"We could spot you all the above." Jeb hesitated for less than thirty seconds. "If Shelby can spare me in the kitchen, then I'll help." He stood so they could get started. "We can find one or two clean blankets and a set of sheets around here. I've got an old electric heater so you won't freeze." Jeb stretched out his hand to shake his dad's across the table. "We'll give this situation a try, but if you drink, one time, you'll leave. If you quit your job or get fired, the same. Fair enough?"

"It's more than." A smile lit Josiah's face. "Thank you, Son, for the chance. I won't let you down."

"I'm not doing it for you, but because of Him." Jeb pointed one finger upward. "All I keep thinking is what would Jesus do? He wouldn't turn his father away."

Whatsoever ye do. Shelby thanked the Lord for Jeb's kindness.

"I'll head over to the barn." Josiah rose from the table after the handshake.

"Have you eaten?" Shelby extended an invitation. "We're having sandwiches, but you're welcome to join us."

The man smiled.

For a moment, he resembled Jeb so much, that Shelby thought her heart would burst.

"I appreciate it, but I ate in town." Josiah rubbed his chin. "I'll haul my stuff, and then if I could get those cleaning supplies, I'll get started."

Jeb sat silent, as his father's footsteps echoed as he exited through the kitchen. He sighed and stood. "Shelby, what have I done?"

"The right thing. I don't know what else you could do." Shelby opened her arms for a hug.

Jeb came without hesitation. "I might have told him to get out and not to come back." His voice muffled against her hair. "Shelby, I loved him so much until he bailed on me."

She imagined the boy, younger than a teenager, who'd felt abandoned, and she understood. "Give him a chance, Jeb."

"I am, honey, God help me. God help us all." Jeb stepped back and ran a hand through his hair. "Let's go eat, and then I'll help him clean."

Shelby kissed his cheek. "Holler at the kids to come down while I make the sandwiches." She spent the afternoon in the kitchen, enlisting the children to assist. Shelby sautéed celery and onions in a skillet and stirred it into the dry bread mixture. She added sage, thyme, a little pepper, and a bit of salt, then combined it with broth made from the turkey neck. She augmented it with canned chicken broth, tasted, added more sage, and covered it with foil. In the morning, she would bake it. She cleaned up the mess.

The kids watched television.

Jeb was in the barn with his dad.

So, she focused on supper. Shelby wanted to keep it light, since they would feast tomorrow, so she baked salmon fillets and fixed rice pilaf. If she needed to stretch the meal, she could add one of the loaves of bread she had baked.

Jeb passed through twice. On the first pass, he grabbed an armload of bedding, and on the second time, he carried a portable heater. He paused for a brief kiss.

"How's it going?" Shelby brushed her fingers across his cheek.

"Better than I expected." He wobbled his hand back and forth. "We're talking, some."

Since there would be five, not four for the meal, Shelby asked the kids to set the dining room table for supper.

Lexi placed the napkins.

Levi brought the silverware. "Who's eating with us?" He positioned a fork, knife, and spoon at each place with precision.

"Jeb's father, but they haven't seen each other for a long time." Shelby hurried back to the kitchen to fetch a pitcher of iced tea.

"Why not?" Levi trailed her.

"I don't really know. Jeb's dad left after his wife, Jeb's mother, passed away. His grandparents finished raising Jeb here, in this house." Shelby had no explanations and wasn't about to try to make any.

Her own emotions were mixed. While Shelby believed Jeb did the right thing, as a Christian and as a son, she wondered how the addition of Josiah Hill would affect their status quo. No matter what happened, the life they'd been sharing would change. Her stomach churned with nervous agitation.

At supper, things went well. Josiah asked them all, including the kids, to call him Joe. He praised the simple food and joined the conversation. No one touched on any heavy subjects, but after the meal, Joe retired to the barn with thanks.

Once the kids had been bathed and tucked into bed, Shelby sat with Jeb in the living room. He remained pensive, although when she settled into her usual corner of the couch, he smiled and parked beside her. "It's been a day."

His sigh echoed through the room as he rubbed his temples. "I never expected him to come back, especially sober. I can't believe he gave me most of the money back. That's a first."

"It's good, though. Do you have a headache?" Shelby laid one hand across his forehead.

"Yeah, I do. I'll take something before I go to bed." He shut his eyes for a moment.

"Come over here and let me massage your head." Shelby patted her lap.

Jeb stretched out on the couch and rested his head

on her knees.

She used her thumbs in a circular motion as she worked out from the center of his forehead. After fifteen minutes, Shelby sighed. "Better?"

"Oh yeah, lots. I'm gonna fall asleep here if I don't get to bed." He yawned as he sat.

They climbed the stairs together and parted with a kiss.

Thanksgiving dawned bright and clear. Temperatures were moderate, and Shelby had a song on her lips as she baked chocolate chip muffins for breakfast.

Jeb wore a smile when he came downstairs.

So did his dad when he joined them for breakfast.

"Tell me what I can do to help around the place." Joe dunked part of his muffin in his coffee. "I'm open to anything."

"I forgot to buy whipped cream for the pies." Shelby smiled. She'd figured she would have to make a quick run into town or ask her mom to bring some.

"I can get it, no problem." Josiah picked up his truck keys and donned his threadbare jacket.

Knowing the kids watched the annual Thanksgiving Day parades on television, Shelby cooked with Jeb's help. "Your dad seems sincere."

"He does." Jeb glanced up from the knife he was sharpening. "He wants to go to church on Sunday with us."

"Wow. Did he used to attend Faith Church, too?" Shelby stirred the bubbling green beans and added dried onions.

"Yeah, back in the day. Miss Bessie and Homer will be surprised to see him. They'll both remember."

Jeb ran his finger over the knife blade and shaved fine hairs from his arm to test the sharpness.

Shelby prayed it would be fondly.

The guests arrived on schedule. Coats were placed in the guest bedroom. At two o'clock, all nine diners gathered around the table. They linked hands, and Jeb asked the blessing in a hushed tone. After he said "Amen," he invited everyone to join him in a family tradition. "When I was growing up, we always went around the table so everyone could name something they're thankful for. Dad, I thought you might remember and want to start us off." Jeb gazed at Joe.

"I do." Joe nodded. "I'm grateful to be home and glad my son's giving me the chance to be here." He stared at his plate as he spoke.

Homer Anderson didn't hesitate. "I'm thankful I was invited to this dinner and glad to see Joe again. It's been a long time, brother."

"Amen." Miss Bessie folded her hands together upright in prayer. "I'm grateful to still be alive and going strong."

"I'm delighted my cousin has come home and recovered from his accident." Addison threw in her opinion. "Jeb, I'm happy for you."

Shelby's heart brimmed full as everyone gazed at her. "I'm thankful to have a roof that's still standing over my head. I'm grateful for my children, my mom, and for Jeb. God brought him into my life, and he's a blessing."

"I didn't say mine yet, but I will now." Jeb twined his fingers through Shelby's. "I'm glad I'm on the mend and thankful I'm done with rodeo. I enjoyed the sport and made my living for many years, but it's good to be home. I'm glad to have Shelby, Levi, and Lexi in my life. Y'all mean everything to me. I'm glad my dad's back. He was gone too long." To his surprise, he meant every word, even about rodeo and his father. *Maybe I've finally come to terms with giving up bronc riding.*

Lexi piped up. "I'm grateful to live in a big, warm house, and have lots of food to eat, and to know Jeb."

Levi stood when he spoke. "I'm thankful for this home, for my mom, Jeb, being close to my grandma, and maybe getting a grandpa."

Jeb started at the idea and glanced at Joe.

Josiah bowed his head as if in prayer and flushed.

Shelby's mom had the last turn. "I'm grateful for all of you, and everything." Delia blotted her eyes with a paper napkin.

The turkey tasted tender, not dry, and delicious. Every side dish from the dressing to the sweet potatoes to the pumpkin pie and gravy turned out perfect, which was one more reason for Shelby to be thankful.

Although they ate too much, everyone present enjoyed the meal and the day. All the women banded together to clean the kitchen in record time.

Joe drove Miss Bessie and Homer home.

Addison had to report for work, but she thanked Shelby for the fine meal. She turned to Jeb for a hug. "Tell Uncle Joey, it was good to see him." Addy headed out the door.

"I need to go home, too." Delia stood and stretched. "Since I work at the high school cafeteria, I get time off whenever school's out. I might get up early to hit all the Black Friday sales. Shelby, do you want to go?"

"No way." Shelby made an exaggerated shudder. "I don't like Black Friday. Too crowded for me."

"But the bargains!" Her mom's face lit up. "I love shopping!"

"I never have the money, and they never have anything I want on sale." Shelby hugged her mom. "Good luck." She handed Delia leftovers to take home and put the rest of the food away.

Joe returned from dropping guests off and the children went to bed. "I'm headed to bed, unless you need anything else."

"Nah, we're good. Good night, Dad." Jeb smiled. His old man had been helpful.

"It's not bad outside. Come sit on the glider with me for a few?" Jeb stretched out his hand in invitation.

They didn't bother with the cushions but cuddled close, rocking back and forth in an easy rhythm. Jeb put his arm around her shoulders.

She leaned against him. "Did you have a good Thanksgiving?" She savored his firm shoulder beneath her head.

"Yeah, everything I hoped for, and more. Did you? I hope you're not worn out from cooking." He brushed her hair back with a gentle hand.

"I'm fine. I enjoyed having decent food to fix. I had a wonderful day." Shelby turned to kiss his cheek.

"Just wait until Christmas. It'll be even better." Jeb stroked the spot her lips had bussed.

She made no comment. Christmas had always been a disappointment in her life. Shelby had never received the gifts she wanted as a little girl, which was one reason she didn't encourage her children to have unreal expectations. Santa Claus didn't come through for her, and her kids didn't even believe the old elf existed. As an adult, she struggled with money for gifts and to have a decent meal. Shelby's dad had died close to Christmas when she lived in southern Missouri, so the holiday's wonder and magic became muted. She often had said, "I don't believe in Christmas" and meant it. "Aren't the stars awesome, Jeb?" Shelby gazed into the heavens. Here on the farm, away from the lights of town, the stars sparkled like glitter scattered across the night sky. "They're beautiful."

"So are you, honey." He caught her face between his hands and kissed her, sweet, long, and properly.

Shelby might not believe in Christmas, but her faith rested with God and her heart in Jeb.

The holiday might disappoint, but she prayed Jeb never would.

She loved him too much to believe anything else.

Chapter Fourteen

The unexpected return of his dad unsettled Jeb. He hadn't figured Josiah would be back for months, maybe years, and only when he needed money. Instead, Dad showed up at the back door, sober, clean, and repentant on the day before Thanksgiving. Jeb's first thought had been to ask him to leave, but he didn't. He couldn't claim a Christian walk if he lacked forgiveness in his heart. If it hadn't been for Shelby's hand on his arm, or her soft words about the least of his brethren, he might have sent Josiah packing. Jeb listened to Shelby and to the still, small voice in his heart urging him to forgive not seven times, but seven times seventy.

On Friday, after coming to terms with his dad's homecoming during the long night, Jeb decided to offer his support. Over scrambled eggs and toast, he glanced across the table and cleared his throat. "How did you sleep?"

"Fair enough." Joe laced his fingers around his coffee mug. "I appreciated your help yesterday, son. I'd like to do a few more things to improve space, if you don't mind. I'd like to hang up a blanket or two to cut down on the draft. If you have a spare lamp, I wouldn't mind using it."

"Sure, no problem." Jeb swallowed around a lump in his throat. "I can lend a hand, and if there's anything you need we don't have, we can run into town."

"On Black Friday?" Shelby grinned. "The stores will be crazy."

Jeb shrugged. "If we have to go, we'll deal."

"I'd appreciate it, Jeb. I made a small list." Joe pulled a scrap of paper from the front pocket of his shirt.

"Let's go then and get it over with." Jeb's chest ached with either hope or the beginnings of indigestion. He wasn't sure which.

On the way into town, the men talked. As they had made the room livable and clean, their conversation had centered on the task, and not the past. Jeb hadn't been ready for more, but now, as his dad drove, he couldn't hold back the question he'd carried since he was twelve. "Why'd you leave?"

"I couldn't stay." Josiah kept his gaze on the road. "You have a right to ask, so I'll try to explain. I loved Daffy, your mom, so much. Watching her die came close to killing me. It broke my heart. I didn't want to stay here without her. I knew I'd see her in every corner and listen for her voice. I knew I couldn't handle the grief. I turned yellow-bellied and split."

"Daffy?" Jeb gripped the dash with both hands.

As an eighteen-wheeler roared past, the driver blasted the horn.

Jeb jumped. In a seventy-mile-per-hour zone, Joe drove eighty, but the truck had to be hitting ninety. "Mom's name was Beth."

Joe sighed and slowed his speed. "I know. It's a nickname from an old Hank Williams song, "Setting The Woods On Fire." It was way before our time, but ol' Hank sang about Daffy and Dilly ordering up two bowls of chili. It started out as a silly joke, but we adopted them as our private names for each other."

Shock rippled through Jeb's mind. *I never thought about my folks as a couple or in love. They were just Mama and Daddy to me.* He shuddered with the sudden revelation. Since the day Jeb stood at the front door and watched his daddy drive away, he had burned with resentment. Anger had fueled his actions and hardened his heart toward Josiah. For the first time, Jeb realized his dad had been grieving. Mourning didn't excuse his actions, but it explained them. "I never heard those nicknames, and I didn't understand, Dad. I do now, partly because of Shelby." Jeb wiped away a few tears trickling down his cheek.

"I thought she was your home health nurse." Josiah frowned as he turned toward Jeb. "You told me so the first time I came."

"Shelby started as my nurse, but she's everything to me now. Dad, I love her. She doesn't know yet, but I'm going to propose on Christmas. I want to get married, raise her kids, and have some more." Getting married hadn't been on Jeb's radar before his injury. A sense of shock and awe rattled him. Things had changed with speed, but he had no regrets. If he'd ever been sure about anything in his life, it was Shelby.

"I kinda thought so by the way you look at her." Josiah stopped for a turn and continued into the nearest retail store parking lot. "One of the reasons I quit drinking and headed back is because I want to see you happy. I thought they might be your kids, when I came back on Wednesday, and I hated to think I missed out on grandkids. It's bad enough I wasn't there for you."

His dad's confession rocked Jeb to the core. He clutched his throat with surprise as his breath came short. Words tangled on his tongue, but Jeb spit them out anyway. "You're here now, and they *are* my kids in my heart. Dad, why now, though, after so many years?"

Josiah took a long time before he replied. He circled the parking lot and pulled into a spot, then sighed. "When I heard how badly you got hurt, I thought how I'd feel if I lost you. I know I ain't seen you for too long, but I always loved you, son. You're all I have left. I remembered the good times between us, before Daffy got sick, and everything changed. I'm not young anymore, and I'd like to be in your life. I hope to make amends for bailing on you. That's not all."

"What else?" Jeb prayed for strength he could handle more.

"Back then, I turned my back on the Lord and everything I knew to be true. I got angry He didn't save your mother, so I went off the deep end. Instead of clinging to my faith, I poured myself into a bottle. I drank so I wouldn't think or remember. It was wrong. I've repented and gone back to Jesus. I'll be in church every Sunday, and I'll go to meetings for alcoholics like me." Joe paused and sighed. "Even if I never take another drink, I'll be an alcoholic until the day I die. Since God has forgiven me, I might be able to forgive myself one of these days. I just hope you can." Josiah rested his forehead against the steering wheel.

"Oh, Daddy." Jeb reverted to his childhood name for his father. "I'm glad you came back. I never thought I could, or would, but I forgive you. I'm happy you'll be here for Christmas. I plan to have the best one ever, for Shelby's sake. She's not much on Christmas, but I hope to change her point of view."

"I'll pray you can, Son." Joe Hill raised his head

and turned toward Jeb for an awkward hug.

"Let's go face the crowds and get what you need." Jeb used his coat sleeve to wipe tears from his face. "Maybe we can grab some lunch before we head home."

"I'd like that a lot, Son. Let's do it." Josiah stepped out of the truck into the discount store parking lot and stuck the keys into his pocket.

Let's do it. Jeb remembered the phrase. His dad had spoken it often, usually before they headed out together for a fishing trip, to a major league baseball game in Kansas City, or for an adventure. He steeled himself not to weep. Much more emotion and he would bawl like a baby. He still hated the way his dad had left, but he understood, at least a little. "Count on it, Dad."

With speed, they grabbed the items on Joe's list: a small table lamp, a battery-operated radio, a couple of paperback books, and packaged cookies. Navigating through the crowds proved as difficult and annoying as expected but they managed. Afterward, father and son shared a pepperoni, hamburger, mushroom, and onion pizza at a local eatery. The combination brought back memories. The pizza place had been Jeb's childhood favorite. Even the familiar restaurant hadn't changed in decades. Each table still boasted a red-and-white-checkered cloth, and the place smelled of rich sauces. The meal tasted good and proved priceless as Jeb got reacquainted with his father.

After Thanksgiving, the Christmas season kicked into high gear. Dr. Guiseman gave Jeb the go-ahead to drive during the first week of December. Jeb got his wheels back in time for the season and his birthday.

Although Shelby didn't make a big deal about his

birthday, she got the recipe for his favorite cake from his aunt and baked one.

The kids and his dad sang "Happy Birthday"—the first time anyone had in longer than Jeb remembered.

Shelby fried two chickens for a special meal and bought a gift.

He treasured the hand-carved cedar cross she found and wore it on a heavy chain around his neck every day.

"It's been almost twenty years since I was with you on your birthday." Joe handed him a small pocketknife. "I didn't spend any money or wrap it, but I wanted you to have Pop's knife. Happy birthday, Son."

The gift touched Jeb's heart, and he valued the heirloom. "Thanks, Dad. I'll keep it forever." After his birthday, Jeb's focus returned to the festive season. Most evenings after supper, they, including his dad, gathered in the front room to watch old classics including *Rudolph The Red-Nosed Reindeer, Frosty The Snowman,* and *The Year Without A Santa Claus.* Jeb bought DVDs of his favorite, *The Little Drummer Boy,* and the original cartoon, *How The Grinch Stole Christmas.* They also watched movies with a holiday theme, including *It's A Wonderful Life, Miracle On 34th Street,* and *The Santa Clause.*

Jeb loaded the stereo in the house and in his truck with his favorite holiday tunes. He sang along with Elvis, Johnny Cash, Nat King Cole, and other greats. His most cherished Christmas CDs had music from the 1940s, 1950s, and 1960s. His grandparents had enjoyed the older songs, and so did he.

At his suggestion, Shelby requested time off until January.

After a long discussion, her boss granted the

request.

The insurance money from her house would cover her most pressing debts, and she no longer had to pay utilities.

Jeb would help Shelby shop for a newer, dependable car after the holidays. He prayed daily she wouldn't find a new place to live. By New Year's Day, he hoped they would be engaged.

Shelby still used his truck to take the kids back and forth to school.

Sometimes, Jeb rode along, sometimes not. Occasionally, he drove. Few of his health restrictions remained. According to Dr. Guiseman, he still couldn't lift anything over twenty pounds or ride horses. Physical therapy would continue once a week into January.

Jeb ordered more books and movies for the children, bought flannel shirts, jeans, and boots for his dad, and discovered small trinkets for Shelby. He looked forward to the annual church candlelight service on Christmas Eve. Although he hadn't in years, Jeb planned on making one or two trips to see the Christmas lights. Krug Park in town put together a major light display, and he anticipated the delight it would bring Shelby's kids.

On a chilly December evening, everyone donned their coats and loaded the truck, including Joe, for the elementary school holiday program.

Delia met them at the school.

Although the kids could sing about Santa, but not the Savior, each class sang or put on a skit. Lexi's kindergarten class offered a delightful rendition of *Santa Claus Is Coming To Town* and *Jingle Bells.* Each child in the front row, including Lexi, carried a bell to ring.

Levi's classmates put together a fun skit with a Western theme. A lost cowboy seeking a Christmas tree searched the prairie and range without success. He brought a tumbleweed back to the bunkhouse instead.

They stopped for hot chocolate after the program.

"I can hardly wait until we get a tree." Levi's eyes sparkled as he sipped his. "How do we pick one?"

"We'll go this weekend and find the prettiest, straightest, tallest one." Jeb grinned, happy with anticipation.

On the third Saturday in December, the planned tree-finding mission shifted to Sunday afternoon.

Delia bought tickets for a special production of *The Nutcracker* in Kansas City and took the kids.

Jeb lacked interest in the musical performance.

Shelby didn't seem to care, and when her mom asked if the kids could spend the night at her place afterward, she agreed. Shelby's mom picked up Levi and Lexi, and they headed for the urban scene. Jeb puttered around the house. He had no interest in choosing a tree without the children, and he missed them. He decided this would be the perfect time to enjoy Shelby's company.

Joe headed into town to work an extra half-shift, then catch a meeting.

So, they had the house to themselves. Jeb grabbed a notebook and sat at the kitchen table. "What do you want for Christmas dinner, honey? We need to think ahead and make a list. It's ten days from tomorrow. I thought we'd run to town and pick up some groceries."

"I haven't given it a thought. I always fixed

whatever I could. Sometimes, it was a roast or maybe meatloaf or ham." Shelby massaged her forehead. "My grandmother always made a boneless pork loin for Christmas Day and ham on New Year's."

"I like a ham on Christmas." He craved a big bone-in traditional one. Granny had always served a shank half, and Jeb wanted to keep the tradition. "Let's plan on roast pork with dressing and black-eyed peas on New Year's Day."

"Black-eyed peas?" Shelby stuck out her tongue. "I don't know if I like them, or if I've ever eaten any. Why?"

"Gotta have some for good luck." Jeb wouldn't dream of taking a chance. Even alone, he'd bought a can, seasoned them with bacon, and cooked the peas.

"Okay, we'll get some. I'm tired. I need to figure out what to make for supper." Shelby covered her mouth and coughed hard.

"We can have something easy, honey. It'll just be me, you, and Dad. I'm not picky." Jeb noted the dark smudges beneath Shelby's eyes and her deep fatigue. Her barking cough also concerned him. "I can cook if you want, or we could open a can of ravioli. What about Sunday dinner?"

"I don't know." Her shoulders sagged. "I'll get something out of the freezer later."

"Sure. Will Delia bring the kids back in time for church, or are they going with her again?" Jeb liked attending as a family, but he also could roll with the flow.

Shelby shrugged. "I forgot to ask, Jeb."

"It works as long as they're home by dinner. I thought we'd find a Christmas tree tomorrow afternoon.

I want to wait for Levi and Lexi." Jeb rubbed his palms together.

"I'm sure they'll have a blast." Shelby paused for another round of harsh coughing. "If you plan to go to St. Joe tomorrow, why not get groceries then instead of today?"

"We could." Jeb hitched one shoulder in a half-shrug. "How about I buy you lunch instead? We could get some barbecue or those street tacos you like."

"Not today, Jeb, thanks." She wrinkled her nose. "I'm so tired."

He wasn't excited about choosing from the sandwich fixings and leftovers in the fridge. "C'mon, honey. Dad's at work, and the kids are with your mom. We could have a date."

Shelby rubbed her arms and shivered. "I wouldn't enjoy it today. I don't feel the best, and this cough is wearing me out."

Jeb stretched out his hand. "Let's go to the living room and get comfortable. We can forget about wrapping and just hang out."

Her face lit with a small smile. "I'd like that."

In the front room, Jeb considered playing the piano but decided against it. Shelby didn't look well and might not appreciate the noise. He scrutinized her. Her eyes drooped, and he'd never seen her so pale. "Are you sick, honey? I can take you to the doctor. There's more than one urgent care center in town."

"What for?" Shelby wrapped in a soft blanket and curled into the corner of the couch.

"If you're coming down with a bug, maybe they could prescribe something to help you feel better or ease that cough." He touched her forehead, but it remained cool.

"Don't fret, Jeb. I'm only tired." She huddled tighter into the covers. "Put on some Christmas music, and I'll rest."

Jeb nixed his notion to hunt down a Christmas tree on Sunday. Maybe he could search on Monday after school. He settled into his recliner with a book and put holiday tunes on the stereo. When Shelby fell asleep, he didn't wake her, and when he offered a sandwich at lunch, she declined. He talked her into sharing a can of soup. Jeb got some wrapping done.

But Shelby had no interest or energy to help.

Joe arrived home from work.

Jeb warmed up ravioli for a simple supper. He found some frozen garlic bread to serve with the pasta.

"This ain't bad at all." Joe filled his bowl with seconds. "I never had parmesan cheese to sprinkle on top, but it adds some flavor." After the meal, Joe challenged Jeb to play cards. "We could play a few hands, unless you've forgotten how."

Jeb laughed. As a little boy, Joe had taught Jeb to play more than one card game. "Not hardly! Playing cards helped pass a lot of empty hours while I was rodeoing." He located a deck of cards in a kitchen drawer and settled at the dining room table.

Shelby watched for thirty minutes, but she continued coughing. "I'm heading up to bed. I'll see you in the morning, but I probably won't go to church."

Jeb rose for a kiss.

But Shelby turned away. "I might be coming down with something, and I sure don't want to give it to you. Good night, Jeb. Good night, Joe.

"Sweet dreams, sugar. I hope you feel better." He

blew an air kiss in her direction.

"Me, too." Another bout of harsh coughs racked her as she walked away.

He watched her climb the steps with a slow tread and frowned.

"Is she sick? She doesn't look so hot." Joe glanced up from his cards.

Jeb shrugged. "I think she might be. If she doesn't go to church, I'll stay home, too. Are you going?"

"I wouldn't miss it, son. I need the lift I get every week. Fact is, I'm bushed, so I'll head out to my room, too."

"Good night, Dad." Jeb picked up their cards, washed up the bowls and spoons used at supper, and retired for the night.

Jeb rose early, concerned about Shelby. He hadn't slept well but resisted the urge to check on her. He made coffee and decided he'd fix breakfast when she came downstairs. He could prepare lunch, too, and remembered he'd better call Delia to find out what time the kids would be home.

His dad appeared, but Shelby didn't. Joe looked good dressed in a button-down shirt with blue jeans and a sport coat. *You'd never think he lived a hard life all those years and drank himself halfway to the grave.*

"I'm off. If you need anything, call me after church, and I'll pick up whatever's needed." Joe made the offer as he headed out the door.

"Thanks, Dad. Will do." Jeb rose and poured a second cup of coffee. He had decided to nuke some frozen pancakes when he heard Shelby's footsteps. He hurried to meet her. "How are you, sugar?" Jeb reached to hug her.

But she stepped away. "Jeb, I'm really sick." Shelby bent forward as she coughed hard. "I feel awful. I think I have a fever. I should go back to bed."

Jeb placed the back of his right hand across her forehead. "You're burning up. Do you have a thermometer?"

"I did, at my house, so it's gone. I'm so cold. Why isn't the heat on?" Shelby shivered as she slumped into a kitchen chair.

Jeb frowned. He'd been comfortable in shirt sleeves. "It is, and it's not chilly in the house. Let me see if I can find a thermometer." He located a glass mercury one and took her temperature. It registered one hundred and one degrees. Fear cut through him like a sharp knife. "I'm gonna take you to urgent care."

"No, you're not." Shelby put her face in both hands and shuddered. "I've got the flu. I'm a nurse, I know these things."

"What if it's COVID-19" Jeb hadn't had it, but he knew folks who had. Two of his older rodeo pals, men in their late fifties, long retired from the circuit, had died. Both had other medical issues, but COVID-19 scared him.

"It's not, but if you want to make sure, I've got tests in my nurse bag." Shelby coughed. "After I take one, I need to rest, Jeb."

He brought her a test.

She swabbed herself.

Jeb winced as she stuck it far up her nose. Twenty long minutes later, he frowned and asked about the results. "Is it positive?"

Shelby squinted at the small square and shook her head. "No, I told you I don't have COVID-19."

Thank God. Flu's bad enough. "Do you want coffee? You ought to eat something." He hovered, helpless, and uncertain what to do.

"No coffee. I'll drink tea if there's any in the cabinet. I can't eat right now. Will you bring it to me on the couch?"

"You bet." Jeb brewed a cup of the lemon tea Shelby liked. He brought it to the living room, along with a dose of acetaminophen. "Here, honey. I'll carry you back upstairs if you want after you drink that."

Shelby shook her head. "Uh-uh. You'd wreck your back. I can walk." Another round of coughing wracked her slender body.

"Then you can use the guest bedroom." Jeb brushed her hair back from her face, frowning at the fevered heat of her skin. "I want you close, so I can take care of you."

Her eyes glittered in her pale face. "Okay. I feel too terrible to argue."

"What are your symptoms?" They might have ruled out COVID-19, but Jeb wanted to make sure it wasn't anything worse than influenza.

"Horrible headache, I ache all over, my throat hurts, and I can't stop coughing." Shelby shook with chills. "And I'm cold, so cold, but I know I've got a fever."

"I'm sorry, sugar. Let me get the bed ready." Since he'd last slept there, Shelby had put on fresh sheets, but he added extra pillows and pulled blankets from the cedar chest at the foot of the bed. Jeb turned on a small lamp and fetched Shelby. He put an arm around her for support as she hobbled into the room. Jeb tucked her into bed and covered her. "Are you comfortable?"

"As much as possible." Shelby grasped his hands in hers. "I'm sorry I'm sick, Jeb. I know you wanted to go to church today and pick out a Christmas tree. Go ahead if you want."

"I'm not going anywhere." He perched on the edge of the bed. Her skin blazed beneath his touch. "What do you need?"

"I don't know, Jeb." Shelby groaned and covered her eyes with one arm.

Jeb wasn't a nurse, and he'd never taken care of anyone in his life. When he got sick, he holed up in bed like a hibernating bear and slept. Jeb fetched a washcloth from the bathroom, soaked it with tepid water, and returned. He bathed her forehead and cheeks, then laid it across her head. "Does this help at all?"

"A little." Shelby opened her eyes with a long sigh. "Jeb, tell Mom not to bring the kids home. I don't want them to catch this. Flu can be rough on little ones."

He waited until she fell asleep and called Delia from the kitchen landline.

She answered on the second ring. "We're on our way. We just left town."

"Don't come." Jeb leaned against the fridge for support. His show of bravado with Shelby vanished once he was alone and didn't need to keep up a brave face for her sake. He couldn't remember the last time he'd felt so incapable. "Shelby's come down with the flu, and she's really sick. She wants you to keep the kids, if you could."

"Oh, no." Delia cried. "Poor Shelby. Of course, they can stay with me. They certainly don't need to catch a bug. I can drop them at school before I go to work tomorrow. Lafayette High School isn't far from their elementary school, so I can pick them up, too. This is the last week before Christmas break." Delia spoke fast, with her words running into each other. "Do you need me to bring anything over?"

"Thanks, but Dad can fetch whatever we need. He went to church this morning, so he's out and about. Tell the kids not to worry." Jeb straightened several fridge magnets.

"Will do. Keep me posted on how Shelby's doing, all right?"

"Absolutely. I'll talk to you later." Jeb ended the call and then dialed Joe. The early service should be over by now.

"What do you need, son?" Josiah answered immediately.

"Shelby's got the flu, and she's extremely sick. Can you pick up one of those digital thermometers?" Jeb tried to think about what else might be handy. "Maybe get orange juice and a box of the lemon tea she likes. I'll send you a picture of the package. I don't know how many cans of soup are here, so pick up a selection including chicken and beef broth. Whatever else you might think. I really have no clue, Dad."

"I'll take care of it, Jeb. I'd best get some stuff for me and you to eat, too. What about Shelby's kids?" His dad's voice echoed, strong and full.

"They're staying with Delia." Jeb would miss them, but if they remained in town, they wouldn't get sick. "I hope they don't get upset." It wasn't comparable, but he remembered how he'd felt when he realized his mom was ill.

"Best place for them. I'll be home quick as I can. If

you think of anything else, give me a ring." Joe ended the call.

Jeb checked on Shelby, who still slept. He brought the rocking chair from the living room so he could sit beside the bed. Concern gnawed at him, and he felt useless. A memory rushed into his head. He'd had a severe bout of flu when he was fifteen, and Granny had put him to bed in this very room. *I don't know what to do for a sick person, but Granny did. Remember, Jeb.*

His mind flashed back sixteen years. Granny had bathed his forehead, just as he had Shelby's. She coaxed him to eat but didn't push. *Feed a cold, starve a fever,* she'd said. Every little thing she did for his comfort came back now, and Jeb vowed he would do the same for Shelby.

The Christmas tree could wait. Jeb had the stockings and what he needed to fill them. Additional gifts were due to arrive any day, and he'd get them wrapped eventually. He might not be able to bake cookies, but he could buy them. A thought struck. Christmas dinner! They hadn't shopped yet, and the holiday was ten days away. Enough time remained to plan and procure. Shelby should be on the mend by the twenty-fifth. Dad could always pick up the groceries in a pinch.

Jeb groaned aloud. He hadn't bought the ring. Without it, his planned proposal in front of the glittering tree wouldn't be the same. He wanted to make Christmas merry for all of them, especially Shelby. Jeb decided he'd carve out time to visit a jewelry store. "It's too soon to give in to the Grinch or Scrooge," he muttered aloud as he sat beside the bed.

Shelby stirred. "What?"

"Never mind, sugar." He kissed her forehead. Jeb thought the fever might be down a little, because her skin didn't seem as hot. "Can I get you anything?"

She shook her head. "Socks. My feet are like ice."

Until now, he hadn't realized she wasn't wearing any. "I'll fetch some." Jeb dashed upstairs, grabbed a pair from her dresser, and brought them. He pushed back the covers at the foot of the bed and slid her cold feet into the stockings. "Better?"

"Warmer." Shelby wiggled her toes as Jeb covered her feet. "Thanks."

"No problem. Honey, I'd do anything so you'd feel better. If I could, I'd take the flu so you wouldn't have to be sick." He smoothed the blankets over her and did his best to plump the pillows to make her comfortable.

Her fever-bright eyes met his. "I believe you would. It's funny, but Jimmy always stayed as far away as possible if I became sick."

"I'm not Jimmy." The more Jeb heard about the man, the less respect he had for him.

"I'm sorry I've messed up Christmas." She scooted onto her side and faced him.

"You haven't. It's ten more days. We'll keep Christmas, and I promise, it'll be wonderful." He meant every word. His plans, though, were in jeopardy with Shelby's illness. As long as no one else came down with the flu, Jeb thought he might still pull it off.

He would need a little bit of Santa Claus and a lot of Jesus to get it done.

Chapter Fifteen

Josiah came through. He brought home a thermometer, tea, soup, over-the-counter meds, a cough suppressant, and everything else Jeb requested. He also carried in several flavors of sherbet—oranges and lemons, a half-gallon of chocolate chip ice cream, a stack of frozen meals, a bag of still-hot fried chicken, biscuits, wedge potatoes, three kinds of lunchmeat, microwaveable burgers, potato chips, and heat-to-eat sausage biscuits. Joe brought two boxes of cereal and a gallon of milk, plus orange juice and clear soda.

"I figured Shelby might like the sherbet in a day or so. It goes down easy." Joe put the items away with familiarity. "I work tomorrow and every day this week except Thursday and Sunday. If you think of anything else, I can head back to town."

Jeb nodded. This was the dad he remembered from early childhood. Back then, he had been a kind man who always delivered what was needed. He'd been responsible, and until his mom got sick, Jeb had relied on his dad. If he needed something, then Dad provided, whether it was material items or words he needed to hear. His dad's support vanished when Joe left. For years, Jeb harbored resentment and lived with simmering anger in his gut. Both were gone, and he hoped neither would return. Hope replaced both, along with a love for his dad he realized he'd never lost. "I appreciate the help. Thanks." Jeb inhaled the fried chicken's aroma with delight, and his stomach rumbled. A cookie had been his breakfast. "Shelby's asleep, so let's eat while the food is still hot."

"Good idea." Joe sat at the table and bowed his head as he spoke a simple blessing.

Jeb devoured two pieces of chicken, a couple of biscuits, and some wedge potatoes. He savored each bite. He finished with a single scoop of ice cream. "That hit the spot. I needed food."

Joe smiled and polished off a drumstick. "Of course. Best keep your strength up. I pray you don't come down with the flu."

Shelby had a coughing fit, audible in the kitchen, so Jeb hurried to the bedroom. He carried the thermometer and the cough suppressants. "Hey, honey."

She half-sat, body wracked with hacking, one hand pressed to her chest. "Jeb," she croaked. "Where were you?"

"Helping Dad put away things from town. We have a good thermometer now. Let me take your temp." Jeb touched the device to Shelby's forehead and frowned. "One hundred and three. If it doesn't come down, I'll need to get you to the doctor."

"I'm a nurse." Her voice cracked as she spoke. "I don't need to get checked out, because I know what's wrong. It's the flu. Jeb, I'm thirsty."

"Do you want water, orange juice, or soda?" Jeb pushed hair away from her face with a soft touch. "I've got cough suppressants and plenty of acetaminophen."

"I'll take some orange juice." She coughed hard, then sighed. "I'll try the cough tablets and the pain reliever. I'm not able to rest when I can't quit coughing."

Shelby drank a little juice under Jeb's watchful gaze and took the meds. He plumped her pillows and straightened the bedding as much as he could. "Do you feel like eating?" Despite what Granny taught about starving a fever, Jeb knew Shelby needed sustenance to fight the virus. "I'll fix anything you'd like."

She shook her head, then winced. "I can't eat right now. Maybe I will later."

Although worried, Jeb didn't want to argue. "All right, sugar."

"Will you be in here?" Although she huddled beneath the blankets, Shelby extended her left hand and grasped his.

"Of course. If I step out for a moment, holler for me or…wait!" Jeb had an idea. "I'll be right back." Granny had collected bells, and they remained on a shelf in the front room. Jeb considered the choices. He picked up a small silver bell etched with flowers. He'd given it to his grandmother for her birthday several years before she passed. He rang it and approved. The sound would carry, so he returned to the guest room. "If you need me, ring this, and I'll come on the run."

"It's pretty." Shelby took it and tested it. "Okay. Hey, Jeb?"

"What?" He plopped into the rocker. Jeb stroked back a stray lock of her hair from her face.

"I really love you, babe." She caught his hand and touched her lips to it.

"I love you, too, honey." Her pronouncement pleased him, and the endearment touched Jeb's heart. She hadn't used one before. "Rest."

The next few days were rough. Shelby remained sick, and her fever spiked every evening. Jeb hated seeing her misery so he did his best to alleviate it. When she shivered with chills, then he covered her with more blankets. He provided lemon tea or juice when she became thirsty. Although she didn't want to eat, he talked her into sips of broth and a little soup. About the time Jeb began to wonder if she would improve without a trip to the doctor, her fever lessened.

Shelby perked up enough to lie on the couch instead of staying in bed.

He offered to carry her, but she refused, so he supported her as she made a slow walk to the living room. "Why's the couch moved?" She glanced around the room. "It's next to your recliner now."

"I made a spot for the Christmas tree." Jeb's dad had done the heavy lifting at his direction. "It's less than a week until the twenty-fifth."

"Just skip a tree this year." Shelby waved one hand. "I'm too tired, and the kids don't know any different. We can do one next year."

Although her expectation they would be together for the next Christmas delighted him, Jeb would have a tree this year, regardless. "I want a tree, honey. You won't have to do a thing but admire it."

She sighed. "I won't be helpful wrapping presents, either. I'm so tired and weak, Jeb. I'm supposed to be taking care of you, not the other way around."

He sat on the floor beside the couch and held her hand. "I'm all right, and you'll get stronger. Do you really feel better?"

"I do, mostly. I still cough without taking the medicine, though." A whine crept into her voice. "And what about Christmas dinner? We never went grocery shopping."

"Dad said he'd go tomorrow on his day off. I'd like to go with him, but I'd rather not leave you alone." Jeb planned to buy the ring, too, but he wasn't about to spoil the surprise.

A faint smile lit her face. "I bet you've got cabin fever. You should go."

"I might ask your mom if she'll come out to stay." He'd spoken with Delia each day, often more than once. "School ends today for the holiday break. I think the kids would like to see you." Shelby talked to them most days on the phone, but it wasn't the same.

"Maybe."

"Don't be silly. You know they want to see you. If you're up to it, then she can bring the kids home." Jeb crossed his fingers because the house wasn't the same without them.

"I do miss them, and I'd like that. If Joe makes the trip to town, then you should go. I'm glad you've stayed home while I was ill. It helped, knowing you were here." Shelby tightened her grasp on his fingers.

"There's no place else I'd rather be, Shelby, especially when you're sick." Jeb kissed the back of her hand. "Want soup for lunch? Dad brought home more last night, so there's chicken noodle, sirloin burger, and minestrone."

"I'll try sirloin burger, if I can eat at the table." Shelby stirred from the couch and made her way to the dining room. Once there, she ate more than she had since she came down with the flu.

Jeb paired his soup with a thick bologna sandwich. For supper, he planned to heat up chicken and dumplings the pastor's wife had delivered after hearing Shelby had the flu.

On Saturday, Delia brought Levi and Lexi home.

The kids ran straight to the living room where Shelby rested in the recliner.

Although she still wore her robe and nightgown, she'd brushed her hair and pulled it up with a claw clip. Ice water, a small cup of orange juice, and a bell were within reach.

"Mama, Mama, you're alive!" Lexi dived at her mother with arms spread wide.

Jeb caught her and put his arms around her. "Go easy with your mama. We need to use care and go easy. She's still recovering."

"Grandma told you the same thing, Lexi." Levi rolled his eyes. "Can we hug you, Mama?"

"As long as it's gentle." Shelby embraced her son and kissed his cheek. "C'mere, Lexi."

Her daughter flew into her arms.

Shelby held her close.

Lexi knelt and laid her head in Shelby's lap. "I worried, Mama. I got scared Christmas might be canceled."

Jeb's heart twisted. "No one ever cancels Christmas. Everything we talked about is still happening."

Levi faced him. "There's no tree. You said we'd have a tree."

"We will. Dad and I are heading to town this morning, and a tree is on the list." He fist-bumped the kid. "We're ready to roll now."

Shelby held her hand out to Jeb. "Be careful and hurry back."

Jeb kissed Shelby's cheek. "I will, honey. I'm glad your mom's here. She didn't leave, did she?"

"No, I'm right here." Delia strolled into the living room. "Take all the time you need, Jeb."

Joe offered to drive so Jeb shrugged. "Sure, if you want."

"Where all do we need to go? I'm guessing more than just the supermarket." Joe eased the old truck down the driveway. "I heard something about a tree."

"Definitely a tree, although I'm not sure how good the selection will be this close to Christmas." Jeb would settle for any halfway decent pine. "I bought lights, but I guess we still need ornaments, garlands, and stuff."

"Ma's Christmas decorations boxes should still be in the attic unless you moved them. I know exactly where to look." Joe pulled on sunglasses as he reached the main highway.

"I didn't know. I'd like it if you can find them." Jeb hadn't set foot in the attic in years. It wasn't a full third story but an unfinished space with boards laid down, instead of a solid floor and low-hanging eaves. "I might grab a few more ornaments, just in case."

"Tree lot, discount or department store, then groceries." Joe ticked off each stop. "Anywhere else?"

"First on the agenda is a jewelry store." Jeb blurted out his mission. "If I'm gonna propose, I need the ring."

"Definitely!" Joe slapped the steering wheel and laughed. "We'll find somewhere you can buy a ring."

"Thanks, Dad. Will you help me pick one?"

"I'd be happy to, Jebediah." Joe scratched his cheek with one finger. "I'm no expert, but I'll tell you which one is pretty."

"I have one more favor to ask." Jeb drew a deep

breath. "Will you stand up with me, as my best man?" *If she says* yes *and there is a wedding.*

Josiah pulled onto the shoulder and stopped the truck. He extended his right hand and shook Jeb's left. "I'll be honored to, Son."

Jeb embraced his dad. *Forget shaking hands. It's time for a hug.*

In town, they hit the mall but had no luck choosing a ring. Next stop was a national chain jeweler. Jeb had a few ideas about what he wanted, but he didn't see anything close. At the third jewelry store, he found the perfect match. The Art-Deco style white-gold ring featured a central diamond flanked by four smaller stones, two on each side. Crisscrossed loops like a basket decorated the band. Tiny diamond chips sparkled. The matching wedding band boasted the same style and fit into the engagement ring. "This is the one." Jeb lifted the ring to catch the light.

"It's beautiful. Now you need one for you," Joe told him.

Jeb chose a plain white-gold men's band. He paid for the rings and asked for a pair of jewelry boxes. "Now let's find a Christmas tree."

As he feared, none of the tree stands had many trees left. One tree lot had already closed for the season. On the advice of the second tree lot attendant, they headed for a traditional grocery store deep in town. Woodbury's Market still had some fir trees, although Jeb couldn't decide if they were Douglas or Noble variety. He stood several specimens up, considered, and rejected them. Each was too tall or short, too fat, or too skinny.

"Best choose one, Son. I doubt you'll find much

selection anywhere else. It doesn't have to be perfect." Joe pawed through the possibilities and held them out for Jeb's approval. "Once it's decorated, it will look beautiful."

Jeb decided on a six-foot-tall, slender Douglas fir. It wasn't perfect with a few bare spots, but once decorated, it would be pretty. Jeb and Joe wrestled the tree to the truck. They wrapped it with a faded blanket from behind the seat to protect the fragile branches.

At one of the discount stores, Jeb picked out a few garlands, a box of ornaments, and a wreath for the door. He bought coloring books and crayons for both kids, bike helmets he'd forgotten until now, a stuffed dinosaur for Levi, and a big plush puppy for Lexi. On impulse, he picked out flannel pajamas for Levi and a granny gown in the same buffalo plaid for Lexi. When he realized the PJs also came in adult sizes, he bought the same style for himself and Shelby. Jeb chose a pretty blouse for her, too, and a warm robe to replace the threadbare one she'd been wearing.

"I thought you already had all the gifts." Joe snorted as he rolled the shopping cart through the store.

"I did." Jeb grinned. "It just seems like maybe I haven't bought enough."

"You come by it honest. Daffy was the same way." Joe wore a small smile, and his eyes danced. "Let's get the groceries and get out of here. The store's too busy for my taste."

Every aisle teemed with shoppers. The two men bought the biggest bone-in ham in the case, fixings for scalloped potatoes, frozen vegetables, slice-and-bake cookies, packaged hot rolls, and ice cream. Jeb picked up a selection of convenience foods, in case Shelby didn't feel up to cooking a huge holiday meal.

"I'll buy you a burger if you want, before we head home." Joe made the offer at the checkout.

"Sure, I'd enjoy one." Jeb gathered up the bags and headed toward the parking lot.

After lunch, on their way out of town, Jeb picked up take-and-bake pizzas to serve at supper.

At the farmhouse, the kids sat on the floor with one on each side of the recliner.

Shelby, fighting a nagging cough and still hoarse, read from a book of fairy tales. "And they lived happily ever after." She closed the volume and set it aside.

"Can you read one more?" Lexi clasped her hands together.

"Your mama's tired." Jeb hugged the girl. "I'll read later. Did you guys have lunch?"

"Grandma made sandwiches." Levi moved to the couch. "Mama didn't eat, though."

Jeb knelt. "Do you want me to warm up some soup or nuke a frozen entrée?"

"I'm ready for a nap." Shelby took his hands and smiled. "I'm not hungry, Jeb."

"Sugar, you need to eat something." Jeb worried because she'd lost weight during her illness. She had been too skinny before. "C'mon. I'll fix whatever you want, then you can sleep."

"What are the choices?" Shelby coughed and covered her mouth.

"Pot pies, lasagna, chicken and rice, Salisbury steak, chicken *alfredo*, and Mexican dinners." He'd picked up a wide variety.

"I'll try a chicken pot pie, I guess. Did you get a tree?" She glanced at the vacant space in front of the window.

"Of course. I'll go heat your lunch." Jeb rejoiced she was willing to eat without a lot of coaxing. "Kids, ask Joe to show you what we brought home. It's in the barn."

Both children looked at their mother.

She nodded. "Go ahead."

"Where's Delia?" Jeb hadn't seen her or noticed if her car remained parked behind the house.

"Upstairs, putting clean sheets on my bed. I want to sleep there tonight." Shelby tossed off the blanket. "Then you can sleep in your own room."

Jeb laughed. He had been dozing in the rocker in the guest bedroom or sleeping in his recliner. He didn't think she'd known. "Busted. I'll be glad to be back in my bedroom upstairs, though. If you'll be down the hall, then I'd rather be close."

She shuffled into the dining room to eat. After lunch, Shelby had more color in her face. She coughed.

Jeb offered her a cough tablet.

Delia came through the room. Her arms were filled with bedding. "Your bed's made, Shelby. I thought I'd toss all this in the washer. Are there more dirty clothes?"

"We've kept up with the laundry. Let me carry those." Jeb took the items and headed for the laundry room. "I'll start a load."

"Thanks. I'm heading back to town. I've got a little shopping to do myself. It's the season." Delia winked at Jeb.

"Don't spend much, Mom. Plan on dinner here on the twenty-fifth. I should be up and around to make it." Shelby rose and stood, wobbling more than a little.

"I'll help, sugar. So will the kids. Do you want to go upstairs and rest?" Jeb took her arm so she wouldn't topple.

"Please." Shelby leaned against him. "I could use a nap."

He cradled her close and supported her as they climbed the stairs. He made sure Shelby was situated in bed and propped against pillows. Jeb opened the drapes so she could look outside. "Want me to stay?"

Shelby yawned. "No, I'm okay. Turn on the baby monitor."

Jeb already had it in place. "You bet. I'll check on you in a little bit." He kissed her lips in a slow brush. It was the first real kiss since she became sick.

"I guess your dad took the kids to see the tree in the barn." Shelby yawned as she scooted deeper beneath the covers.

"Yeah. We won't decorate it until tomorrow or Monday, though. Dad's gonna hunt down my grandmother's decorations."

"Why am I not surprised?" Shelby laughed, light and low.

"Because you know I'm stubborn, and I really want a tree." He turned off the overhead light. "Love you, honey. Try to sleep."

Delia stayed longer than intended and traipsed up to the attic with Joe. Together, they located the boxes marked *Xmas* and brought them to the living room. Two contained vintage ornaments, another had the narrow glass tree topper he remembered, along with other holiday knickknacks, and the last held a tree stand.

"That's what we forgot to buy." Jeb picked up the

ancient device. "I'm glad you found this."

Joe nodded. "You bet. I'll get the tree in the stand. It's better if it stands upright for a day or so to let the branches stretch out. Then we'll bring it inside and decorate. Delia, want to give me a hand?"

Shelby's mom blushed. "Sure, I've got time. The stores aren't going anywhere. Levi invited me to stay for supper. I hear there's pizza."

"You bet. We grabbed a pre-made salad, too. Let's go to the barn and get the tree standing. Kids, are you coming?" Joe pulled on his worn coat. "If so, let's go."

Jeb shook his head and grinned as he watched them go. He didn't know Delia well, but he liked her, and from what he could tell, his dad did, too. Over the absent years, he had no idea if Joe had had any relationships, but now Jeb wondered. He'd like his dad and Shelby's mom to be friends, but he wasn't sure about anything more.

He reclaimed his recliner so he'd hear Shelby over the monitor. Jeb shut his eyes and felt relaxed but not drowsy. Christmas was coming together, but there might be a complication or two along the way.

If so, Jeb prayed everything would turn out well, no matter what, and that they all stayed healthy. He couldn't think of anything which might go wrong, but he knew all too well, things often happened.

Chapter Sixteen

On Sunday, Shelby woke early. She savored the warm comfort of bed for a bit longer, then rose. For the first time since she came down with a violent case of flu, she decided she was finally on the mend. Although she'd slept well and long, fatigue and a nagging cough remained. She had little-to-no appetite, which bothered Jeb. As a nurse, Shelby didn't expect to be hungry yet.

Jeb's tender care during her illness deepened her love. No one, not even her mom, had ever nursed her with such devotion or kindness. Shelby prayed he wouldn't come down with the flu, and so far, God had listened. If she'd fallen sick as a single parent, her illness would have been much rougher. She would have been too ill to care for her kids. *Thank goodness for Jeb and Mom.*

In slow motion, Shelby changed from her nightgown into sweatpants and a long-sleeved T-shirt. She put on clean socks and slid her feet into fleece-lined slippers Jeb brought from town. She brushed her hair into a ponytail. She washed her face in the bathroom and frowned at her pale reflection. *I look like a ghost. Maybe the Ghost of Christmas Present.*

The thought didn't bring a laugh. Shelby feared her illness had wrecked Jeb's dreams of a wonderful Christmas, something she didn't believe existed. To her, it was just another day, and the birth of Jesus was the only reason to celebrate. Jeb had other ideas, though, and after his long, lonely years, he wanted to experience a joyful day. She understood but didn't share his desire.

I never bought Jeb a present. The realization thudded into her brain, and she sighed. Shelby had intended to go shopping and had considered gift options. If she had the funds, she would buy the horse he wanted, even though his doctor hadn't cleared Jeb to ride. A horse, however, was far beyond her budget, so she dismissed the thought. Her other ideas were a fishing rod with a quality reel or a decent tacklebox. If she didn't do any shopping, Shelby could make up for it with a New Year's gift.

Shelby tiptoed down the stairs, uncertain if anyone else was awake. All the bedroom doors remained closed. She gripped the banister for support and took slow steps. At the bottom, she paused to catch her breath. A cough tickled her throat, and she hacked. She inhaled the pungent scent of fresh pine and noticed the tall fir tree in the front window. It *was* pretty, even unadorned. Shelby smiled because Jeb had his Christmas tree. The rich aroma of coffee wafted through the house. Shelby moved toward the kitchen and almost ran into Jeb as he exited the room.

"Shelby, you're up!" His face lit with a smile as he put his arms around her. Jeb kissed her, sweet and slow. "You look a lot better."

If her appearance had improved, she must have looked like a hag before. "I'm feeling less rough, Jeb. Could I have coffee?"

"You bet, honey. Come and sit while I pour it." Jeb hovered as she settled in a chair.

Shelby sipped the rich coffee, sweetened with the right amount of sugar, and a splash of milk. "Oh, this is good."

He slid in across from her. "Enjoy. When you want to eat, I'll make something."

"Maybe." Her tummy rumbled with hunger, which was a good sign for recovery. "Are the kids still asleep?

Jeb shook his head. "Up hours ago. They've gone to church with your mom and my dad."

"What time is it? I thought it was earlier." She squinted at the clock. It was after ten. "Which church?"

"Faith. Your mom liked Miss Bessie and Homer." Jeb stroked the back of Shelby's hand as he spoke. "She wanted to see more of the church Levi and Lexi told her about."

"I'm surprised." Shelby took another sip of coffee. "Mom's always been fond of our church on Savannah Avenue."

Jeb shrugged. "Maybe she's ready for a change. Faith is small, and you get to know everyone. Delia might like it."

Shelby nodded. "I wish I could have gone."

"It's a little too soon, honey." Jeb lifted her hand to his lips and kissed it.

"I know." Getting out of bed, dressing, and coming downstairs had sapped her energy. "Maybe I can on Christmas Eve."

"We'll see. What do you want for breakfast?" He pushed back his chair and rose. "Scrambled eggs? Oatmeal? Toast? A sausage biscuit?"

"Oatmeal. What flavor?" Shelby didn't want to get too wild with her first meal. "I like brown sugar and maple."

Jeb sorted through a variety box and plucked out an envelope. "Got it."

Although he'd already eaten, Jeb sat with Shelby as she downed a little hot cereal.

"What's the plan today?" Shelby savored the quiet calm, but it wouldn't last once the kids returned.

"I promised your mom I'd put dinner in the oven. She made meatloaf." Jeb eyed the kitchen clock. "I'm planning to wrap the rest of the presents while Levi and Lexi are at church. They want to decorate the tree after dinner. I might play the piano."

"Wow. Busy day." His plans made her head spin. Shelby craved relaxation while she recuperated. "I could help wrap."

Jeb laughed. "I can use your assistance. I'm all thumbs. We'll use the dining room table."

Shelby sat and waited as Jeb brought the presents.

He also carried an armful of brightly colored holiday paper, two pairs of scissors, tape, tags, and gifts. "Some of these are for your mom and my dad. The rest are for the kids. I've already got your gifts wrapped."

"You shouldn't have bought me anything." Shelby wanted to cry. Jeb provided so much, and she didn't want him to spend more on silly trinkets. "I haven't been able to buy you a present."

"Honey, you're all the gift I need. If you want to pick up something later, it's fine, okay?" He rolled out a length of paper decorated with dancing Santas and cut a piece.

"Sure." His understanding and casual love sent a warm wave through her. "What's the first thing to wrap?"

"Flannel shirts for my dad." Jeb tucked them into a box, placed it on the center of the wrapping paper, and taped the corners in a clumsy fashion. "I got him jeans and footwear, too. Do you want to wrap the boots?"

"I can." Jeb's acceptance of his father's return delighted Shelby. So far, Josiah had proven himself clean and sober. He pitched in like family, which he was.

They finished before the others returned from church. Jeb stowed the presents in the guest bedroom closet, although he'd placed his dad's and her mom's under the tree. He'd brought out both the old and new decorations. "Let's get you settled, before Lexi and Levi come in," Jeb laughed. "They'll want hugs."

Comfortable in the recliner, Shelby sighed with pleasure. She noticed the couch now sat against the open staircase. The piano rested against the open doorway into the dining room. "Who moved the furniture again?"

"Dad did, and I helped. Before you ask, I didn't hurt my back. I was careful." He shot her a wide grin.

Voices heralded the churchgoers return. The kids pelted through the house at top speed but braked when they spotted her.

"Hi, Levi. Hi, Lexi." Shelby opened her arms wide.

"You got dressed." Lexi put her arms around Shelby's neck and hugged tightly. "Mama, I haven't seen you in clothes for so long."

"Only because we were at Grandma's most of the time." Levi came forward for his embrace.

He handled Shelby as if she had been fashioned from fragile glass, which pleased her.

"Jeb said we can decorate the tree today."

"I heard." Shelby eyed the boxes of decorations. "I'll supervise."

"Can we start now? Please!" Lexi clasped her hands and tilted her head.

"First, we'll eat dinner." Jeb set the rules. "Lights have to go on first, and I'll do that once the kitchen is clean."

"Or I will." Josiah walked into the room. "Either way, though, kiddos, Jeb's right."

Joe grinned at Shelby. "Good to see you up and around."

She returned the smile. "I'm glad to be out of bed."

Lexi handed Shelby a crayon drawing of the nativity scene. The star and stable were recognizable. "I made the picture in Sunday School."

"It's pretty." Shelby resolved she'd hang it on the fridge and probably keep it to display every December.

Levi rubbed his tummy. "I'm hungry. When do we eat?"

"Dinner's almost ready, if I can get someone to set the table," Delia called from the kitchen.

Ten minutes later, they gathered. Two sliced meatloaves rested on a platter beside a big bowl of mashed potatoes and another brimming with brown gravy. Packaged hot rolls and frozen corn rounded out the meal.

After the blessing, Delia turned to Shelby. "Is this all right for you? I can fix something else, if it's not."

"Mom, it's fine and looks so good. I won't each much, but I'll try a little meatloaf and a small serving of potatoes." Shelby would love to eat a full plate, but she wasn't sure how her stomach would take it. She'd rather go slow and eat a little than overeat and get sick.

Josiah sat at the head of the table, once his usual spot, and her mom at the other end. Shelby took her place beside Jeb and with the kids across the table. She listened as they chattered about Sunday School and church. Shelby savored the familiar cadence of their voices and tuned out everything else until Joe's weather discussion caught her attention.

"…winter storm watch through Christmas Day." Josiah waved his hands as he spoke. "I hope the weatherman's wrong on this one. They're saying possibly two or three feet of snow, accompanied by subzero windchills."

"I took some trash out earlier, and it's like springtime. That surely can't be right." Jeb frowned.

"I don't know, Son. Mild weather in December often comes right before a big snow. I've seen it happen." Joe filled his plate with a second round of everything. He added gravy to his meat and potatoes. "Sounds like we might get snowed in, so if there's anything we need, I'd best head into town to fetch it."

The idea of snow sent shivers through Shelby. The white stuff might be nice, if she'd ever had the luxury to stay home and keep warm, but she'd always had to go out. Her job took her over rural roads and into the backcountry as often as not. The warmth she'd gained this morning faded, and she shuddered.

"What's wrong, sugar?" Jeb focused his attention on Shelby.

"I don't care for snow. Thinking about it makes me cold." She rubbed her arms through the long sleeves of her shirt. Her uncertain appetite vanished, and she pushed her half-eaten dinner away.

"Mama, it might be a white Christmas!" Lexi

giggled. Her eyes twinkled.

"I'd rather it's not." Delia finished her meal. "But if it is, we'll manage."

Tears filled Shelby's eyes. Although she knew her reaction was over the top, she couldn't help it. "I hate getting out in the snow. Ice is worse."

Jeb scooted his chair closer and put an arm around her. "Honey, you won't need to go anywhere. None of us will. School's out. If necessary, Dad or I can buy anything else we might need before the weather gets here. It's not expected just yet, but I'd rather be stocked up if we get snowed in."

"Mom might get stuck in town. And Joe has to work, doesn't he?" Shelby realized she might be unreasonable but couldn't control her emotions. She'd almost bought into Jeb's happy Christmas dreams, and now, thanks to winter, her fragile hopes shattered.

"Delia's welcome to bunk here, anytime. We've got room. What's your schedule this week, Dad?" Jeb turned toward his father.

Joe pulled out his phone to check. "I work tomorrow and Christmas Eve, then I'm off for a couple days. If the roads get bad, I'll call in. I ain't risking my life, not now when I finally got something to live for."

"Good." Jeb nodded. "Since it's predicted to be bitterly cold, you ought to go ahead and move into the house. You can have the guest room."

Joe's face lit brighter than stars in the night sky. "Do you mean until it warms back up?"

"No, Dad. I meant for good." Jeb's voice cracked.

"I will then, thanks. Do you mind, Shelby?" Joe glanced at her and waited.

"I think it's a wonderful idea. I've wondered if you

were comfortable out there in the barn." Shelby had never seen the room Joe occupied. She hadn't even realized it existed.

"That room's nicer than a lot of places I've bunked." Joe reached for one more hot roll and buttered it. "I'll like being in the house better, though."

Jeb assisted Shelby into the recliner and tucked a blanket over her lap. He planted a kiss on her lips. "We'll start decorating the tree soon. I'll help your mom clean the kitchen first."

"Can't we start *now*?" Lexi danced in circles around the room. She paused to bang on the piano keys.

Shelby covered her ears at the discordant sound. "Stop! You'll give me a headache!"

"If you want to learn to play, I'll teach you, but not right now. Your mama doesn't want or need the noise." Jeb led Lexi away from the piano. Come help Levi get the wreath ready to hang." He dug out a wreath made of silver bells and trimmed at the top with a red bow and faux holly.

Shelby hadn't seen it until now. "How lovely."

Jeb shook it so the bells tinkled. "Sounds pretty, too."

Shelby laughed with her good mood restored. Maybe it would snow, maybe not, but Jeb brought sunshine into her life no matter what the weather did.

By early evening, as dusk fell, the family finished decorating the tree. It sparkled with miniature lights in a variety of colors. Vintage glass ornaments hung beside vintage silk balls. Angels danced from the branches, and Santas swung from others. Snowmen held places of honor on the tree, along with cowboy-themed ornaments. Shelby suspected Jed had collected those—

a single black boot, a cowboy hat, two horses, and a bull. Tinsel garlands in silver, gold, and metallic red wrapped the tree. Candy canes dangled throughout, offering a sweet promise to taste later. A fragile glass spire topped the fir, reminding Shelby of a castle.

"Granny always said it's Russian. A friend of her dad's gave it to them when she was little." Jeb touched it with a light fingertip. "I always thought the topper was special."

"Very." Shelby admired the tree. Her mom left for town, his dad had retired early because he worked in the morning, and the kids went to bed.

Jeb turned off all the lamps.

The sparkling tree and the bright illumination lifted her dark mood. "It's beautiful."

Jeb sat at her knees, at the foot of the recliner, his back leaning against her.

Shelby liked the casual intimacy, and she brushed her fingers through his hair. "You need a haircut."

"I do. I haven't had the time, honey, or even thought about it. I'll go after the holiday." He tipped his head back to look at her.

"I can't decide if I should cut mine or grow it long." Shelby shook her head until her ponytail bounced.

"Let it grow, sugar." Jeb reached back and stroked her hair. "I like it, and I'd love it halfway down your back."

"Maybe." She stretched. "It's so good to feel better."

"I'm glad you're improving." Jeb shifted his position so he could face her, cross-legged on the floor. "I really worried about you. You were so sick."

"It was just the flu." Shelby grasped his hand.

"People sometimes die from influenza." His blue eyes met her gaze without blinking.

"Not me." As a nurse, she knew the stats but didn't want to think about them. "How's your back?"

"It's been good. Gives me a twinge once in a while, that's all." He shifted position and grimaced. "Hurts now."

"Poor Jeb." Shelby leaned forward and cupped his upturned face in her hands. She kissed him. He tasted like peppermint, and she savored the sweet flavor. "I'm supposed to be the nurse."

He shook his head. "We take care of each other, honey."

"I like that idea, Jeb, so very much." Shelby wanted to spend her life with this sweet man, but he'd made no commitment. He loved her, and she loved him, but she didn't know if it would last. Right now, she had no other home, but Jeb made her feel cherished. With the kids, they made a family. If Shelby had a Christmas wish, it would be that this love, this powerful connection, would last forever.

"I love you." Jeb came to his feet and offered a hand so she could rise. He maneuvered and changed position until he sat in the recliner with Shelby across his lap.

Her momentary protest ended when she realized his arms were safe and comfortable.

He cradled her close.

She rested her head on his chest. His steady heartbeat resonated, and she drew breath in tandem with Jeb.

He began to sing, his voice true without music,

traditional Christmas carols. Jeb sang of the birth of a Savior with old words familiar since childhood. His tenor tones rose in "Away In A Manger" and in the classic "Silent Night."

Shelby might have sung along, but she listened, caught in the magical moment loving the man and his tender songs echoing softly in the night.

Forecasters called for a chance of snow. The future loomed uncertain. Christmas might disappoint, but nestled in Jeb's lap, with his arms around her, and his voice in her ear, Shelby didn't care.

She loved Jeb Hill, and she had no doubt he loved her. No matter what happened in the future, this memory would last a lifetime.

Shelby had almost fallen asleep, content in Jeb's lap, when someone pounded on the door and shouted. She roused, agitated, and worried as Jeb rose to answer the door.

The peace shattered, and the everyday world crashed back down, hard.

Chapter Seventeen

With Shelby in his lap, Jeb tasted a rich happiness he'd never known. He had meant to play the piano and sing carols, but instead, he held her close. Jeb sang without music as he cuddled Shelby. He had the ring box tucked in his front jeans' pocket, and for a moment, he considered asking Shelby to become his wife now. The quiet contentment ended when someone with a heavy fist beat on the door and shouted.

Shelby slid from his lap and sat on the couch, twisting her hands.

Jeb padded barefoot to the front door and swung it open with trepidation. "Better be a good reason to nearly break down the door this time of night."

Two men, wearing cowboy hats, stood on the porch.

Jeb flipped the outside light on to see if it was friend or foe. Frigid air rushed around him into the house. Once he recognized the visitors, he grinned. Davy and Waylon Jones, a pair of cousins he knew well from the rodeo circuit, stood there.

Davy clutched a box in his hands and wore a huge grin.

"We were heading home for the holidays when Davy remarked he didn't think we were all that far from where you live. I told you at Thanksgiving we might stop by one of these days, and this is the day." Waylon removed his hat.

"I tried to tell him it's getting late, and you might be in bed." Davy, always the straight man to Waylon's jokes, poked his head forward. He passed the mysterious container to his cousin.

"Since you're here, you might as well come in for a minute." Jeb took a step back to let the men enter. He shivered from the chill night temperature. "All the warm air is going outside."

"Nah, we cain't stay. We're trying to get home before this snow gets here." Waylon shifted the box from one hand to the other. "Met up with Rob, and he told us you ain't riding rodeo anymore."

"I'm not. Docs don't recommend it after the spinal fracture I had." Jeb stated the fact in a calm tone, although it still gave him the willies to think he could have ended up in a wheelchair. "I'll miss it, but I'm settling into life fine. It's good to be home." And in his heart, Jeb knew he spoke the truth. He'd always miss rodeo, but his restless heart had returned to where he began. Acceptance had taken months, but he had finally got there.

Davy slapped Jeb's shoulder. "I imagine so, with a pretty gal. She looks like a keeper."

Shelby stood beside Jeb and leaned against him, her head on his shoulder.

"She is. Shelby's my…" Jeb paused. He wasn't sure what to call her. Until he asked and she accepted his ring, he couldn't say *fiancée*. "My lady."

"Pleased to meet you, ma'am." Davy nodded toward Shelby.

"It's a pleasure." Waylon paused. "We need to get on down the road, but we brought you a Christmas present." He thrust the box toward Jeb, who accepted it. "It's a holiday food gift collection. It has hickory-smoked bacon, peppered bacon, smoked sausages, and ham. There are four different cheese spreads, fancy crackers, and two dozen petit fours. Enjoy it, man, and stay healthy. Come watch us ride bulls, if you get the chance."

"I will. Thank you! We'll enjoy this." Their gesture, and the effort to deliver the gift, pleased Jeb. Rodeo friends were buddies for life. "Be safe driving home, especially in the snow."

"Will do. We won't keep you." Waylon offered a hand to shake.

Davy followed suit.

Waylon leaned forward and cupped a hand around his mouth. "Invite us to the wedding. Looks like there's fixing to be one."

Jeb grinned but didn't confirm or deny. He watched them leave and told Shelby. "They're old friends of mine. Look at this gift box. The kids are gonna love it."

"They will. I was afraid someone at the door this late might be bad news, but everything turned out good." Shelby yawned. "I'm ready for bed, Jeb."

"Me, too, honey." He wrapped an arm around her waist as they walked upstairs. Jeb left her with a kiss at her bedroom door. Jeb didn't sleep well. He felt uneasy about the impending weather. He woke early and flipped on the television for the latest predictions. The winter storm watch had been upgraded to a more dire warning, which concerned him.

"A blizzard warning means winds of at least thirty-five miles per hour, and we're looking at forty or more," Skip Jacket, one of the local weathermen for years, emphasized to viewers. "Once snowfall begins, we expect drifting and blowing heavy snow. Visibility will drop to less than a quarter mile. According to radar, it's a slow-moving system and is expected to arrive later today. The Midland Empire might receive up to thirty-six inches of snow over the next few days. After the system moves out, temperatures will plunge to near zero with subarctic wind chills. It's going to be a cold Christmas, folks. Santa better bundle up tight."

Temps had already dropped from the day before, and now hovered in the upper twenties, which was ideal for snow. Jeb dressed in old jeans, a flannel shirt, and worn boots. He stepped outside beneath heavy grey skies and shivered as wind blew over the farmyard. His dad's truck wasn't in place, so Josiah had already left for work. Jeb's bad knee, from a long-ago rodeo injury, twinged. Most of the time, his knee was a better barometer than the weather service.

In the kitchen, Jeb made coffee and plugged in the waffle iron. As it heated, he followed the package directions from the boxed mix and stirred together a bowl of batter.

Shelby entered the kitchen with her brows knitted with a frown.

He paused in his task and opened his arms for a hug. "Good morning, honey. Are you feeling all right?"

Shelby rested her head against his chest. "I am, but I'm worried about this weather. What if we run out of food or the storm causes a power outage?"

"We won't. There's plenty to eat, but I'm going to town before long to get some stuff. If the electricity fails, we have several battery-operated lamps and at least four coal oil lamps. I need to get more fuel if we want to use them. We'll be warm, regardless." Jeb kissed her after she sank into a chair.

"Will the heater run when it gets so cold? Is it gas or electric?" Shelby rubbed her arms.

"Propane and the tank's full. Besides, there's an outdoor wood-fired furnace around at the back corner of the house. Pop had it put in years ago. Once we get a fire going, the heat from it uses the same duct work as the main furnace. Since the weather will be cold, we'll rely on the wood heat, not the propane furnace." Jeb rubbed her tight shoulders. "Don't worry, honey, we'll be fine."

"Is there enough wood?" Shelby sighed as he massaged.

"Dad said there are two cords around behind the shed. It'll be well-seasoned, which is good. I'll move it closer." Jeb's back ached at the thought, but the chore was necessary.

"Don't hurt yourself!" Shelby turned and caught his hands in hers.

"Sugar, I won't. I'll use the wheelbarrow, and once Dad gets home from work, he'll help. Do you want coffee or your lemon tea?" He rose and prepared the waffle iron. Jeb filled the kettle and put it on the stove.

"Tea sounds good, Jeb. I'm glad we'll be warm, no matter what." Shelby offered a small smile. "Do you need me to go to town with you?"

"No, honey." If the weather hit sooner than expected, he wanted Shelby safe at home. Recuperating from the flu, she shouldn't risk getting chilled. "I might see if Levi wants to go, though."

"What about Lexi?" Shelby smiled. "She'll want to

go if Levi does."

"I'd like her to stay with you. Dad's at work, and your mom's in town." Jeb planned to offer to bring a treat for Lexi, maybe her favorite cookies or cheese popcorn, to compensate. "I won't leave her out. I'll bring her something special."

Shelby steepled her chin on her hand. "I know. I just don't want her upset."

"Upset about what?" Levi hovered in the doorway. "What happened, Mama?"

The kid's as bad as Shelby to think worst-case scenario. Jeb put a tea bag to steep. "It's gonna snow, Levi, so I'm making a short run to town. I thought you'd like to go, but I want Lexi to stay here with your mom."

"Sure!" Levi grinned. "When do we leave?"

"After breakfast. Want sausage and a waffle?" Jeb poured batter onto the hot waffle iron. He heated the ready-to-eat sausage patties in the microwave.

"Oh, yeah! Want me to get Lexi?" Levi edged toward an exit.

"Yes, but don't tell her about town, not yet." Jeb would rather deliver the news himself to avoid ruffled feathers.

After dining on crisp waffles smeared with butter and drizzled with syrup, Jeb insisted Shelby find a cozy spot.

She curled up on her favorite corner of the couch. With the room rearranged to accommodate the Christmas tree, she had a better view of the TV.

"If there's something else you'd like to watch, use the TV in my bedroom." Jeb pointed upstairs.

"I'm fine here. We'll watch Christmas videos."

Shelby smiled. "Lexi's idea, not mine."

"We won't be gone any longer than necessary. Stay there, look pretty, and don't overtax yourself." Jeb delivered a quick kiss and headed out with Levi in tow.

Two days before Christmas with impending weather, the roads teemed with traffic, and the stores would be crowded.

Levi bounced from one spot to another in the truck.

Jeb insisted he sit still. "Fasten your seat belt!"

They picked up multiple bottles of lamp oil, a box of thick household candles, kitchen matches, and a couple of disposable lighters. If the power went out, the electric well pump wouldn't work, so Jeb bought three cases of bottled water and four gallons. Other customers also bought water, so he patted himself on the back for buying before supplies ran low. He also bought a huge pack of toilet tissue, a jar of old-fashioned popping corn, Lexi's cheese popcorn, two pounds of butter, and a couple of canned hams. He picked up several rolls of slice-and-bake cookie dough. Jeb didn't worry much about keeping food cold, because he could always set it on the back porch where it wouldn't spoil. "Can you think of anything else?" Jeb maneuvered the cart toward the checkout.

Levi scrunched up his face and frowned. "Will we really need all this stuff?"

"I hope not." Jeb shrugged. "It's better to have it, just in case. Anything I'm missing, for the snow or Christmas?"

"Mama usually makes cinnamon rolls for Christmas, but she might not feel like it this year. We could pick up a package while we're here." Levi eyed the bakery and smacked his lips. "Maybe one of those

Christmas cakes, too?"

A variety of decorated sheet cakes with poinsettias, wreaths, snowmen, and Santa figurines were on display. Jeb liked the idea. "Pick one out, Levi, while I grab some rolls."

The boy chose a half-sheet cake with white icing. Green frosting depicted multiple evergreen trees, dusted with snow, with an icing border of poinsettias, pine cones, and holly branches. The bakery goods completed their shopping.

With their purchases tucked into the truck, and the cake carefully placed so it wouldn't slide, Jeb had one more stop. He pulled into a florist's shop near the main highway.

"How come we're stopping here?" Levi's eyes widened. "This is a flower place."

"I'm getting a bouquet of roses for your mama." Jeb decided to present her with flowers, the ring, and other gifts. "Do you think she'll like them?"

"I bet she will. I don't know if she's ever had more than a single flower before, though." Levi took a deep breath and turned toward Jeb. "Why are you buying Mama roses?"

Jeb hesitated. He'd wondered if he should tell the children his plans, hoping they would approve, but he hadn't. Kids couldn't keep secrets very well, and he didn't want Levi to blurt his plan to Shelby. Choosing his words with care, Jeb ruffled a hand through his hair. "I love your mother, Levi."

"I kinda thought so." Levi's cheeks turned crimson. "Does that mean we get to keep living with you?"

Kid doesn't pull any punches. "I hope so. Can I trust you to keep a secret?"

Levi nodded with a vigorous motion. "I promise, cross my heart, and hope to die." The boy used his fingers to make the vow across his chest.

"I'm asking your mom to marry me." Jeb grinned as he spoke. He thought his heart might burst with joy. "I want to propose on Christmas Eve or Christmas Day."

"Awesome opossum!" Levi grinned. "I hope she says *yes*!"

Jeb chuckled until it became a belly laugh worthy of St. Nick himself. "Me, too, Levi."

With a dozen red roses trimmed by baby's breath and evergreen sprigs tucked into a silver gift box, they headed for home. Snow flurries began falling as "It's Beginning To Look A Lot Like Christmas" played over the radio.

"Jeb?" The kid tapped him on the arm. "Does anyone else know?"

"My dad, and now you but that's it." Jeb had kept it close. His friends last night, knowing him well, had guessed. "Let's keep it that way, okay?"

"Okay." Levi hummed along with the carol. "I won't even tell Lexi."

Jeb took the next exit and pulled into a convenience store. He dialed his dad's phone, and as soon as Josiah answered, Jeb spoke. "Dad, it's starting to snow. From the forecasts I heard earlier, it'll turn bad quickly. What time are you leaving work?"

Joe chuckled. "Already did, Son, so no worries. Need anything from town?"

"Levi and I just left the store, so we're good." Jeb wondered if he should call Delia. If she didn't leave soon, she might miss her chance to spend the holiday at the farmhouse. "Are you on the way home now?"

"I am as soon as I pick up Delia. I figured she might get nervous driving on slick roads. Soon as I have her in the truck, we'll head that way. How about I pick up fried chicken for an early supper?"

Behind his father's voice, Jeb caught the faint sound of holiday music. "That would be perfect. Thanks, Dad." Jeb's throat was clogged with tears. He'd forgotten, but as a little boy, a family tradition had been to get fried chicken, then eat dinner in the shadow of the Christmas tree, while Pop read from the Book of Luke. They had always done this on December twenty-third. "Be careful, you hear?"

"Same back at you." Josiah ended the call.

The light flurries dancing across the windshield soon turned to large flakes cascading from the sky. By the time Jeb reached their road, he had trouble seeing through the heavy snowfall. He took the driveway slowly and easily before parking near the back door. "Distract your mom, while I sneak the roses inside." Jeb tucked the flowers under his coat. He hid them in a cupboard in the laundry room, adjacent to the back porch.

Levi took several bags and headed for the house.

Jeb entered the kitchen and halted. The aroma of chocolate and rich peanut butter floated in the air. Shelby sat at the table with a smile bordering on a smirk as she finished icing a two-layer cake.

"Nice cake." Jeb eyed the confection with interest. "We bought a big one at the store, so we'll have plenty for dessert."

"It was Lexi's idea," Shelby explained. "We decided to do some cooking."

"What did y'all do besides bake?" Jeb made a quick mental inventory and laughed. Between what she baked and the things they bought, no shortage of sweets existed.

"We made fudge, too!" Lexi cried. "Jeb, there's two kinds, and I helped."

As he imagined the rich taste of chocolate, sweet on his tongue, Jeb's mouth watered. "Cool. Lexi and Levi, go watch for Joe's truck. He should be coming soon, and he's bringing a surprise."

Lexi's eyes widened. "Santa?"

Shelby hid her smile. She had taught Lexi that the generous old elf wasn't real, but at six, the little girl wanted to believe in the magic.

"Not quite. Wear your coat, though, it's getting colder." Jeb turned to his lady and shook his head. "Shelby, couldn't you take it easy while I was gone?"

"I wanted to make fudge. There's not enough days left to bake dozens of cookies like my mom used to, so I made candy. It wasn't hard and I went slowly." Shelby's smile widened. "I did it for you. Joe said your granny always made fudge for the holidays, and you loved it."

"She did, and I did. I appreciate it, but you're not doing another thing today. Maybe you didn't bake dozens, but I see some cookies." Jeb wagged a finger at her. "Dad's bringing home supper."

"Isn't it a bit early?" Shelby sipped from a cup of tea.

Jeb turned the oven on low. "We can keep it warm until time to eat. We've got a Christmas Eve Eve tradition to keep."

"Christmas Eve *Eve*?" Shelby questioned.

"The eve of Christmas Eve." He had produced the term when he was in first grade, and the family had adopted it. "December twenty-third."

"Jeb always called it that because he couldn't wait and jumped the gun on Christmas Eve." Joe entered with Delia and the kids behind him. "I picked up a stranger on the way home."

Delia entered, holding hands with her grandchildren. Beneath the knit scarf wrapped around her head, she beamed. "Hello!"

Shelby gasped, but her eyes lit up. "Mom!"

"Joe offered to give me a ride. My suitcase is in his truck. I don't know where I'll sleep, though." Delia unwrapped her scarf and hung her coat.

"Lexi has a double bed. You can bunk with her." Jeb took the huge bucket of chicken from his dad, spread it into a roaster, and slid it into the oven. He put the containers of mashed potatoes and gravy in the fridge to heat closer to supper, but the wedge fries went onto a cookie sheet beside the chicken. "Apparently, we've got fudge for dessert."

Jeb insisted Lexi return to the front room with the women, while he and his dad toted in their purchases. He stacked the cookies and cinnamon rolls on the counter near the fudge. The bakery cake sat beside the homemade one on the table.

Jeb tasted a small piece of the candy and moaned with delight. It melted in his mouth. Fudge would always be his favorite, but he liked peanut clusters, too. Shelby wouldn't know because he didn't list it on his hospital food favorites. He doubted Dad would remember, but he might.

Dark fell early with the heavy snowfall. Jeb peered

out through the windows but could see little. He ventured out onto the back porch and stood still. Snowflakes swirled around him, as thick as feathers from a pillow. He couldn't even see the barn. Shivering, he went back inside and found Delia heating the side dishes.

Joe filled up the wood furnace outside and brought two wheelbarrows filled with wood to the site. "Snow's really coming down." He rubbed his hands together as he warmed up with a cup of coffee at the kitchen table. "I'm glad we're all here, snug and warm."

"Me, too, Dad." Jeb never dreamed he would spend Christmas with his father again or could have guessed how much he enjoyed his company. "When's the last time you spent Christmas here at the farmhouse?" He expected his dad to name the one before Jeb's mother died.

After a lengthy silence, Joe stared down at the floor. "I came home the last year my daddy was alive. I didn't stay but a day, but I was here. You wasn't."

Jeb tried to remember. Pop died ten years earlier and Granny five. "That had to be the year I went to Texas for the holiday with Davy and Waylon. They're good friends of mine. That's who brought the gift basket by late last night."

"I didn't know anyone had." Joe ran his hands through his short, cropped hair. "It doesn't matter now, though. I'd hoped to spend the day with you. Since you weren't around, I got to drinking. Ma told me to leave, so I did. I came back for your grandpa's funeral, though."

"I remember." Jeb did. "You didn't make it to Granny's service."

Josiah put down his head and stared at the table. "I didn't hear in time, Son, or I'd been here. I've made mistakes, and failing to be here when they buried Ma was a big one. I did watch you ride a few times, sitting up in the stands proud to be the Hillbilly Hotshot's dad. I wasn't always just there to beg some bucks. No matter how messed up I got, I was always proud of you."

"I wish I'd known." If he had, it might have made a difference. Jeb's heart had been set against his father for years. "If wishes were horses, beggars would ride. We can't look back, Dad, so let's move forward. You're here now, and I'm glad."

Joe grasped his son's hand tightly. "So am I, Jebediah."

They feasted on fried chicken with all the trimmings and shared the rich fudge. Jeb insisted on paper plates, so nobody would have kitchen duty after the meal. Once finished, the leftovers were put away in short order.

"Let's hear the Christmas story from Luke. Daddy, would you read, like the old days?" Tears burned in Jeb's eyes as his childhood name for his father emerged, but he blinked them away.

Joe grasped Jeb's hand and held it tight. "I will." He released his grip. "I'm honored."

The kids sprawled on the floor beneath the Christmas tree, Shelby sat in the rocker, and her mom took a seat on the couch beside Joe.

Jeb sank into his recliner.

Joe picked up his Bible and turned on the nearest lamp. He dug in his shirt pocket for a pair of reading glasses.

Those had to be new. He didn't remember his dad

ever needing spectacles.

Joe opened the Good Book to the second Chapter of Luke. He cleared his throat and began. "'And it came to pass in those days…'"

Key phrases stood out as his father read with a steady and true voice. If Jeb closed his eyes, he could be six or ten years old, sitting in this same room.

"'I bring you good tidings of great joy…on earth, peace, good will toward men.'"

Great joy. Jeb had joy in his heart, brimming full, and running over. His Savior was part of it, but so was the reunion with his father, along with his love for Shelby. After Joe read, no one wanted to watch television.

Instead, Jeb sat at the piano and played carols. He didn't sing about reindeer or toys, but about Jesus, Bethlehem, the stable, and the star. On the majority of tunes, they all sang, but sometimes, Jeb was solo. They munched on popcorn made on top of the stove in a skillet, nibbled more fudge, and devoured cookies. Jeb would have brought out the cheese spreads and crackers from the gift box.

Shelby shook her head. "Save those for New Year's Eve."

The pastor phoned, apologized for the late hour, and informed them the Christmas Eve service had been canceled due to the weather. "I know it wasn't scheduled until tomorrow night, but I wanted to let folks know."

"It's for the best." Jeb hung up and spread the word. "We wouldn't be able to get there, anyway."

"What will we do instead?" Levi frowned with a

sigh.

"I brought the DVD of *The Christmas Carol*." Delia held it up. "I always liked this version best. We can drink hot chocolate, eat cookies, and watch it until bedtime on Christmas Eve."

Jeb gave the idea a thumbs-up. It could be a new tradition in the farmhouse. After the kids were in bed, he could stack their gifts under the tree. Although neither child professed a belief in Santa, thanks to Shelby's previous disdain for Christmas, Jeb wanted to surprise them. From hints Lexi dropped, he thought she ached to think Santa Claus might be real. Jeb loved her innocent hope. Once the gifts were placed beneath the tree, Jeb might pop the question, or he could wait until Christmas Day.

It depended on whether or not Jeb wanted an audience, but everything would hinge on the proposal. The mood and moment had to be right, and he would do his best to make the magic happen. Snowbound during a blizzard, with or without electricity, he planned to ask. His Bible said there was a time for every season, and as far as Jeb could determine, the time had come.

The outcome rested on love and his heart. And Shelby. If she declined his proposal, he would be devastated. *I have to hang on, wait, and believe.*

Jeb couldn't handle any other outcome. He wouldn't turn to alcohol like Joe had, but he would go off the deep end, one way or another.

Chapter Eighteen

The snow didn't stop but continued through Christmas Eve. By the time it slacked off, two to three feet blanketed the ground with higher drifts as tall as six feet. Bitter cold descended in the snow's wake, but the house remained warm so Shelby was satisfied. Jeb's efforts to make Christmas delightful were working so far. The house was more than large enough for all to be comfortable.

Shelby hadn't enjoyed the holidays as much since the year her dad died in December. His death overshadowed Christmas. She had also lost her grandmother in December, during her kindergarten year. At five, she didn't remember much about the holiday that year, but she recalled poinsettias had flanked the casket. Most people had sent the seasonal favorite in traditional reds, pinks, and whites. The same happened after her dad died. She had hated the flower ever since. The so-called Christmas spirit had long been absent in her heart. Later, her lack of money diminished any good feelings she had for the holiday. Shelby didn't look for the joy but focused on the crowds, lack of money, and her losses—until now.

This year, Christmas enchanted her. Jeb's enthusiasm proved contagious. Although she hadn't put up a tree in three years, Shelly loved the fir tree fragrance wafting a crisp aroma through the house. She admired the beauty of the evergreen decked out in baubles and balls and sparkling with light. She could sit and gaze at it with wonder for hours.

She had feared her illness might ruin the holidays, but it hadn't. Shelby got caught up in the magic and wished she could do more to prepare for the big day. Still weak from the flu, she knew she wasn't up to baking dozens of cookies, but she had made the effort to stir up fudge, for Jeb.

When Josiah read from Luke in his family tradition, Shelby almost wept. As Jeb played the piano and led them singing carols, she did cry. She believed in her Savior with all her heart, but for the first time, Shelby realized she'd shortchanged Him with her bad attitude about Christmas. The seasonal joy long absent from her heart surged back in a powerful rush.

She woke late on Christmas Eve morning and headed downstairs.

Delia had the dinner well in hand and had prepared the ham to bake on Christmas. She greeted Shelby with a smile. "Breakfast is simple today: hot or cold cereal. Jeb made coffee, but if you'd rather have tea, I'll fix you a cup."

Delia wore an apron Shelby had never seen embroidered with holly leaves. "Coffee's fine. Where's Jeb?" Shelby glanced around the kitchen, but he wasn't present.

"He went with Joe to stoke the furnace." Delia placed a cup on the table. "Joe called in at work and told them he can't make it with the snow. Jeb thought to save the propane we should heat with the wood-burning furnace. I like it. It's a dry heat, and I love the smell of wood smoke."

So did Shelby. "And the kids?"

"Jeb let them go outside. They won't stay long, but they begged." Delia chuckled. "I watched them floundering in the snow from the window."

The old Shelby would have complained and called them inside. Christmas Shelby smiled. In the rare moment alone with her mother, she pulled a question from her heart. "Mom, do you think I'm on the right track?"

Delia glanced toward her daughter and frowned. "In what way?"

"Everything. My job, home, and family." Shelby sighed.

Delia put her hands on her hips. "You're a nurse. It's a great career. You have two wonderful kids, and you've met a fine man."

"Jeb really is—I've never known anyone like him." Her mom's compliment brought Shelby joy. "I just don't know where we're going from here."

"Who does?" Delia shrugged. "I don't. Just take one day at a time."

Shelby accepted her mom's words and nodded. "What's up today? I know we'll watch your movie tonight." Charles Dicken's famous story had always been Delia's favorite. Every year while Shelby was growing up, they watched one of the versions of the classic tale. Delia had read it to Shelby, too, long ago. Delia preferred Patrick Stewart as Scrooge, so his would be the version they watched.

"I'm baking cookies." Delia placed a bowl, spoon, cereal, and milk before her daughter.

Shelby fixed her gaze on the bakery cookies Jeb brought home and raised an eyebrow.

"I know, I know. We have store-bought cookies, and you baked some yesterday." Delia giggled. "There are also slice-and-bake cookie rolls in the fridge plus ready-to-bake sugar cookies. I might as well use them." Delia plucked a bakery cookie from a package and sat with a fresh cup of coffee. "I don't imagine they'll go to waste."

Levi burst into the kitchen followed by his sister and the two men. Snow dropped from their feet and legs onto the kitchen floor, and a sharp chill accompanied them.

Jeb paused to kiss the back of Shelby's neck with cold lips.

"You're freezing." Shelby shivered, but she smiled. If he hadn't kissed her, she would have been disappointed. "Go change into something warm and dry, all of you."

"Yes, Mama." Lexi raced through the house with Levi. Their footsteps echoed as they climbed the stairs.

"I'm good." Jeb plopped into a chair across from Shelby. "I'll warm up quickly."

"I don't want you to get sick, so go." She aimed a playful swat at him. Her attention shifted to watch her mother with Jeb's dad.

Delia cupped Joe's cheeks between her hands. "Your face is like ice, Josiah. Go change. I'll give you a cookie straight out of the oven when you come back."

"I'll do it, but I'll need more than one." Joe grinned. "I'll negotiate for a couple."

Shelby stared after him, then gazed at Delia, who blushed. *I've been too sick and preoccupied to notice, but I think maybe my mom is into Jeb's dad."*

"I'll be back for my cookies." Jeb winked.

Did she mind? A relationship between Joe and Delia might be an unexpected twist of fate, but if their parents became a couple, Shelby wouldn't object.

By late afternoon, the cookies were baked. Delia whipped up two loaves of pumpkin bread, an old favorite. The ham rested in a large roaster, ready for the oven tomorrow. Sweet potatoes and scalloped potatoes were also prepped. Jeb had brought home hot rolls for Christmas dinner. Other menu items would include frozen peas and homemade corn pudding.

"I'll make the ham glaze tomorrow morning." Delia wiped her hands on a kitchen towel. "I'll be finished in here after supper."

"Keep it simple, Mom." Shelby anticipated another pleasant evening.

"I'm making little smoked sausages and fried potatoes. Hearty but not too heavy." Delia sliced potatoes as she spoke.

"Sounds good." Jeb offered Shelby a hand. "Come to the front room. We're in the way in here." He paused in the dining room, pulled her into a tight hug, and kissed her with deep tenderness. "I've been waiting all day for that."

Shelby rested her arms against his shoulders. "You seem edgy and high-strung. Are you okay?"

"I've never been better, sugar. I'm happy about the holiday, and all of us being here together." His lips tickled hers in a second kiss. "How's your Christmas so far?"

"I like it, Jeb, more than I dreamed I ever would. I love you for showing me what it could be like." She stroked his cheek.

He'd moved the rocking chair beside his recliner.

She eased into the rocker. "I'm glad I arranged to be off from work until January. I would have hated venturing out in the snow."

"Would you have had to go?" Jeb frowned. "Your car couldn't get around in this mess, and neither could my truck."

"They would have expected it." Shelby shrugged. "People at home still need their treatment or meds. I've done home health for three years and never had the company cancel because of weather."

"That doesn't sound right. What about the holidays?" Jeb leaned closer to bridge the slight gap between the chairs and draped an arm across her shoulders.

Shelby sighed. "I always had to visit patients. I was here on Thanksgiving, wasn't I?"

"That's different." His arm around her tightened as he shifted closer. "We're…"

She waited for him to define their relationship, but he didn't, which bothered her. She had noticed the way Jeb groped for a word when his friends asked about her. He'd come up with *my lady*. It might mean more than *girlfriend*, but Shelby couldn't be sure what Jeb intended. She had no idea where she stood with him or what would happen in the future. *I'd like to stay here and be Jeb's wife but if he's not willing, then I'd better start looking for another house or an apartment soon. If nothing changes, I'll do it right after Christmas.*

Shelby expected to return to her job after New Year's Day. The kids would go back to school soon after. She had to decide if she wanted them to stay at their current school, in St. Joe, or enroll them at Savannah. If she kept them in town, she'd have to use her mom's address, since no house stood at the former location. Shelby didn't know if Jeb expected her to stay indefinitely or what. If the roof hadn't collapsed, she would have moved home once the job ended. *I don't want to take advantage of Jeb, and I can't. I won't. Maybe I can find a place to rent in Savannah.*

If Jeb asked, then she would stay. Shelby loved the big farmhouse and his family history here. If she remained, however, what would be her role? She didn't know. A platonic love affair wasn't her desire, but she had morals. Shelby wouldn't be in Jeb's bed, unless she had a wedding ring on her finger.

Since his life was also in transition, she hated to ask. After years making his living in rodeo, one severe injury ended his career. Jeb had talked about running cattle on the place, but so far, he hadn't done anything to get started. To be fair, he'd been recovering and still was. Then Shelby got sick. *I love him and he loves me. It's wonderful, but it's not enough. I have to build a life for my kids, solo or with Jeb.*

Shelby resolved to ask him after the holidays what he wanted. Before she went back to work, or the kids returned to school, she had to know where they stood. The uncertainty made her stomach ache, so she said a silent prayer. *Lord, let me find out his heart and his plans. I trust You to lead me on the right paths but right now, I don't know where that might be.* She picked back up the thread of conversation. "We're what? Jeb, I don't know what we are."

"We're Jeb and Shelby." He wrapped his fingers around her hand. "I love you, sugar."

"I love you, too." If she didn't find answers today, she would enjoy Christmas and deal with reality later.

"Tell me what we're doing after supper." Jeb broke the silence.

"We'll watch the Scrooge video my mom brought, make popcorn again, and go to bed." Shelby kissed his fingers.

"After we get the gifts under the tree." Jeb offered a reminder.

"Right." Shelby had forgotten because she usually had no more than two or three gifts per child. "We'll be the last ones to sleep."

"And the first ones up in the morning." Jeb adjusted his shirt collar and undid the top two buttons.

"We will?" Shelby yawned. She became tired so easily.

"Don't you want to watch Levi and Lexi run down the stairs, shouting with excitement because they see presents under the tree?"

"I do." She hadn't thought about it until now. *Maybe I cheated them out of the whole Santa and Christmas thing until now.* A touch of guilt saddened her.

"Besides, I need my coffee before we open presents. I might even sneak a cinnamon roll." Jeb licked his lips. "Maybe a cookie. So, we have to be the first ones up and downstairs."

The family gathered around the dining room table for supper. Afterward, they headed into the living room to watch the holiday classic.

Shelby had seen it numerous times and so had her children. Watching the tale now, Shelby realized she had much in common with the fictional Ebenezer. He didn't keep Christmas and didn't think anyone else should, either. Scrooge was a mean-spirited miser, which Shelby didn't think she had ever been. She was known to pinch pennies, however, primarily because she never had enough money.

Like Scrooge, she had failed to see the glorious side of the holiday—the love, laughter, and joy. The Cratchit family was portrayed as poorer than Shelby with a sickly but beloved child. They still made merry. Three Ghosts of Christmas, past, present, and future, were needed to turn Scrooge's heart. *I'm glad I didn't need the same experience to find my way.*

When Tiny Tim, crippled and able to walk only with a crutch, cried, "God bless us everyone," Shelby echoed the sentiment in her heart. She'd forgotten parts of the film might seem frightening to kids, especially the future ghost in a long black robe with no visible features.

Lexi shifted from her place on the floor into Shelby's lap and hid her face.

She stroked the child's hair in an absent-minded fashion. "He knew how to keep Christmas well," Shelby repeated the line as the movie ended. "So do you, Jeb."

Her man grinned. "I try."

Josiah donned his coat and knit hat to stoke the furnace one last time.

Delia and the children marched upstairs to bed.

After Joe returned, Shelby and Jeb brought out the gifts so they could retire, too. Jeb filled the stockings with an orange, assorted candy, and two holiday pencils each. Together, they arranged the packages under the tree. The presents spilled out across the floor.

Jeb rolled the bikes in from the back porch. "Do you think they'll know who gets which?"

"One's pink and one's blue. I think they can figure it out." Shelby sighed. "Jeb, you bought way too much stuff."

"Nah. I might have eaten more fudge and cookies than I should have, but you can't ever buy too many presents." He chuckled and patted his belly. "I could stand in for Santa. I'd love it."

"You're too skinny." Shelby laughed. "Speaking of Santa Claus, do you want the milk and cookies the kids set out?" Although her kids didn't believe, Delia had suggested Levi and Lexi follow the custom for fun.

"No, thanks. I'm good for tonight. I already ate way too many sweets. If I have more, I'll get a stomachache. Let's listen to Christmas tunes, then turn in for the night."

Shelby dimmed all the lights except for the tree and tuned in carols on the radio.

Jeb sat on the couch beside her, and they nestled together.

She dozed but woke around midnight. "Jeb, we need to go to bed!"

He roused and shook his head. "Yeah, we'd better. Morning'll come early. Do you want me to wake you, or just let you get downstairs on your own?"

"I'll come downstairs early. If the kids wake up first, though, all bets are off. They will beat me down here. I can't control that, I'm afraid but it won't matter, as long as I get to catch a glimpse of their excited faces." As long as she didn't miss the moment her children saw their gifts, it would be fine.

"It matters to me." Jeb's smile vanished, replaced by a frown. "Sugar, I want it to be the two of us first thing in the morning. It's important to me."

He's holding back or keeping a secret. "Why?" Her uncertainty returned. Surely, he wouldn't tell her to move on Christmas Day. If he did, Shelby had no place to go. She would have to hustle to find a place in town. Most of the insurance money from the house had gone to pay old bills. She hoped to buy a car with what remained, but the funds wouldn't stretch far enough for a deposit and rent payment on a house or apartment.

Jeb kissed her, his mouth slow and sweet on her lips. "You'll find out. Don't look sad. It's nothing bad, Shelby. I just want to ask you something."

Her heart plummeted. "Just ask, or tell me now, Jeb." If she had to wait, she probably wouldn't sleep.

" 'Joy cometh in the morning.' " He quoted from Psalms. "Trust me, sugar."

The plaintive note in his voice touched her. Shelby nodded. "All right, Jeb."

"Good night and Merry Christmas. It's after midnight. Should I turn off the tree?"

If the kids came downstairs and saw the packages, they would flip. They might rouse the household, so they could dive in and open their gifts. "Yes. If Levi and Lexi see all this, they won't go back to bed."

Jeb knelt and unplugged the lights. He offered her his hand to mount the stairs. They walked to the top and parted at her bedroom door.

"Good night, Jeb." Shelby managed to keep a quaver out of her voice.

" 'Night, honey. Don't fret. Get a good night's sleep. Tomorrow's gonna be a big day."

She watched him open his bedroom door, walk into the room, and close it. For the first time since she'd come to the farmhouse, Shelby cried herself to sleep.

Before Jeb, before this job, it had been a common occurrence. With bills mounting faster than she could pay them, lonely in her solitary life, and always worried about her children, she often wept before she slept. Once the tears were shed, a rush of love for Jeb filled her heart. Fatigue and recovery brought wild thoughts. Scrooge's movie must have upset her emotional balance. Shelby reached deep inside to recapture the joy of Christmas she'd found this year. She caught a flicker of it before she said her prayers. By the time she finished, the time was after two.

A still, small voice spoke to her soul. *Trust Jebediah. Give him your heart. He won't break it.* Shelby already had. If Jeb disappointed her, she would never believe in anything ever again. Christmas would lose its sparkle, and she would live out her days, sad, lonely, and solitary.

Chapter Nineteen

Jeb lay awake. He wished he'd proposed to Shelby on Christmas Eve and hadn't waited. Although he didn't understand why, Jeb suspected he had upset her. Hopefully, whatever it was would be forgotten and forgiven when he asked the question. The moment he knelt to propose had to be perfect, so he planned each step.

Once downstairs, he would light the tree, make coffee, and set the scene. Jeb would have the roses and the ring in hand. Shelby would join him, and Jeb would drop to his knees. By then, she should have a fair idea of what he intended. He'd memorized the words he wanted to say, and he went over them again, more than once.

Long before the first light of dawn crept into the sky, Jeb slipped down the hall to the bathroom. After a long, hot shower, he shaved. Jeb slapped on his favorite musky cologne. He combed his hair, then padded back to his room to don Western-cut slacks. Jeb chose his favorite black long-sleeved, snap-button shirt, decorated with rich green embroidery. The same details accented his cuffs. He dropped the cross Shelby bought him around his neck, then slid his stocking feet into his best boots.

Jeb studied his reflection in the mirror. He would have worn the outfit to church, if it hadn't been canceled. He tucked the ring box into his pocket and descended to the front room with a soft tread. The last thing he wanted was to wake the kids.

He retrieved the roses from the enclosed back porch. The flowers had remained fresh, and he savored their fragrance. Jeb made coffee and brought his mug into the living room. He carried the roses in his free hand.

Once the tree sparkled with light, Jeb shifted the furniture to center the rocking chair to face the tree. He settled down in the recliner to wait. Although tired, he didn't doze. Jeb didn't expect Shelby to turn him down, but his nerves were on edge. Jeb worried the kids might rise before Shelby and ruin his plan. If so, he would adjust, but Jeb wanted to propose to Shelby without distraction or an audience.

At the stroke of six, Shelby came downstairs. Like him, she had dressed up for the day. She wore a dark-red velour dress with long sleeves, a V-neckline, and a full skirt descending past her knees. Jeb grinned. He had expected her in nightgown and robe, but he liked her outfit. He crossed the room to meet her at the foot of the steps and extended his hand. "Good morning and merry Christmas, Shelby. You look beautiful."

"Good morning. You're very handsome this morning, Jeb. I love the shirt." Her cheeks flushed as a small smile flirted with her lips.

"It's my favorite." Jeb swept her close for a long, delicious kiss. "Come sit."

"Jeb, I don't understand. What's all this?" Her eyes swept over the room, the tree, and the new position for the rocker.

"It's Christmas, honey. I have a question to ask."

Jeb inhaled her pleasant floral perfume. "That's a pretty dress."

"I've had it forever." Shelby shrugged. "I thought it might be festive."

He nodded. His throat became dry since the moment had arrived to propose. "Sit and close your eyes, honey, just for a moment."

Shelby hitched her long skirt into place as she eased into the rocking chair. She lowered her lashes and waited.

Jeb brought out the roses. He took the ring box from his pocket, then knelt.

"Can I open my eyes yet?" Shelby smoothed her skirt.

"Yes, sugar." Jeb opened the box, removed the ring, and held it high between the fingers of his left hand.

The only illumination in the room came from the lighted tree. Shelby blinked and gazed at him. "Jeb…"

"Hush, Shelby." If he didn't speak the words he had committed to memory, he'd lose them. "I love you more than I ever thought I could love a woman. When the bronc threw me last summer, I knew my rodeo career might be over. I figured it was a disaster, and the worst thing that could have happened. Without the injury, I might have had five good years left busting broncs, so I felt pretty sorry for myself. I'd even say I thought I'd been cursed. I came home, because I had no place else to go, to lick my wounds like an old hound."

Jeb paused to draw a deep breath and made a conscious effort to slow down, so he wouldn't babble. "Instead of cursing me, the Lord blessed me. If I hadn't got hurt, I wouldn't have met you, and I'd never known how much I could love. I thought you were the prettiest thing, even the first night they carried me in from the ambulance. I decided you were the kindest when you returned, on your own, because I needed you. You're the best nurse I've had, and trust me, I've had quite a few over the years, since I got hurt more times than I can count. You cooked for me like I was family, and your kids turned out to be a delight."

"Jeb..." Her voice shook, and her brown eyes met his. "Jeb, what are you saying?"

"Let me finish." He touched one finger to her lips. "I took the time to figure out what I wanted to say, and I'd like to speak my piece. I knew we could be friends, but it wasn't long until I wanted more. I loved you before that day at Corby Pond, but when you told me you cared. I had to share what was in my heart. I loved you then, and I love you now."

Jeb cleared his throat. "I believe you'll do me good, not evil, all the days of my life. I want to love, cherish, and take care of you forever. I'd like your kids to become mine. Their father's dead, and I'd like to be their daddy. It only works, though, if you become my wife. Shelby, will you marry me?"

She gasped, and her hands flew to her cheeks. "Is this for real? Do you mean it, Jeb?"

"Of course, I do. It's not a joke, sugar. Will you?" If he stayed on his knees much longer, he might topple like a tree in a windstorm. "I bought this ring in case you said *yes*."

Shelby remained silent, but her gaze stayed steady as she looked him in the eye.

Jeb's chest tightened, and he had trouble drawing breath. He figured he might be on the verge of a panic attack.

"Yes. I will. I love you, Jeb, and I want to be your wife." Tears slid down her cheeks, but Shelby smiled. "Oh, Jeb. Jeb."

"Don't wear my name out, sugar. Let me see your hand." Relief flooded him as he took a deep, long breath. Jeb slid the ring onto her left hand. The circle fit and sparkled in the reflected glow of the Christmas tree.

Shelby lifted her hand and gazed at the diamonds. "It's the loveliest ring I've ever seen."

Jeb laid his head in her lap, weak with relief because she hadn't turned him down. He savored the feeling as Shelby mussed his hair with her fingers. "I got scared you might tell me *no*." He mumbled against her skirt. "I'm glad you didn't."

Her fingers raked through his hair. "Jeb, don't be mad, but I need to tell you something. I worried yesterday maybe you didn't want us together for the long haul. I never doubted you love me, but…"

Jeb raised his head. "That's why you acted weird last night?"

She nodded. "I know better now."

"I'd hope to shout." He rose from the floor and placed the roses in her outstretched arms. "I almost forgot these."

Shelby lifted one and inhaled the sweet fragrance. "No one ever bought me roses before. Will you tell the kids or should I?"

"Levi already knows." Jeb chuckled. "I got the flowers in town the other day, and he wanted to know why. I told him I love you and planned to ask you to be my wife. He seemed happy."

"What did he say?" Shelby stood, cradling the

roses like a beauty pageant queen.

"Awesome opossum." Jeb laughed, remembering. "We're getting married!"

"First, let's keep Christmas." Shelby laid the roses beside her chair and wrapped her arms around him. "You made me believe in you and Christmas. It'll always be merry now because I'll never forget this. Kiss me, please."

Jeb captured her mouth with his, as he slid the posies out of the way. His lips drank from hers, nourished and enriched by the connection. " 'Kiss me with the kisses of your mouth.' " He referenced the Song of Solomon. "Let's get some caffeine before anyone else gets up."

After tucking the roses into an old vase of his grandmother's, Jeb and Shelby drank coffee together in the kitchen.

Joe stumbled into the kitchen, wearing faded jeans and a flannel shirt.

"Merry Christmas, Dad." Jeb rose to pour a third cup for his father.

"Back at you. I'm looking shabby compared to your finery." Joe eyed them with a grin. "Am I missing something?"

"Just this, Dad." Shelby thrust her left hand forward to show off the ring.

Jeb loved the way she called Joe *Dad*.

"Oh, my. Congratulations. I knew Jeb planned to ask, but I'm delighted it's official." Joe shook Jeb's hand, then hugged him. "This is wonderful news!"

Upstairs, a burst of noise indicated the children were awake. Jeb grabbed Shelby's hand. "Let's head back to the front room. I don't want to miss their faces when they come downstairs and see the tree with all the presents."

Shelby sat in the rocking chair.

Jeb stood beside her. He flicked on a lamp, so they wouldn't miss a single expression. One moment the kids were in the upstairs hallway and then they galloped down the steps.

Lexi giggled as she descended.

"Bikes! I see two bikes. Totally fantastic!" Levi whooped and rushed to the blue model.

Delia followed at a sedate pace and joined Joe on the couch. Both beamed.

"I see I should have dressed for the occasion, whatever it is." Delia tittered.

"We're celebrating." Shelby lifted her left hand, and the light caught the ring. The center diamond twinkled like a winter star.

Delia gasped, then grinned. "Oh, Shelby!"

Levi offered a thumbs-up. "Way to go, Jeb!"

"Mommy got a pretty ring!" Lexi clapped her hands together.

"It means they're getting married. We get to live here for real and forever." Levi ruffled his sister's hair.

Jeb stepped forward, then knelt before the children. "It means more than that. Come here."

The kids moved closer.

Jeb put one hand on Lexi and the other on Levi. "Your mama's agreed to become my wife, but that's not all. I want a family." Jeb paused and swallowed hard. He didn't want to sob and give the wrong impression. He wasn't sad. His emotions overwhelmed him, but the children might not understand. "Levi, Lexi, will you take me as your daddy? I'd like to raise you and give you my last name, Hill. Will you be my kids, not just your mom's? Can we be a family?"

Levi didn't crack a smile. He met Jeb's gaze and returned it. After consideration, he nodded. "Yes, Jeb. I'd like you to be my dad. I want us to be a forever family."

Lexi didn't hesitate. She leaped toward Jeb and almost knocked him over as she hugged him. "Me, too, Jeb. I love you. Can we call you daddy?"

Tears streamed down Jeb's face above his smile. "You bet."

Shelby joined him on the floor. Together, she and Jeb folded the kids into a four-way hug.

Jeb laughed as tears ran down his cheeks. "This is the happiest day of my life. I love all of you so much." His knees ached, and he wasn't sure how much longer he could hold the position.

Shelby slipped one arm around his waist as the kids pulled free.

Jeb shifted to a cross-legged position and handed Levi a gift. "Let's open presents!"

During a wild half-hour, the gifts were unwrapped, and paper strewn in every direction. Each time Levi or Lexi opened something new, they exclaimed with delight. The race car model proved to be a hit, but so did the stuffed dinosaur, the miniature garage set, and everything else.

Lexi insisted on dashing upstairs to fetch her favorite doll, so she could push Janie in the new toy buggy. With Joe's help, she unpacked her play dishes and hugged the plush dog until Jeb feared the seams might burst.

Joe's face lit when he unwrapped his new shirts,

jeans, and boots. "I'll be in style wearing these. I can't remember last time I got gifts at Christmas. Thanks, son."

"No problem." Jeb grinned. "I'm so glad you're with us, Dad."

Delia put on the warm robe and spritzed a little perfume on her wrists.

Shelby fussed when Jeb handed her six packages. In addition to the pajamas that matched the kids and his, he'd given her an e-reader, fancy, scented soaps, a hand-knitted shawl, and a new Bible, because hers had a broken spine and was missing multiple pages.

Jeb had bought books for the kids, too, ones they could read on their own and others for the family to read aloud. After breakfast with cinnamon rolls and bacon from the holiday gift package his friends brought, Jeb picked up discarded wrapping paper. His heart sang with joy, and he couldn't keep from crooning his favorite carols as he worked. The house smelled wonderful with delicious aromas from the baking ham. Jeb joined Shelby in the kitchen. For now, he moved the new bikes to the back porch. He was as disappointed as the kids since they couldn't take them out because of the snow.

"Man, I wish I could ride my bike today." Levi gazed out the window with a sigh. He snitched a cookie.

Shelby swatted his hand, laughing "Save your appetite for dinner. You've never ridden a bicycle. You'll have to learn, but we'll wait until the snow melts."

"Daddy said he'll teach me." Levi grinned.

Jeb's joy overflowed, and his eyes leaked to hear

Levi use the title. He vowed he would be the best father possible to both kids. "I will, soon as possible."

At dinner, they joined hands as Jeb asked the blessing. "Dear Lord, on this blessed Christmas day, when we remember Your birth, thank you for this feast spread before us, bless the hands which prepared it, and thank You for each person around the table. I came home in defeat, but thanks to Your love and mercy, I am a happy man, with joy unspeakable. Thank You for my bride-to-be Shelby, for my children, and for our parents. Bless and keep our family. Amen."

Jeb had never tasted more delicious ham, but the side dishes could have been made from sawdust for all he noticed. His gaze was on Shelby, and he couldn't wait to plan a wedding. Whether she wanted large, and lavish, or simple, and sweet, Jeb would make sure she had the ceremony of her dreams.

"Shelby, have you thought of a date for the wedding?" Delia passed the sweet potatoes for another round. "I think a spring wedding would be lovely. Your flowers could be lilacs, daffodils, peonies, and tulips. Summer would be wonderful, too. The kids will be out of school, and your flowers might be lilies, or daisies, or even roses. Maybe you could get married outside. And, for fall, there're chrysanthemums, asters, or snapdragons."

Shelby exchanged a smile with Jeb. "Mom…"

Delia steepled her chin on her right hand. "I doubt you'd want to wait almost a year, but I always thought a Christmas wedding with evergreens and poinsettias would be beautiful."

"Mom, I'm not waiting to marry Jeb." Shelby reached for Jeb's hand and held it. "I want our wedding right away."

Everyone glanced at Jeb.

He shrugged. They hadn't had time to consider a date, and he would be happy with any date Shelby chose.

Delia plucked a hot roll from the basket and buttered it. "Spring, then. The weather might still be cold in March, but April…"

"Mom." Shelby turned in that direction. "I'd like to get married on New Year's Day, at Faith Church, in a simple candlelight ceremony. Jeb, what do you think?"

He grinned while mouths dropped open around the table. "Fine with me, honey, the sooner the better."

Levi and Lexi clapped.

Joe whistled.

"That's in a week!" Delia twisted a napkin between her fingers. "I don't know if we can put together a wedding so quickly."

"We can." Jeb had no doubts. He'd looked up the requirements for Missouri marriages, and no waiting period was necessary. "All we need is a license. Then we have to check with the pastor, get flowers, candles, and a cake."

"And a dress." Shelby grasped his hand. "I need a wedding dress."

"We'll get one, sugar." Jeb gazed into her eyes. In this moment, no one else existed for him.

"I have a dress in mind." Delia's lips lifted in a smile.

Shelby shifted her gaze to her mother. "Tell me! I have an idea I know the one you're talking about."

Jeb hoped the gown wasn't one his bride-to-be had worn at her first wedding. He wasn't superstitious, but the idea had bad vibes.

"I don't know if it would fit, Shelby, but you can try it on. It really should be cleaned." Delia clasped her hands together.

"What dress is it?" Jeb laid down his fork. Curiosity overcame his appetite.

"Mom's great-grandmother's wedding dress from 1912. It's very pretty, but not too fancy. I think it's perfect." Shelby's eyes sparkled.

"What about a veil?" Delia used her hands to mime placing one on her daughter's hair. "The original crumbled years ago."

"I want to wear flowers in my hair, and nothing more." Shelby patted her head.

"As soon as the snow melts, we'll go to the courthouse, get a license, and figure out what else we need," Jeb announced his plan. If Shelby wore the vintage gown, then maybe Jeb wouldn't need to rent a tuxedo. One of his Western-cut suits might do.

"Perfect." Shelby planted a kiss on his cheek. "It will all come together."

Long after everyone else had retired for the night, Jeb held Shelby on his lap in his recliner. They both wore the buffalo plaid pajamas he'd purchased. He snuggled her, dropping little kisses on her face and neck at will. He was happier than he'd ever been.

The Christmas tree shimmered, and the lights sparkled as he realized he had truly come home. After years of traveling the rodeo circuit, wintering on the farm, and leaving each spring, Jeb would stay where he belonged. He sang the refrain from the old song "Home For The Holidays" for Shelby.

"We're both home."

Her words whispered softly against his cheek.

"Our hearts are home."

"Amen to that." His injury-forced homecoming had transitioned into something wonderful. Jeb had anticipated the holidays with gladness, but now, he envisioned a life waiting to be lived, a wife to be loved, and a family to raise. If the Lord was willing, Jeb wanted more kids to fill the old house with laughter and life.

The Hillbilly Hotshot had come home, in many ways, for the holidays and forever. In one week, a new chapter in their lives would begin, and Jeb praised God with a whole heart in silent joy.

" 'My beloved is mine, and I am his,' " Shelby quoted from the Songs of Solomon.

"Always, honey." Jeb sealed his promise with a kiss.

Chapter Twenty

Dusk came early on New Year's Eve. At the farmhouse, the family celebrated the New Year with roast pork, dressing, and several side dishes tonight, because the wedding would take center stage on January first. No one stayed up until midnight, and although the mood throughout the farmhouse was happy without a party. The celebration would follow the wedding.

In keeping with tradition, Shelby spent her wedding day with her mom in town.

After the snow melted, Delia had moved back home.

Lexi joined Shelby at Delia's, but Levi remained with Jeb and Joe.

Early in the afternoon, Delia and Shelby headed to the church. With Lexi's help, they decorated the sanctuary before Shelby prepared for the ceremony.

Delia prepared the punch, but Joe promised to deliver the cake to the church hall.

Shelby donned her great-great-grandmother's vintage dress with care, in one of the Sunday School classrooms. She brushed her hair until it shone, then pulled it into an updo, and added a rose behind her left ear.

"Are you nervous?" Delia tugged the gown into place with gentle fingers.

"Not one bit." Shelby couldn't wait to walk down the aisle and become Jeb's wife.

"You're beautiful, Shelby Jo." Delia stepped back and offered a smile to her daughter.

"You look pretty, too." Her mother wore a dressy, soft gray mother-of-the-bride dress. The tea-length skirt swirled around her legs. At seven p.m., Shelby took her place at the rear of the church and clutched her bouquet of white and red roses trimmed with evergreen. Since her father had died long ago, Delia would walk her down the aisle to give her away.

The small country church had never been lovelier than by candlelight. Two candelabras, with tall, burning tapers, stood on either side of the pulpit. Each side window held a lit white pillar candle. Their soft vanilla fragrance wafted through the church. A white bow decorated the end of each pew, and a basket of flowers, matching Shelby's bouquet, rested in front of the altar.

Miss Bessie played the piano in a rendition of *Love Me Tender* to set the mood.

Shelby watched her children lead the way down the aisle with measured steps. Levi carried the wedding rings on a satin pillow and wore a suit cut the same as Jeb's. Lexi dropped rose petals from a basket with precision. She wore a new black velvet dress with a lace collar.

Jeb waited at the altar in his best Western-cut suit and a brand-new shirt.

Josiah stood at his side, more dressed up than Shelby had ever seen him.

Pastor Burnett waited in the center, ready to officiate.

When the music shifted into *The Wedding March*,

Shelby and her mom stepped forward. Shelby focused on Jeb. Her handsome groom met her gaze and grinned. Once she reached him, she handed her flowers to Delia. She and Jeb faced each other, hands linked.

"We are gathered here today, in the sight of God, to join this man and this woman in Holy Matrimony." Pastor Burnett wore a brilliant smile. "Jeb, you grew up in this church, and your family are long-time members. Shelby, we're glad you and the little ones found a church home with us. The church family is happy to share your blessed day."

Jeb spoke his vows first, using the traditional words, which resonated over the years. "I, Jebediah, take you, Shelby, to be my wife, to have and to hold from this day forward, for better and for worse, for richer, and poorer, in sickness, and in health, to love, and to cherish, until death do us part. I give my solemn vow."

Although Shelby knew Jeb expected her to respond with the same promise, she had chosen something else. She spoke the words Ruth used for her mother-in-law, Naomi. Over the centuries, Ruth's promise had often been used as a marriage vow, and Shelby decided it fit how she felt. " 'Entreat me not to leave you or return from following after you. For whither thou goest, I will go, and where thou lodgest, I will lodge. Thy people shall be my people, and thy God, my God. Where thou die, I will die, and there will I be buried. The Lord do so to me, and more also, if aught but death part thee and me.' " She had committed the words to memory and spoke with a clear voice.

A single tear slid down Jeb's cheek, but his smile increased, brighter than the candles.

"Do you have a ring for your bride?" Pastor Burnett asked.

Joe handed the ring to Jeb, who slid it onto Shelby's left hand. "With this ring, I thee wed."

Shelby stared at the lovely ring, overwhelmed by what it meant. She wore her engagement ring on her right hand for the ceremony. On impulse, she moved it above the wedding band, then took Jeb's simple ring from her mom. "With this ring, I thee wed."

The pastor grinned. "By the power invested in me by the State of Missouri, and the Lord God Almighty, I pronounce you to be husband and wife. Jeb, you may kiss your bride."

Jeb took her into his arms and kissed her, his lips tender and sweet on her mouth. Shelby locked her arms around his neck and gave back the kiss.

Applause rippled through the church, and from the back pew, where Jeb's rodeo buddies sat, someone yelled. "Congratulations to the Hillbilly Hotshot and Mrs. Jeb!"

Pastor Burnett faced the gathered guests. "May I present, Mr. and Mrs. Jeb Hill! There will be a reception in the church hall immediately following. Please stay and join us."

Hands clasped, Jeb and Shelby walked down the aisle joined by the children. Levi took Jeb's left hand, and Lexi took Shelby's right. As a family, they walked to the back of the sanctuary, accepting congratulations as they did. They retreated to the hall, where a three-tiered cake trimmed with red and white roses waited.

Shelby joined her husband behind the table.

Joe took photos as they cut the first slice, then the newlyweds fed a tidbit of the sweet cake to each other.

Shelby cut the pieces, and Jeb handed them out to each guest. They saved the smallest, top tier to share on their first anniversary. As everyone enjoyed the cake, Jeb leaned over to whisper in Shelby's ear. "Check out my dad and your mom."

Joe and Delia sat cozily in one corner, intent on their conversation and oblivious to the rest of the room.

Shelby smiled. "I believe they like each other."

"I think it's a little more than that. I wouldn't be surprised if we see another wedding before long." Jeb grinned at the possibility.

Shelby took a second look. "You might be right. Mom hasn't even dated in years. She quit trying because she met so many duds."

"I wouldn't know about Dad, but he hasn't gone out with anyone either, not that I'm aware about. If they do get together, I'd call it a blessing."

"Grandma and Grandpa," Shelby tried out the titles. "It works, even if one's from my family, and the other is from yours."

Their parents would stay at the farmhouse, while the newlyweds spent a night at a historic bed-and-breakfast inn in St. Joseph. Housed in a one-time mansion, the romantic getaway would be ideal for a brief honeymoon. Jeb had tried to convince Shelby to go farther afield, to Kansas City, or even St. Louis, but she didn't want to leave the kids very long.

"Take a look." Jeb nudged Shelby to focus on their parents.

Josiah tucked a strand of hair back from Delia's face, then presented her with a stray rose. Her mom's face flushed pink. Joe cupped Delia's cheeks with both hands and kissed her.

"Oh, my!" Shelby turned her attention elsewhere.

Jeb chuckled. "I give them until June to get married."

Although they had requested no gifts, a pile of presents waited. They opened and exclaimed over each one. A hand-embroidered framed Bible verse from Miss Bessie, gift certificates for area restaurants from Pastor Burnett and his wife, bath towels, a crystal vase, a cast iron skillet, and a hurricane lamp were a few of the items they received.

"Thank you." Shelby grinned as she unwrapped each gift. As much as she enjoyed her candlelight wedding and the simple reception, Shelby craved Jeb's solitary company.

Delia packed up the presents. "I'll carry them to the house and put them on the dining room table. You won't have to mess with them tonight."

Shelby prepared to toss her bouquet. Once she did, the result surprised everyone, Delia most of all, when her mom caught the flowers.

Shelby hugged her kids.

"Can't we go, too?" Lexi asked.

"We'll take a family vacation when it's warmer." Jeb had already considered a trip to Branson or even to Disneyland. "And we'll be home tomorrow."

"Behave for your grandparents." Shelby kissed the top of Levi's head. "Watch after your sister."

They dashed outside in a shower of birdseed and good wishes to Jeb's truck.

Jeb assisted Shelby, hindered by her long skirt, into the passenger seat. When he pulled away, he heard tin cans clattering behind them.

"I don't know who put those there or when."

Shelby laughed.

"I don't either, but we'll stop down the road to undo them. I'm not driving into town with all the noise."

At the majestic bed and breakfast, Shelby drew a long breath.

The large stone mansion remained decked out for the holidays.

"It looks like a castle."

"All the houses on this street do," Jeb commented.

"They call it Millionaire's Row" Shelby referenced the rich local history.

He picked up the large suitcase they packed to share for the night, then paused. "Can I carry you over the threshold, honey?"

"No way, Jeb. I don't want you to hurt your back. We'll walk inside together, just like we'll face life."

The former home featured colorful stained-glass scenes, vintage wallpaper, and incredible original woodwork. As they climbed the stairs to their suite, Shelby couldn't resist touching the priceless antiques they passed. Inside the honeymoon suite, a huge four-poster bed complete with a canopy rested against the wall. The windows offered a fabulous view of St. Joseph, but Shelby could see it tomorrow. Tonight, she wanted Jeb. Within the bathroom, she changed from her bridal finery into a full-length satin nightgown with matching robe. The dusky rose color favored her brunette hair and brown eyes.

Jeb's eyes glistened when she emerged. "You're beautiful, Shelby." He took her into his arms and kissed her.

Neither would ever forget their wedding night in

the lovely mansion.

Over the next few weeks, they settled into life at the farm as a family. Shelby transferred the children from the St. Joseph public schools to the Savannah district. Each morning, she or Jeb saw them down the driveway to catch the school bus. They met the kids when they returned at the end of the day.

Jeb began the process of adopting Shelby's children. Since their birth father had died, no parental permission was necessary. The court appointed a guardian ad litem to make sure the adoption would be in the kids' best interest. Levi and Lexi both talked so much about Jeb, the guardian had no trouble approving the adoption. A social worker visited the farmhouse for a home study, and then they went before a family court judge. Levi and Lexi emerged as Hills.

"Do you want to work?" Jeb asked Shelby in the first weeks after the wedding. "You don't have to, sugar, but if you'd rather, it's fine."

She had resigned her home health nurse position, instead of returning. Shelby laughed. "I've got a secret, Jeb. I applied to be a substitute nurse for the Savannah district, and I'm hired. I'll work when one of the nurses at any of the schools is absent. It's enough for me. I want time to spend with you and our family. I'll be home every night in time for supper."

"I like it, and I love you." Jeb kissed her. "You can be a farmer's wife and help me, too."

By March, he acquired a herd of Angus cattle. Fifty cows and two bulls seemed enough to begin. He bought a tractor, and in the spring, he would plant hay in two pastures. He decided to wait on a horse for now. Jeb didn't want to risk his back or his newfound joy.

Just before Easter, and right after her birthday, Shelby realized she was pregnant.

"How do you feel about the number five?" Shelby asked her husband on a spring night when the lilacs beside the front porch were in bloom. Their delightful fragrance permeated the evening. She held back a giggle, so excited and delighted her joy threatened to erupt before she shared.

"It's a good one. Why?" Jeb rocked the porch swing with a gentle rhythm.

"We'll be a family of five around Thanksgiving. I'm carrying our child." She took his right hand and placed it over her still-flat stomach.

Jeb grinned. "Boy or girl?"

"Too early to know, and I'd rather not until the baby's born," Shelby told him. "We'll have to think of names."

"Luke for a boy." Jeb spoke without hesitation. "Laci for a girl."

Shelby shivered. *Synchronicity.* "I've thought about those names, too."

"Then those are the names." Jeb nodded. "We'll use one, then the other next year."

In July, not June, as Jeb predicted, Josiah married Delia. He moved into her small house, but they often visited the farm on weekends. The guest room became the grandparents' room.

Luke Elijah Hill arrived on Thanksgiving morning at six a.m. Jeb ate turkey and dressing in the hospital cafeteria.

Delia promised to make a true feast when mother and son came home.

Almost two years later, Laci Elizabeth arrived at

the end of February and missed being a leap-year baby by four short hours.

On a clear night when stars spangled across the night sky, Jeb Hill stood on his farm and gazed upward. His heart brimmed full of joy. In August, he'd mark three years since he took a spill from a bucking bronc, suffered a spinal fracture, and thought life as he knew it had ended.

He had feared a lonely existence and worried without rodeo he might become bitter. Instead, the Lord blessed him with the best wife a man could have, four beautiful children, and a prosperous life. Jeb spoke aloud, words from Psalm 16, " 'I have set the Lord always before me, because He is at my right hand, I shall not be moved. Therefore, my heart is glad and my glory rejoices.' "

He would rejoice always and love his family more than life. Jeb Hill, the Hillbilly Hotshot, had come home to stay.

Praise for Lee Ann Sontheimer Murphy

"Jebediah Hill, known as The Hillbilly Hotshot, finds himself broken and busted up in the hospital. Fearful that his future as a top-notch bronc rider is over, he refuses to accept his fate. When Shelby Thacker, a kind and dedicated home health nurse, enters his life to care for him, Jeb gains a new purpose beyond healing his body. Shelby and her two children need a secure future, but she puts that aside to fulfill her duty of helping Jeb heal. Together, Jeb and Shelby discover the mysterious ways in which the Lord works miracles. This is a touching story of healing broken hearts from the past."
~Karen Jennings, author

~*~

"I enjoyed this heartwarming Christmas tale very much. Lee Ann has a good one here."
~John Hornick

~*~

A charming holiday story set in the Heartland. Tugged at my heartstrings from page one to the end.
~Jan N.

~*~

"Beautiful from beginning to end. I love the sweet romances. Jeb and Shelby both find a new way to move ahead in life in this Christmas story set in my home state of Missouri!"
~J.A. Hayes

A word about the author…

From an early age, Lee Ann Sontheimer Murphy scribbled stories, inspired by the books she read, the family tales she heard, and even the conversations she overheard at the beauty shop where her grandmother had a weekly standing appointment.

As an author, she has published more than sixty novels and novellas writing as both Lee Ann Sontheimer Murphy, Patrice Wayne and Liathán O'Murchadha.

She spent her early career in broadcast radio, interviewing everyone from politicians to major league baseball players and writing ad copy. In those radio years she began to write short stories and articles, some of which found publication. In 1994 she married Roy Murphy and they had three children, all grown. Lee Ann spent a number of years in the newspaper field as both a journalist and editor and was widowed in 2019.

In late 2020, she hung up her editor's hat to return to writing fiction. A native of St. Joseph, Missouri, she lives and works in the rugged, mysterious, and beautiful Missouri Ozarks.

https://leeannsontheimer.blogspot.com/
Other Titles by this Author
The Cowboy's Last Chance
The Scarred Santa

Thank you for purchasing
this publication of The Wild Rose Press, Inc.

For questions or more information
contact us at
info@thewildrosepress.com.

The Wild Rose Press, Inc.
www.thewildrosepress.com

Milton Keynes UK
Ingram Content Group UK Ltd.
UKHW010233111224
452348UK00011B/740